Plantation Shudders

Plantation Shudders

A Cajun Country Mystery

Ellen Byron

CROOKED
LANE

NEW YORK

Copyright © 2015 by Ellen Byron

All rights reserved.

Published in the United States by Crooked Lane Books, an imprint of The Quick Brown Fox & Company LLC.

Crooked Lane Books and its logo are trademarks of The Quick Brown Fox & Company LLC.

The Library of Congress Cataloging-in-Publication Data is available upon request.

ISBN (hardcover): 978-1-62953-250-9
e-ISBN: 978-1-62953-251-6

Cover design by Jennifer Canzone.
Book design by Jennifer Canzone.

Printed in the United States.

www.crookedlanebooks.com

Crooked Lane Books
2 Park Avenue, 10th Floor
New York, NY 10016

First Edition: August 2015

10 9 8 7 6 5 4 3 2 1

Dedicated to the two loves of my life, Jerry and Eliza.

Also to my beloved mother, Elizabeth, and my deeply lamented late father, Richard Seideman.

Chapter One

Maggie flew down southern Louisiana's River Road in the red '64 Falcon convertible that she'd inherited from her late grandfather. Strands of brown hair from her thick ponytail whipped her face, but after a day spent flouncing around in a polyester plantation belle gown as a tour guide at Doucet Plantation, the wind's attack felt great.

The familiar scenery followed a pattern: bucolic countryside, hideous industrial plant, an empty field, hideous petrochemical plant. This was the schizophrenic nature of what the legendary road had become—one plantation after another either demolished or demoralized with a monstrous neighbor. But there were some gorgeous survivors, like Doucet—and Crozat.

As Maggie crossed the Mississippi and drove toward Bayou Beurre, she thought of tales her family told about love-struck suitors who swam across the mighty river, braving its wicked currents for the chance to woo her great-great-great-grandmother,

Ellen Byron

Magnolia Marie Doucet. It sure beat the "whassup" texts Maggie got from her last boyfriend.

The river receded into the background, and gradually the ratio of countryside to industrial complex tilted in countryside's favor. She slowed down as she passed the large "Welcome to Pelican" sign that featured a fat grinning pelican playing an accordion under the town motto, "Yes, We Pelican!" It was a clever way of reminding the world that local pronunciation required emphasis on the last syllable of the town's name, not the first. But Maggie preferred her personal slogan: "Pelican: The Town People Are Smart Enough to Come Home To or Too Dumb to Leave."

Rather than make a left into Pelican, she stayed on course. A white fence appeared on the left side of the road, its long reach broken in the middle by an open gate. She turned and entered the property, driving down a hard-packed dirt road under a canopy of pine and oak trees. The trees forked left and right to embrace their prize: Crozat Plantation.

While the Doucets, her mom's family, had long ago donated their historic cash guzzler of a plantation to the state, the Crozats, her dad's family, had clung to their ancestral domain, which they now operated as a gracious bed and breakfast. It wasn't the largest plantation in Louisiana, but with its classic Greek Revival architecture, Crozat was one of the most iconic. Thirty-two majestic square columns encircled the entire mansion. A second floor balcony also ran its circumference, and each floor featured a wide, welcoming veranda. Crozat was more human than house to Maggie, pulsing with life drawn from the generations of strong and

2

quirky inhabitants it had sheltered for almost two hundred years.

As much as Maggie got a kick out of working at Doucet Plantation and entertaining visitors with her personal connection to it, Crozat was home. But it was a home she envisioned visiting during holidays or for the occasional getaway weekend from New York. It was not a place she planned to slink back to as a thirty-two-year-old whose personal life and career both hit a wall. The Brooklyn art gallery that Maggie and her boyfriend of six years had cofounded was now being run by her ex and the woman he'd married instead of her. She had returned to Louisiana searching for the inspiration she needed to ignite her own career as an artist, but success was proving elusive. Maggie feared that she disproved her own slogan—maybe it wasn't so smart to come home to Pelican.

"No," she shouted into the air. She stopped the car, stood up, and shook her fist at the heavens in her best Scarlett O'Hara-reaches-the-end-of-her-rope imitation. "As God is my witness, I will not have downer feelings today." Maggie resumed a leisurely drive toward the plantation, and her melancholia melted away as she absorbed the lovely view of Crozat. She searched for a new perspective on the old home that she could bring to life through oil paints or vibrant watercolors, perhaps even pastels.

Then she suddenly shuddered as a chill ran through her lithe body on the warm August day.

People in Pelican took "the shudders" seriously. Whenever they struck Maggie's Grand-mère Crozat, she drawled dramatically, "Someone's walkin' on muh graaave." This was followed by a heated family debate over whom that might be until everyone agreed that it was a case for the town voodoo priestess, a woman respected both for her psychic abilities and for the fact she was the first local merchant to download the app that enabled her cell phone to take credit cards.

Maggie searched her mind for what could have spooked her but came up empty. Maybe this was just one of those rare cases where a chill was just a chill, she shrugged. Still . . . it made her nervous.

She drove past the plantation into a garage placed at the far end of the property, where guests wouldn't notice its peeling paint. The Crozats were still playing financial catch-up after Hurricane Katrina, so repainting the family garage was on hold until possibly forever. Maggie parked, got out of the car, and walked to the family's organic garden patch, where her mother, Ninette Doucet Crozat, was gathering vegetables. The family's beloved Basset hound rescue, Gopher, was by her side. He was in his favorite position, head and torso resting on the ground, catching rays while the lower half of his body cooled off in a hole he'd dug—hence the name Gopher.

"Need some help, Mom?"

"I'm good," Ninette said, pushing her baseball cap back to dab at a few drops of perspiration. Her tiny figure disguised a will so strong that it had powered her through a bout of Hodgkin's lymphoma in her early twenties. "Your dad may need help, though. We had a few last-minute reservations come through. I think we're finally full up for the week."

"Excellent. I was getting worried."

"We all were, honey. Now, why don't you take this kale into the kitchen?"

Maggie took the basket of kale from Ninette and headed for the plantation kitchen, her steps lightened by the relief of a "No Vacancy" sign. Late summer bookings had been hurt by a national trend toward starting the school year in August rather than after Labor Day. But if there was one time of year that every hostelry in Pelican should be booked up, it was the week of Fet Let.

Louisiana abounded with festivals celebrating its unique blend of cultures. They ranged from New Orleans's world-renowned JazzFest to Pelican's Fete L'ete—Fet Let to Pelicaners—a casual event that honored the end of summer. Businesses and families set up stands around the town square where they sold crafts and fantastic homemade food made from recipes handed down through generations. Singers sang, fiddlers fiddled, and there was the requisite bounce house and petting zoo for the kids. To capitalize on the popular event, Maggie had suggested a Fet Let end-of-summer special, offering a discounted room rate plus breakfast, dinner, and happy hour for guests who booked August's last full week. She was happy to see that her brainstorm had paid off.

She put the kale in the industrial-size refrigerator. Then she walked into the back parlor where her father, Thibaut "Tug" Crozat, worked at a computer housed in a nineteenth-century secretary. Grand-mère Crozat, clad in pale blue linen pants and a crisp white blouse, her soft gray hair meticulously coiffed as always, sat on a nearby wingback chair. She had an iPad with an attached keyboard perched on her lap.

"Are the reservations confirmed? Can I update our page?" Grand-mère asked her son. Gran' had become the family social media maven, a poster girl for the computer-loving seniors who were chasing teens off Facebook.

"All confirmed. Update away, Mama."

As Gran' gleefully posted on the plantation's Facebook page, Maggie peered over her father's shoulder at his computer screen. Tug's red-gold hair took on a metallic glint in the evening's setting sun. "What's the breakdown?" she asked.

"Two couples, one of them honeymooners; some college boys here to fish; a single male; a family from Australia; and four women who are the executive board of a group called the Cajun Cuties, a national group of Cajun wannabes," Tug said. "They usually meet at Belle Grove Plantation to plan the year's activities, but Belle Grove's guesthouse flooded this morning and they rebooked them to us."

"Thank you, Belle Grove's antiquated plumbing," Maggie said.

"Amen to that," Tug seconded. "Should be an interesting week."

Maggie and her dad shared a grin. Then she shuddered again.

Tug looked at her, concerned. "You okay?" he asked.

"Yes. I don't know where that came from."

"Oh, dear," Gran' said. She pursed her lips. "Shudders. That's not good. Not good at all." She made the sign of the cross and her son shook his head, amused.

"No need to get melodramatic. Right, Maggie?"

"Right." Still, Maggie couldn't help notice her father surreptitiously crossing himself as well. Tug was the Crozat least susceptible to local superstitions. Something had spooked him, which only made Maggie more nervous.

*

Later, as soon as Maggie finished a dinner that was heavy on kale, she drove into Pelican's Historic Business Center—a lofty name for what was essentially a sleepy village. Its picturesque center featured four blocks of two-story buildings with wrought iron balconies that framed a town green, an unusual feature for the area and the pride of Pelican.

Maggie parked in front of two shops, Bon Bon Sweets and its sister store, Fais Dough Dough Patisserie. She grabbed some boxes from the Falcon's backseat and walked through Bon Bon into the workroom that it shared with Fais Dough Dough. High school student Briana Poche, her brother Clinton, and a few friends sat at a table stuffing small gauze bags with various herbs, roots, and talismans. Supervising them was Maggie's cousin, Lia Tienne. Although Lia was seven years older than Maggie, the two had grown up together and were bonded like sisters. Lia's late father was of Franco-African heritage, which had blessed her with café au lait coloring and the bone structure of Nefertiti. She was recognized as the Pelican town beauty, which mortified her.

Lia smiled when she saw Maggie, who put her boxes down on a workbench. "Hey. Whatcha got for me?"

"Mugs, plates, mostly," Maggie said. She had started a small side business making souvenirs that featured her artistic take on local landmarks. Instead of the historically accurate but dull illustrations usually featured on such mementos, hers were bold and modern. They had yet to generate a profit, but she took comfort in the fact that at least she was breaking even.

Lia reached into one of Maggie's boxes and pulled out a black mug that featured a stylized white illustration of a dilapidated plantation. "Oooh, I love this."

"My SOS series—Save Our Structures. A portion of sales go to the historical society so we can save the buildings that are falling apart." She pointed to the cup in Lia's hand. "That's Grove Hall. If the Durands don't do something with that place soon, there's not gonna be anything left to save." She then eyed the gift bag assembly. "What exactly are you doing?"

"A bride-to-be from Metairie ordered two hundred gris-gris bags for love as wedding favors."

Maggie held up a silvery gauze bag imprinted with "Brent and Carolyn: A Magical Evening." "What a great idea."

"Yes, you'll have to remember that," Lia said, grinning.

Maggie shook a finger at her. "Nuh-uh. If my mother doesn't get to nag me about marriage, you don't either."

Maggie joined the teens at the table, and Lia handed her a sharp knife and the ginger root. Maggie started chopping. As each bag was passed around the table, she dropped in a small piece of ginger as another love talisman.

"So, you have a full house?" Lia asked as she carefully packed up completed gris-gris bags.

"Happy to report, yes." Maggie filled Lia in on the reservations. Lia suddenly shuddered, and Maggie gasped. "You, too? The same thing happened to me. That's so weird."

"Something's not right," Lia said, shaking her head. "Just . . . not right."

The kids at the table exchanged concerned looks. There wasn't a generation in Pelican that didn't take stock in omens. "Or," Maggie said, trying to lighten the mood. "Maybe you just shivered because I said that one of our guests was a single guy in his early forties. Just right for you, Leelee."

Lia didn't say a word. Instead, she focused on her task, picking up speed as she packed the box. Maggie felt terrible. Lia's husband Degas had succumbed to leukemia two years earlier. It was a brutal reminder of Plantation Alley's other, darker nickname—Cancer Alley.

"I'm an idiot. I should have kept my stupid big mouth shut—"

"No, it's okay. It's . . . I'm not ready. Honestly, Maggie, I don't know if I ever will be."

Briana's lip quivered and a tear fell on the gris-gris bag she was packing. "Oh, that bag is especially powerful now," Lia told Briana as she gently laid a hand on the girl's shoulder. "You get to keep it." Briana was about to burst into tears when Clinton, a chunky eleventh grader, let out a resounding Coke burp.

"Whoops. Sorry."

Clinton's belch broke the tension, and the kids burst into laughter. Lia took a seat next to Maggie and began filling gris-gris bags. She pulled a safety pin out of a box on the table and then took a tiny black bag that smelled like anise and pinned it inside Maggie's tank top above her heart.

"Oh please, Lia. I am so not in the mood for love these days."

"It's not for love."

Maggie, feeling uneasy, looked at her cousin. "Then what is it for?"

"Protection," Lia said grimly. "From evil."

Chapter Two

The next day, after clocking out from her shift at Doucet, Maggie drove home to help Crozat's guests check in. She parked and walked to the main house, where she saw four middle-aged women who she assumed were the Cajun Cuties extricating themselves from a rented mini SUV parked in front of Crozat. Maggie ran over to help them. All four were clad in leggings and oversized T-shirts, an eighties look that Maggie thought too many women on the flip side of forty still clung to.

"Hi, I'm Maggie Crozat," she said as she grabbed a heavy suitcase and guided a particularly plump sixtysomething out of the car. "Welcome to Crozat Plantation."

"*Laissez les bons temps rouler*," the woman declared in a New York accent as thick as a slice of Sicilian pizza. Her bright, sparkly makeup was as eighties as her outfit, and a quarter-inch of white roots betrayed her hair's black dye job. "Let the good times roll! I'm Jan Robbins and I'm proud to be a Cajun Cutie. But I can see who the real Cajun cutie is here."

Maggie smiled. "To be honest, I'm only half Cajun. My mom's family is, but my dad's side is Creole, descended from French settlers, not Acadians."

"I love it," Jan declared as she made a heavy landing from the SUV. "Hey, Cuties," she called to her cohorts, "we lucked out getting moved here." Marie and Bobby "Bud" Shexnayder, a local couple that the Crozats hired to help during busy weeks, appeared just in time to save Maggie from being swarmed by the enthusiastic group. Marie and Bud piled their suitcases into a wheelbarrow while Maggie led them to the plantation's converted carriage house. As they walked, Jan surprised her with a spot-on recitation of Crozat's history.

"Wow," Maggie said, "You may know more about this place than I do."

"I love this part of the world," Jan said. "Every bayou, swamp, and historical site. That's why I founded the Cuties. We've got about five hundred dues-paying members, all people who love Cajun Country as much as I do."

"Here's hoping that after your visit, you share a love of Crozat with all those members."

Jan gave Maggie a thumbs-up. "*Laissez les bons temps rouler*," she repeated.

The other guests trickled in as the afternoon wore on. Emily and Shane Butler, a couple not much older than Maggie, turned out to be celebrating their fifth anniversary. Emily was fine-boned and petite, and Shane sported stubble and consciously geeky eyeglasses. They both worked for start-up Internet companies and were the archetypal Brooklyn hipster couple. The family from Australia and frat boys from Georgia showed up almost simultaneously. Carrie and Lachlan Ryker were trim and sporty, as were their three kids.

The frat boys were all blonde, over six feet, and virtually indistinguishable from each other. "We did some days in New Orleans and I still got the hangover to prove it," one of them told Maggie as another reached into the back of the car and hauled out garbage bags subbing as suitcases for their belongings.

"I'm all about taking an airboat ride and seeing some gators," the second frat boy said.

The third member of the group nodded enthusiastically. "Yeah," he added. "I'm totes stoked."

Kyle Bruner, the "single guy" from Texas, showed up a half hour later. Handsome and polite, he had salt-and-pepper hair, a tanned face, and was shy of the Georgia boys' height by only an inch or two. But what struck Maggie most about Kyle was the overlay of sadness to him. It was as if he were going through the motions of life rather than actually living it.

"I'm looking forward to my visit," he told Maggie as she walked him to his room. "I've always liked this part of the country."

"Oh, so you've been to Cajun Country before?"

"Yes. I was married in the area."

Maggie was about to ask Kyle where, but the look of pain that crossed his face stopped her. She wondered why his wife wasn't with him and discreetly checked his left hand. It bore neither a wedding ring nor a tan line. Whatever had happened between the couple must have occurred some time ago, Maggie thought, but he's still not over it.

By five o'clock, when everyone met on the veranda for wine and cheese, the only two guests who hadn't checked in were a Hal and Beverly Clabber. As they all snacked and drank, Gran' and Maggie entertained the visitors with local lore. Gopher parked himself directly in front of a box fan, where every so often he'd shake his head to keep from dozing off. Occasionally, a dollop of drool would fall from his mouth's folds and be propelled across the veranda by the fan, narrowly missing a guest. Kyle scored points for helping Tug pass out cocktails. "I'm not very good at sitting around being waited on," he confessed. Then he asked Gran' if she needed a refill.

"Always," Gran' said as she handed him her glass.

"In the morning, I can show you around Crozat and its outbuildings," Maggie told the guests.

"That sounds great, doesn't it, Boo Bear?" Shane Butler said to his wife Emily, who nodded eagerly.

"Fantastic, Boo Bear," she said as she intertwined her fingers with his.

"Why, you two call each other the same nickname," Gran' said. "How adorable. Isn't that adorable? Kyle, be a dear and freshen my drink. I seem to have drained it rather quickly."

"Can we swim in the bayou?" asked Luke Ryker, the Australians' middle child, whom Maggie pegged as about ten years old.

"I wouldn't recommend it," Maggie said. "You can't be sure what's in there."

"Like gators," one of the frat boys jumped in. Unable to keep their names straight, Maggie had secretly nicknamed the group Georgias One, Two, and Three.

"I want to swim with gators!" Luke's younger brother Sam declared.

Their sister Alice, who looked to be around twelve, gave an annoyed sigh. "You are *so* embarrassing." Take away the Aussie accent and Alice could have been any tween in any mall in America.

"We do have a pool," Maggie said. "Dinner's not until seven, you could go now."

The boys raced off to change into swimsuits with their parents on their heels. Alice reluctantly dragged herself behind them.

"I wonder what happened to the Clabbers," Maggie said as she scanned the long driveway that led to Crozat.

"Maybe they decided not to come," Tug said as he handed his mother a martini. Gran' sniffed it suspiciously.

"It better not be one of those awful 'Cajun' martinis. They're the souvenir tea towel of cocktails."

Before Tug could respond, everyone was startled by the sound of a car explosively backfiring. Attention shifted to a circa-1970s Volvo slowly turning into the long Crozat driveway. It inched its way up the driveway at a pace so sluggish that it became hypnotic. After what could have been a few minutes or an eternity, the car pulled up to the front of Crozat. An elderly woman was at the wheel, while a senior citizen who looked more cadaver than man sat in the passenger seat. He hand-cranked his window down with an ancient, wrinkled hand and glared at the group on the veranda. The man's watery blue eyes seemed bleached by the sun. "So far I'm very unimpressed with the service," he said, glaring at the Crozats and their guests.

The newlyweds, Hal and Beverly Clabber, had arrived.

"How about someone helping me with my walker?" Hal Clabber barked at Maggie, Tug, and Bud as they hurried to the couple. Tug pulled suitcases and Hal's walker out of the car's trunk while Maggie helped the old man out of the car and Bud tended to Beverly Clabber.

"Our apologies," Tug said, trying to appease the old crank. "Welcome to Crozat. Can we get you a drink? Some snacks?"

"We'll take wine—red—cheese, and whatever else you're offering, in our room."

"We're on our honeymoon," Beverly Clabber added with a wink.

"Well, isn't that *marvelous*, just *marvelous*," Gran' declared. Maggie bit her finger to keep from laughing. She knew that the more uncomfortable Gran' felt, the thicker her accent became, and the Clabbers were inspiring a drawl so pronounced that Gran' sounded like a hokey Southern dowager from a 1930s B movie.

Hal pushed his walker toward the front steps and stared at them. "The Americans with Disabilities Act prohibits discrimination based on disabilities."

"Translation: get the ramp, Dad," Maggie muttered to her father, who seemed uncharacteristically befuddled.

"Yes, right, of course."

Tug and Bud pulled a wooden ramp out of its discreet hiding place in nearby bushes and placed it over the stairs. Hal carefully pushed himself up it onto the veranda.

"Do you need help, ma'am?" Maggie asked Beverly Clabber.

"I'm fine," Beverly replied. As opposed to her grouchy husband, Beverly hadn't stopped smiling since the couple arrived.

To say she scampered up the steps would be an exaggeration, but she got to the top without a problem and waited for her husband, smile still plastered on her face. Maggie began to wonder if it was the result of nerve damage from a stroke.

"I'll show you to your room," Maggie said, relieved that Tug had serendipitously put them in the one bedroom located on the main floor.

"We requested the first floor," Hal said.

"No you didn't," Maggie somehow managed not to say aloud as she led the Clabbers down the hall to the Rose Room. She opened the ornately carved walnut door and the Clabbers followed her in. With its deep pink walls, white cypress ceiling medallion, and museum-quality furnishings, the Rose Room was legendary among antebellum historians for its pristine Victorian beauty. *Good luck finding something to complain about here*, Maggie thought as the Clabbers took in their surroundings.

"It's lovely," Beverly acknowledged. Hal walkered himself into the en suite bathroom. When he came out, he didn't look happy. He beckoned to Maggie, who gritted her teeth and followed him into the bathroom. Hal pointed to a roll of toilet paper on a vintage-style wrought iron holder.

"This is all wrong," he said. "You unroll from the top, not the bottom. It's much more efficient."

"Thank you so much for pointing that out." Maggie reversed the toilet paper, managing to hide the middle finger she was shooting Hal as she did it. "Marie's on her way with your wine and appetizers. If you need anything else, my cell number's on the information sheet. Please don't hesitate to call."

With that, Maggie backed out of the room, hoping against hope that Hal wouldn't take her up on the offer. Beverly smiled her Joker smile. "You have to understand," she said apologetically. "Hal has a leaky anus."

Maggie couldn't get to the kitchen fast enough. She pulled a bottle of white wine out of the refrigerator and poured herself a full glass. "Ohmygod, ohmygod, ohmygod, ohmygod."

Ninette, who was stirring a large pot of jambalaya, watched with concern as Maggie took a big slug of wine. "Honey, are you okay? You never drink before dinner."

"We never hosted the Clabbers before." Maggie filled her mother in on the conversation, and Ninette burst out laughing.

"Oh, you poor thing, that is truly awful. I swear, there are days when I think we should just donate this place to the state, like my family did."

"No, I think what you do—what we do here—is wonderful. It's the first time that a guest ever brought up leaky anus in conversation. And hopefully the last, although I've learned not to assume anything when it comes to our guests."

*

Maggie managed to avoid the Clabbers the rest of the afternoon. She took a long shower and stretched out the length of time she usually took to apply makeup. She dawdled as she poked through her closet, finally settling on sandals and a coral cotton sundress. Then, steeling herself for the long evening ahead, Maggie walked over to the main house.

She feared what dinner and a few drinks might bring, but the repositioned toilet paper seemed to have mellowed Hal.

His nastiness had disappeared, replaced by a patronizing superiority that she often found characteristic of retired college professors—a bit of braggadocio Hal had already dropped into the conversation several times.

Predinner martinis had made Gran' particularly loquacious, and by the time the main course of chicken and andouille sausage jambalaya was served, she'd enthralled her listeners with tales of Crozat tragedies and triumphs. Duels, star-crossed romances, yellow fever epidemics—Gran' covered it all. "Legend even has it that the notorious pirate Jean Lafitte buried a casket of treasure somewhere deep in the Crozat woods and then stole Felix Crozat's finest steed to escape the army battalion that was tasked with hunting him down," she said in her most theatrical voice.

"It's like a movie," said an awestruck Debbie Stern, who, at somewhere around fifty, was the youngest of the Cajun Cuties. "Tell us more."

"Everywhere around us, families were driven to sell their property or abandon it. And then, just when we at Crozat seemed to be pulling ourselves out of the depths of despair," Gran' intoned, her voice dropping theatrically, "we found ourselves facing the deprivations of war."

"You mean the Civil War?" Debbie gasped.

A spoon clattered into a bowl. Kyle coughed as he tried to swallow a laugh. Gran' instantly sobered up. "My goodness, the doctors are right. The sun really does age a person. No, dear, I'm old but not quite that old. I was referring to World War Two."

"Oh, of course," Debbie said, embarrassed. "I don't know what to say. I just got lost in your stories."

"Well then, that's quite a tribute to my storytelling," Gran'
said, kindly letting Debbie off the hook.

"Tell us about the pirate and his treasure again," Sam
begged. The other diners joined him in encouraging Gran's
return to the buried treasure legend.

The rest of the meal was uneventful. Poor Gran' was
held conversational hostage by Hal Clabber as he boasted
of the expertise in twentieth-century American theater history that had won him tenure at Conway College, a small
school in Nebraska. Maggie imagined that there were a lot
of Conway parents who owed Hal thanks for being so boring that he propelled students out of theater and into more
lucrative fields.

Hal finally dozed off in his chair and was helped to his
room by Bud and Marie. Beverly followed, smiling as always.
As soon as the last guest was gone, Maggie and the rest of her
family retreated to the kitchen to clean up. Tug and Ninette
then retired to bed, and Maggie walked Gran' back to the house
the two shared. It was a shotgun house, the name inspired
by a layout where a bullet shot from the front door would go
straight out the back door. Dating back to the 1820s, it was
the oldest building on the property and the original residence
of the Crozats before they decided to celebrate their sugarcane
wealth with a fancy showplace.

Maggie kissed her grandmother good-night and then
retrieved the oil paints and portable easel that she kept in her
bedroom. With the help of a small flashlight, she made her way
through the dark to woods at the east end of Crozat land, where
a stream fed into Bayou Beurre. Green branches hung heavy

over the lush waterway, and an occasional cypress popped out of the water like an arboreal jack-in-the-box.

As she set up her supplies, Maggie's eyes adjusted to the dark. The outside world fell away as she focused on her canvas. She had taken to painting at all different hours, capturing the way light and dark played with the lush Louisiana landscape. She particularly loved the plantation grounds at night, when clouds, stars, and the moon competed for space in the sky. The evening's full moon provided the scene with highlights and shadows; Maggie filled in the rest with her imagination.

A long gray cloud wandered over the evening's full moon, and she took a brief break to let her eyes readjust. She heard leaves crunch nearby. An animal, she assumed, probably a neighbor's dog. There was another crunch. Then another. And Maggie realized that she wasn't listening to an animal. She was hearing footsteps.

Maggie was no longer alone.

Chapter Three

Maggie froze, heart pounding. *Should I scream?* she wondered. *No. Relax. It's probably just a guest who can't sleep.* She took a few deep breaths to calm herself.

"Hello, who's there?" She called into the darkness. "It's me, Maggie Crozat. Is everything okay?"

The footsteps stopped. Then they resumed at a quicker pace, fading as whoever it was took off in the opposite direction. Maggie packed up her supplies and hurried home. She checked out the main house and outbuildings to see if the late-night visitor might be one of Crozat's guests, but all was still in both buildings. She scurried inside her house, double-locked the door, and rested her ear against it, listening for any sound that indicated movement outside. There was a rustle of leaves, and Maggie tensed. She peeked out the front window and noticed Spanish moss swaying from a slight breeze. *I must have heard the wind picking up the leaves*, she thought. She waited in silence, but there were no more footsteps.

Maggie sat on the couch and tried to calm herself down. The event spooked her. Why would anyone be wandering around Crozat in the middle of the night? And if they weren't "up to no good," as Gran' would say, why was there no response when she called out? Maggie fussed over these questions and more as she readied for bed. She checked to make sure her window was secured, crawled under the bed covers, and fell asleep clutching the gris-gris bag Lia had given her for protection.

*

Maggie woke up a few hours later to find that the weather was growing dark and moody. There was no way the day would pass without a storm, at least a brief one. She decided not to mention what had happened the night before to anyone. She didn't want to worry her parents or Gran'.

The guests slowly assembled on the veranda for the tour of Crozat, yawning at the early hour and limiting their small talk to perfunctory greetings. The only no-shows were the Clabbers. Maggie debated skipping her hostess duty of checking on them, but guilt propelled her down the hall to their room. She could hear the sound of tandem snoring through the door, so she left the couple to their beauty sleep, although in this case the only thing beautiful about it was that it freed her from their company for a few more hours.

Maggie led her guests through the main house, sharing its history as they went. She was so used to giving tours at both Crozat and Doucet that she could cheerfully impart information while thinking to herself, as she was doing at the moment:

How did I go from aspiring artist to plantation guide and maker of cheesy souvenirs?

She took everyone onto the front lawn for a panoramic view of the stately mansion. "Every side of the house has windows almost a full story high," Maggie shared. "When all of them are open, they provide a cross breeze that I'm guessing saved at least a few of my ancestors from death by Louisiana mugginess."

"I think I got a bad case of that myself," Cutie Angela muttered. A stout woman bordering on obese, she wiped perspiration off her second chin before it dripped down to her third.

The group left Crozat's manicured grounds and hiked through abandoned fields where the plantation's slave quarters and sugar mill lay in ruins. The Crozats hoped to have the money to restore the plantation's outbuildings someday, but given the cost of maintaining the buildings that still stood, someday seemed far off.

Maggie stopped in front of what appeared to be a miniature store. "This was the plantation store, which was built after the war. After the *Civil* War," she added for Debbie's benefit. "Postwar, a lot of former slaves returned to their plantations as tenant farmers, so some plantations set up stores where they could buy supplies more easily than going into town. As transportation improved, the stores disappeared. Crozat's has been closed for eighty years."

Maggie took a skeleton key and unlocked the store's old door, which crookedly swung open. Everyone stepped into the space and gazed around the century-old time capsule with fascination. The interior was completely intact, down to a few old cans and other dust-covered items still on the shelves. A turn-of-the-century cash register sat on the counter waiting for what could only be a ghostly transaction at this point. After months of showing off the shop to visitors, Maggie had reached the point where, if she wanted to, she could close her eyes, point to a shelf, and rattle off its faded occupants with 100 percent accuracy.

"Fantastic," Jan said. The other Cuties echoed the sentiment, as did all the guests.

"Oh, Boo Bear, I love it," Emily Butler gushed. "Don't you?"

"Totally, Boo Bear."

Maggie took a moment to enjoy their reactions. Guests' enthusiasm made her efforts worthwhile, especially if they translated into glowing reviews on a travel website. "I always like to finish up my tour here. Now, anyone besides me ready for breakfast?"

The whole group answered in the affirmative, so Maggie brought them back to the main house. Since the Georgia boys were heading off on a fishing excursion and the Ryker family on a swamp tour, Ninette packed their breakfasts to go. The Butlers—who would now forever be known to the Crozats as the Boo Bears—asked for breakfast in bed.

"I didn't know that was an option," grumped Hal Clabber, whose crabbiness had returned. He and Bev had roused themselves and were seated between Kyle and Jan, who Maggie had learned was the Cajun Cuties' board president. While the other guests helped themselves to reasonable portions, Hal heaped his plate with pecan pancakes, scrambled eggs, andouille sausage, cheese grits, fruit, and Lia's delicate croissants, clearly determined to squeeze every last breakfast item out of the complimentary buffet. Bev sported a slightly modified version of her husband's plate. *The couple's eating habits are eating away at our profits,* Maggie thought darkly.

"Everything is delicious," Beverly said, smiling as always. Maggie wondered if she slept with that grin on her face.

"It's predictable," Hal declared. "I'm disappointed in the lack of creativity."

Then stop stuffing your face with it, Maggie wanted to scream. Instead she said, "We'll work on that."

As soon as the guests finished breakfast and left the table, Maggie cleared it. She was about to return to the shotgun when she heard a timid voice behind her.

"Excuse me." Maggie turned to see Cutie Debbie. "We were wondering if you'd like to come into town with us. We want to support the local businesses and perhaps you could fill us in on some of Pelican's history on the way."

Maggie decided to embrace the opportunity to remove herself from the Clabbers' beck and call. "That sounds like a great idea," she told Debbie and followed her to the Cuties' van, where the rest of the group greeted Maggie's addition to their numbers with great joy. She climbed into the front passenger seat of the van, and they took off.

As Jan drove the women into the village, Maggie pointed out the occasional landmark—like an old schoolhouse that still possessed a working bell and a white-columned Jesuit monastery almost two hundred years old.

"You see that alley of trees that ends in an empty field?" she said to the women as she gestured out the window toward the river. "That's where another plantation once stood."

"Petite Chambord," Jan said. "Once the largest in the area, lost to fire in 1871."

Maggie looked at Jan in surprise. "Nice. I'm impressed."

Jan shrugged and grinned. "What can I say? I gotta have something to put in my Cajun Cuties newsletters."

The van made its way into Pelican and found an empty parking spot in front of Fais Dough Dough. Maggie jumped out and was dropping coins into the meter when she saw Rufus "Ru" Durand saunter toward her. Ru was the Pelican chief of police, a patronage job that few residents gave much thought to since crime in the town was so infrequent. Ru, who was the color and shape of unbaked bread dough, was oblivious to his lack of importance. But fortunately for Pelican, his arrogance and sense of superiority were kept in check by what many locals considered a genetic streak of laziness.

"Hey, Maggie."

"Hey, Ru."

Ru took the nightstick he was swinging like a Keystone cop and pointed it at the meter where Maggie was parked. "That got changed, ya know. Only half an hour."

"Yes, I do know," Maggie checked her phone. "It's 8:54. I'll be back at 9:24."

"So will I," Rufus said. "Ready to write you a ticket at 9:25."

Maggie clenched her teeth and managed to refrain from a nasty comeback. She knew Ru was taunting her. Enmity between her family and the Durands went back more than one hundred fifty years. "Not to worry, Ru. I'll be right on time."

"If you say so." Rufus turned to the Cuties. "Enjoy your all-too-brief visit to the bakery, ladies. And Maggie, tell Lia that I think of free coffee and croissants more as a thank-you than a bribe. I'm just sayin'."

Rufus winked at her and strolled off. Jan glared at his back. "In New Jersey, we have words for guys like him."

Maggie laughed. "I bet they're the same words we have in Louisiana. I'm sorry about that. Let's just forget it ever happened and buy us some homemade treats!"

The Cuties happily followed her into the store. They shopped up a storm at both Bon Bon and Fais Dough Dough, grabbing many of Maggie's souvenirs as well as Lia's treats. While they loaded up their baskets, Maggie filled Lia in on the horror that was the Clabbers.

"What did you do when he said breakfast was 'predictable'?"

"I responded politely and then spent the rest of breakfast fantasizing about putting my grapefruit knife in just the right position so that if someone 'accidentally' tripped Hal Clabber, he'd be impaled by it."

Lia laughed. "Oh, it's gonna be a long week. I think you could use some ice cream."

"We all could. I'll take a gallon of Brown Sugar. It'll go great with Mom's Bananas Foster tonight."

Lia tried to press the ice cream on Maggie as a gift, but Maggie insisted on paying her cousin for it. Then she and the Cuties drove home as quickly as possible. Rain was certain to come by afternoon or evening, and she hoped the summer storm wouldn't bring with it a power outage. The Crozats had a backup generator that kicked in pretty quickly, but there was always that transitional moment when guests panicked.

Maggie and Gran' spent the afternoon helping Ninette prep for dinner and sharing notes about the week's guests. All three agreed that the Clabbers were awful, the Ryker kids cute, the Butlers bland, the Cuties entertaining, and Georgias One through Three harmless.

"For my money, the most interesting guest in this lot is the handsome Mr. Bruner," Gran' said. "He's quite refreshing for a Texan."

"What does *that* mean?" Ninette asked as she put a pot of water up to boil.

"He doesn't wear cowboy boots, which even the most sedentary of his fellow statesmen insist on tromping around in. And so many of the Texans who come here can't stop bloviating about how great their state is. Remember that one man? Every time you put out a flower or a piece of fruit, he would say something like, 'We have roses the size of your head in Texas.' Or 'I once grew a cucumber that was as big as a basketball player's forearm.' That was my favorite. I wanted to say, 'Do you live in a state or a nuclear testing site?'"

The others couldn't help but laugh at this. "I'll tell you one thing, though," Gran' continued. "He's got a story, that Kyle. Good looking, obviously successful—he had one of those high-end credit cards, didn't he, Ninette?"

"That's nobody's business, Charlotte," Ninette chastised.

"Well, he did, I saw it. But no wife, no family? And he didn't set off my gaydar. Trust me, there's a story."

Maggie raised her eyebrows. "You know about 'gaydar'?"

"I doff my cap to the Internet."

Maggie excused herself from dinner prep to set the table. At five, the guests assembled for happy hour. Tug mixed Sazeracs, and Kyle once again helped serve.

"Oooh, milady would love a refill," piped up Beverly Clabber, who was buzzing from the first round Maggie had delivered to her mere moments before. She gave her husband a flirtatious poke in the ribs. "What about you, milord?" Hal Clabber grunted what sounded like a yes.

"At the rate those two are inhaling food and beverage, we'll be lucky if we break even on them," Maggie muttered to her father as he mixed the couple's second round. He put a finger to his lips, simultaneously shushing her and suppressing a smile.

Ninette stuck her head in from the kitchen. "Dinner's ready."

A loud clap of thunder startled everyone, and then the skies opened. Rain poured down outside and was hurled against the house by wind gusts. The lights flickered for a moment but then regained their power.

"Fantastic," Cutie president Jan enthused. "Nothing like a Cajun Country summer storm."

Fortunately, despite the initial noisy thunderclap, the storm wasn't as close as it seemed, although Maggie could tell it was heading their way. As they dined, the guests filled each other in on their day's activities. Hal Clabber never said a word, and welcome as his silence was, Maggie began to wonder if something might be wrong with him. Gran' also seemed to notice the change in his behavior.

"Mr. Clabber, you're awfully quiet tonight," she said. The man responded with a grunt.

"Hal's not feeling great," Beverly explained. "The humidity here really gets to him."

"Why don't we have our liqueurs in the front parlor?" Gran' suggested. "It's a bit cooler there."

"Thanks, but we need to get our boys to bed," Carrie Ryker said. Her sons groaned and protested, while their sister snarked her refrain about how embarrassing her entire family was.

"And if it's okay, we're gonna take it to our room," Shane Butler said. Emily entwined her fingers with her husband's. The couple's lust for each other was starting to annoy Maggie, who wouldn't have admitted to her best friend that it had been more than a year since she'd even made out with someone.

The Rykers and Butlers took off, and the Crozats herded the rest of the guests into the front parlor. The storm was moving closer to Pelican, with less and less time between lightning strikes and thunder booms. Maggie could tell that some of the guests were feeling jittery. After about fifteen minutes of forced small talk, all conversation petered out. Maggie chose a soothing classical playlist from the bed and breakfast's iPod, hoping it would distract everyone, but with the storm practically on top of Crozat, even she felt edgy.

"It's not a hurricane, is it?" Suzy asked after a particularly loud boom.

"No, just a typical summer storm," Tug said with a reassuring smile. Suddenly, a fierce crackle and loud explosion of sound made everyone jump, and Crozat went completely dark. The room filled with chatter from the nervous guests.

"It's okay, we have a generator. It'll come on any minute," Maggie called to everyone. But the generator didn't come on, and the guests stumbled around in the dark.

"Dad, what's wrong?" she asked as Tug pulled out backup flashlights that she quickly distributed.

"I don't know. I'll go take a look." Tug left to check on the generator while Ninette and Gran' helped the guests with their flashlights. Georgia One held his under his chin and made a face.

"Arghgh, I'm a zombie."

"Dude, that's awesome," Georgia Two said as he and Three broke out laughing.

"Stop it, that's not funny," Jan snapped.

"Arghggh."

"I said stop it."

"That wasn't me, I swear," Georgia One replied. Maggie flashed her light around the guests and finally landed on Hal Clabber, whose face was purple and hideously distorted. Angela and Suzy screamed, as did Hal's wife Beverly.

"Hal!"

"Arghgh," Hal choked out. Then his eyes rolled to the back of his head, an enormous shudder engulfed his body, and he did a face plant to the floor.

"Everyone, out of the way," Kyle ordered the others, who drew back but didn't leave the room, frozen in either fear or fascination. Kyle dropped to his knees, flipped Hal over, and began performing CPR.

Maggie grabbed the phone and dialed 911. "Help! I'm calling from Crozat, we have a very sick guest."

"Tug, Tug!" Ninette yelled to her husband, who raced back into the house. Moments later, an ambulance roared up to the front of Crozat. Two EMTs ran in and took over from Kyle, but it became clear that lifesaving measures were unnecessary because there was no life to save.

"Hal, Hal!" Mrs. Clabber cried. She grabbed Maggie and drew blood as she dug her long nails into Maggie's wrist. "My pills, in my purse, I need my pills."

Being that Beverly was the kind of woman who never strayed too far from her handbag, it was dangling from a purse holder she'd attached to a nearby lamp table. Maggie fumbled through it and pulled out bottles of Xanax, Zoloft, and Abilify. *No wonder she's always smiling*, Maggie thought, then snapped out of it and handed the bottles to Beverly. The woman's hands shook as she tried to open them.

"Here, let me help." Maggie opened the bottles, and Beverly grabbed them from her. She quickly choked down several pills.

"Wait, you need water." Maggie, guided by her flashlight, found a water carafe on the bar and poured a tall glass. "Here, Mrs. Clabber."

Beverly grabbed the glass with one hand. Then she clutched her chest with the other.

"My heart," she gasped. Then Beverly made an awful choking noise, frothed at the mouth, and collapsed onto the floor next to the late Mr. Clabber. The EMTs instantly switched their focus to her, but it was obvious that the task was equally hopeless. Mrs. Clabber was as dead as her husband. As the EMTs notified the coroner's office, a dazed Maggie realized something.

Beverly Clabber had finally stopped smiling.

Chapter Four

Given Police Chief Rufus Durand's usual slothful gait, it was surprising how fast he and a few of his officers showed up at Crozat.

"Probably to revel in our bad luck," Maggie muttered to Gran' as Tug filled Ru in on the Clabbers' deaths. After discovering that the main house's blackout had been caused by bad fuses and not the storm, Tug restored power. Meanwhile, Ninette tended to the guests in the kitchen. Liquor calmed all of them fairly quickly, helped by the fact that no one really knew or liked the Clabbers, so the general emotion was a surface shock rather than deep sorrow. The Butlers, who'd come downstairs to get flashlights, joined the others around the kitchen's large oak table and were filled in on the night's startling events, as were Carrie and Lachlan Ryker. The Clabbers' simultaneous demise was rapidly turning into the kind of bizarre story that would elevate each guest's vacation anecdotes way above a friend's routine stories.

"Tape off this room and the one where the Clabbers were staying," Ru instructed a rookie officer, as the couple was bagged and loaded onto the coroner's gurneys. "I don't want anyone touching anything until the coroner's report comes back."

"Good heavens, you're being rather dramatic, Ru," Gran' said. "It's tragic those poor people died, but do you really need to turn this into some television episode?"

"Just doing my job, ma'am. Two people dying within minutes of each other could be some kind of crazy coincidence. Or it could be something else."

"What, like murder?" Maggie scoffed. Ru didn't say no and Maggie got a sick feeling in her stomach.

"Stop it, Magnolia," Gran' reprimanded her. "You're being as ridiculous as he is."

"Man, I am working up a powerful thirst here," Ru said as he leaned against a wall and watched his underlings scurry around Crozat.

"Tug, why don't you mix Rufus a Sazerac?" Grand-mère said.

Tug didn't respond, but he fixed a drink for Rufus and handed it to him without a word. Rufus took a swig, closed his eyes, and nodded. "Yeah, that's right good. You keep mixing Sazzies like this and Crozat might come back from the Katrina dead."

Maggie resisted the urge to grab Ru's drink and dump it on his head. She noticed her father clenching and unclenching his fists and hastened to change the subject before either he or she exploded. "Are your guys going to take much longer, Ru? It's been a rough night for all of us."

Rufus held out his glass for a refill. Tug mixed him a fresh drink, and then the police chief motioned for Gran', Tug, and Maggie to follow him out of the room and onto the veranda. The worst of the storm had passed, but a light rain still fell.

"Now, Maggie here happened to mention murder," Ru said as he chomped on an ice cube. Maggie winced. She could never understand how people enjoyed chewing up something that cold and hard. Rufus addressed Gran'. "You may be right, Mrs. Crozat. Me and Maggie may be making a big deal over nothing. On the other hand, what kind of law enforcement officer would I be if I didn't at least pursue that avenue of investigation?"

"This is outrageous," Gran' fumed. "There hasn't been a murder at Crozat in over a hundred years. Well, that we know of. Frederick Crozat was found hanging from one of the oak trees around the turn of the old century, but they never did determine whether that was suicide or Arvin Johnson taking revenge for Fredrick bedding his mistress."

"My concern is the Clabbers," Rufus said. "I'm gonna get the coroner's office to put a rush on the autopsies. In the meantime, no one leaves Pelican until we interview every last guest, and that could take some time seeing as how shorthanded we are at Pelican PD."

"What?" Maggie exclaimed as Tug groaned and buried his head in his hands. "You sonuva—"

"Maggie," her father warned.

Gran' pulled herself up to what was left of her full height, having shrunk by four inches over the years. Still, with heels, she managed to be eye-to-eye with Rufus, who skimmed 5'6" on a good day. "If this is standard procedure, that's one thing, young man," Gran' said. "But if you're milking it to make trouble for us, that is just plain bad manners."

"Thanks to budget cuts, we genuinely do have a personnel shortage at the station, ma'am," Rufus responded. "But I'd be lying if I said I wasn't enjoying this a little."

"You are a giant, steaming—"

"*Maggie*," Tug said, his tone sharper.

"It's all right, Mr. Crozat," Rufus said. "I'll chalk it up to the situation. But like I said before, I got a job to do. Right, Maggie?"

She ignored Rufus, and he took off in his squad car, kicking up dust and gravel. But Maggie knew he had a point. And she also realized Ru was brighter than she usually gave him credit for.

"Well, I guess I better break it to our visitors," Tug said.

"I'd be surprised if any of them were terribly upset," Gran' said. "Especially if they'll be staying gratis."

"Gran', we can't afford to do that," Maggie protested.

"We can't afford not to, chère. How can we charge them for a vacation spent being grilled by the likes of Rufus Durand? Yes, it will cost us, but if our guests make a disgruntled departure, it will hurt us more in the long run when they post unflattering comments on all the travel websites."

"I think you're right," Ninette said. She turned to Tug. "I don't see any other way around this, do you?"

Her husband pursed his lips and shook his head no.

Tug assembled everyone in the parlor and filled the guests in on the police chief's request for their continued presence, leaving out the possibility of murder. Initially, there were a few complaints. "Maybe we should see if they fixed the plumbing at Belle Grove," Angela groused to Jan and the other Cuties.

Gran' jumped in before anyone could respond. "Even if they did, this is Louisiana, honey. Lord knows when they'll get rid of the mold or its awful smell." She turned up the charm as she addressed all the guests. "Y'all seem like such lovely people and I do believe that once we get past this tragedy, you'll have a stay at Crozat that's memorable for the right reasons. I know this experience was not on anyone's itineraries, so we want to make it up to y'all. The rest of your stay will be entirely complimentary. That means a week of beverages, hospitality, and home-cooked meals on us."

That silenced the grumblers. The guests, now bonded by what had become an adventure—and a free one at that—commiserated with each other about the shocking turn the evening had taken. A few made shared plans for the morning and exchanged supportive hugs before retiring to their rooms. Only Kyle remained behind.

"Your offer is extremely generous," he told the Crozats, "but I'd rather book a moldy room at Belle Grove than take you up on it. I'll be paying for my stay." The family protested, but Kyle ignored them and walked out of the room.

"What a kind man," Ninette said.

"He's awesome," Maggie agreed.

Tug smiled at his daughter. "Am I picking up on something?"

"God, no."

"He's not her type," Gran' said. She'd traded her highball glass for a wine goblet. "Too stable. Maggie prefers a man who's a hot mess."

"Oh, nice, Gran'," Maggie shot at her. "And by the way, men aren't called hot messes, just women."

"Not according to urbandictionary-dot-com."

"That's it, I'm cutting off your Internet access."

"Enough, you two," Tug admonished them. "We have bigger problems to solve than Maggie's love life. I don't like what Rufus Durand was intimating."

"It doesn't make sense," Ninette said. "Why would anyone want to kill them, especially poor Mrs. Clabber?"

"I know," Maggie agreed. "I can see people lining up to take a whack at him, but her . . ."

"Maggie, honey," her mother said, "the man may have been a terror, but he is gone. We should show some respect."

"Ugh, Mom, that's so old-fashioned. Why should we show respect to someone who didn't deserve it? Shouldn't respect be earned? Even posthumously? He was a nasty old coot, and I'm not going to say differently just because he's dead."

"Hey, don't you talk to your mother like that," Tug scolded Maggie.

"It's all right, we're all tired," Ninette said with a sigh. "I'm going to bed."

"I am too," Gran' said and followed behind her daughter-in-law.

As soon as the women were gone, Tug focused on Maggie. "You need to be more sensitive to your mother's health,

Magnolia. Stress can make a body do bad things, and with two guests dying plus us having to float the other ones, that's one big bag of stress."

"You're right." Maggie was filled with remorse. "I'm so sorry. That was totally thoughtless of me. I'll do anything I can to help, Dad. And as soon as things are normal around here, I'm going to work on building up my souvenir business, see if I can get more plantations to sell my stuff. Including ours. Gran' has to get over thinking it's 'déclassé' to shill our own merchandise."

Tug looked at her, amused. "Shill?"

"I dated a guy in the garment business when I first moved to New York. And no, he wasn't a hot mess. In fact, *he* broke up with *me*." Maggie paused. "So maybe I'm the hot mess. Or the just plain mess."

Tug opened his arms. "Come here." Maggie shared a hug with her father. Tug sighed. Then he shuddered.

Maggie drew back. "What's wrong?"

"Well . . . there's something I didn't want to mention in front of your mom. Did you happen to notice that the main house was the only one that went dark tonight? When I checked the generator gas line, I saw that it'd been turned off. And I swear I changed those fuses just about a month ago, but the ones that blew were old and worn out. And not even the brand I buy."

Maggie was silent as she digested what Tug was saying.

"Look, maybe I'm the one who's being dramatic," Tug said. "It's late, and my brain is worn out from all this. I'm going to bed. But first, I'm walking you to the shotgun. I'm sure the Clabbers' deaths are nothing more than a tragic result of old age and health issues, but I don't want to take any chances. If Ru's instincts are as sharp as I wish they weren't, we've got way bigger problems than a lack of cash flow."

Chapter Five

Maggie, exhausted by the traumatic events of the night before, overslept the next morning. By the time she got to breakfast, the Georgias were heading out with the Ryker family for a day of "'sploring," as Sam Ryker excitedly called it.

"We thought it was a good idea to distract the kids from those poor people's deaths," Carrie whispered to Maggie. She motioned to Georgia One, who was pretend-wrestling with Luke. "Even the big kids."

Jan Robbins, in her role as Cajun Cuties president, opted not to let the passing of two people she barely knew and liked even less upend her group's agenda. She even convinced Kyle to join the Cuties on a tour of local plantations. "We're checking out some new ones for our convention next year," Jan explained. "We're also going to the African American Museum in St. Martinville." The other Cuties simultaneously nodded agreement as if they were one person. Shane and Emily debated joining the tour group but then opted to stay at Crozat and enjoy some R and R, which Maggie assumed was code for making love.

She had to admit that she was a little jealous of how much sex the couple was having.

"If you'd like, I can pack y'all a picnic lunch," Ninette offered as she entered with a plate of steaming hot beignets. The Cuties brightened, but Kyle demurred. "Lunch is on me, ladies."

"You won't catch any of us saying no to that," Jan said, while the other Cuties once again nodded. They reminded Maggie of the three little maids from Gilbert and Sullivan's *The Mikado*.

"I'm happy to at least pack you a snack," Ninette said.

"No," Kyle responded firmly. "You've got enough going on right now. I'll take care of everything."

Maggie realized Kyle's generosity was inspired by his sensitivity to the expenses the Crozats would be racking up. *He's a catch*, she thought to herself. *Almost too good to be true.* She shook her head as if to erase the thought, upset that recent events were making her unfairly suspicious.

"If anyone's interested, there's also the eleven a.m. Mass at St. Theresa's," Gran' shared as she shook powdered sugar onto a hot beignet. "I may not have liked the Clabbers, but it would be terribly rude not to pray for them. You're coming, aren't you, Maggie?"

"Yes, Gran'." Maggie cleared the table, ran the dishwasher, and then dressed for Mass. Since her wardrobe consisted mostly of T-shirts and jeans, a scoop-neck teal rayon top and black pencil skirt was the best she could do. She flipped the camera on her phone to do a quick inventory. Slim build but with an "ample bosom," as Gran' would say, hair the color of burnt sienna that fell a few inches below her shoulders, a smattering of youthful freckles on the bridge of her upturned nose that contrasted with the fine lines around her eyes. Maggie didn't completely hate what looked back at her, although she would always be bugged by the fact that her 5'4" height, once deemed average, had been reclassified as petite.

As much as she would have preferred to wear the comfy Converse high-tops that she had personalized with quirky drawings, she strapped on a pair of black platform sandals and headed outside. Since her mom, dad, and Gran' had already left in the family sedan, she climbed into the Falcon. Jan honked from the Cuties' minivan. "We're going to Mass before we hit the plantations," she yelled. "We're practically locals now, huh, Kyle?" Jan clapped Kyle, who'd been awarded the front seat, so hard on the shoulder that he flinched, and the Cuties took off behind the Crozats.

*

As Maggie motored toward St. Theresa of Avila Catholic Church, she pondered how best to deal with the Clabbers' passing. The Crozats were in a tough spot. They had to find the right balance between what they owed their guests and what they owed their late guests. A memorial—that's what the situation called for. She'd ask Father Prit if he'd lead a memorial for the Clabbers. That would give everyone closure and allow her to help Crozat's visitors formulate some guilt-free postmemorial tourism plans. This might even create the positive press that the family desperately needed, although Maggie couldn't stop herself from imagining a travel website review that read, "Some nasty old fart and his weird wife died, but the airboat swamp tour was awesome."

She made a mental note to check with Pelican PD in the morning and see if the department had tracked down any Clabber relatives who could share whatever plans the couple had made for shuffling off their mortal coil. At the risk of being insensitive, the sooner they headed to their final resting place, the sooner those at Crozat could move on with their lives.

Maggie pulled into the church parking lot, which was already full of vehicles ranging from brand-new Mercedes to decades-old pickup trucks. St. Theresa's served a tiny parish with a wide range of parishioners. There were Cajun descendants of the Acadians driven from Canada in the mid-eighteenth century by Le Grand Derangement, and Caucasian and African Creole families that could trace their Louisiana lineage back almost three hundred years. More recently, St. Theresa's had welcomed the Vietnamese fishermen and their families who now called Pelican home.

Maggie walked into Saint Tee's, as the locals called it, and settled into the Crozat family pew, inhaling the chapel's unique fragrance of old wood combined with generations of gardenia perfume. Lia slid in next to her. She folded her long legs to one side and adjusted her flowing tangerine summer dress so that it covered them. "How are you doing after last night?" she asked.

Maggie shrugged. "We're okay. There's not much we can do until we hear the results of the autopsy. Oh God, saying that, it really hit me. Those poor people are dead."

Lia put a comforting hand on Maggie's knee. Maggie squeezed it back. Father Prit Vangloo began the service, which was unintelligible to most of his parishioners. Originally from New Delhi, he'd brought a thick accent with him when he came to America barely a year before. Pelican knew its parish was too small to rate an American or even an Irish priest, so they welcomed Father Prit, who was kind and giggled like a besotted schoolgirl whenever he talked about Pope Francis, whom he idolized. Parishioners eventually came up with a way to handle his poor pronunciation. "We just pretend he's leading a Latin Mass," Gran' explained. Maggie, who'd met her share of Sikh cab drivers in New York, had little problem understanding the good Father and often found herself pulled into post-Mass conversations to subtly translate.

Ever the papal fanboy, Father Prit's homily focused on the pontiff's familiar themes of humility and service to those less fortunate. Maggie prayed that the Clabbers had found peace, or at least less to complain about, wherever they ended up. The choir sang, the service ended, and the attendees all poured into the parish hall, where the Hospitality Committee had laid out a postservice spread that was the envy of every church in the area. Tables were piled high with fruits, homemade pies and pastries, and traditional local treats like boudin and fried oysters.

Maggie noticed Kyle staring at the spread. "I've got paralysis of choice," Kyle told her. "I don't know where to begin."

"I'll make it easy for you," Maggie said. She pointed to a beautifully arranged tray of pastries. "These were made by my cousin Lia, the best pastry chef and candy maker in Louisiana, and possibly the world. Lia, come here."

Lia, who was nodding and pretending to understand as Father Prit pontificated about something, excused herself and came over to Maggie. "Lia, Kyle. Kyle, Lia," Maggie said. And in the moment the two shared shy hellos, the electricity between them was so palpable that Maggie could feel it. Even Gran', busy arranging the buffet, glanced up, drawn by the charge. The only thing missing was a chorus of angels or cartoon characters with their eyes popping out on springs as the bubble over their heads read "boooinnng!" A line from Shakespeare's *Twelfth Night*, which Maggie hadn't read since sophomore year of high school, popped into her head: Kyle and Lia "no sooner looked but they loved."

"Lia, you must make a plate of your incomparable delicacies for Kyle," said Gran'. "Oh Maggie, look, there's Renee Harper." Gran' practically yanked Maggie away from Lia and Kyle, who were already so deep in conversation that they didn't notice.

"Subtle, Gran'," Maggie said. She started toward Renee, but Gran' pulled her back.

"Stop, Renee will see you."

"I thought you wanted to say hello."

"Oh Lord, no. I just wanted to get us out of the way so that whatever was sparking between Lia and Kyle could catch fire. That Renee Harper is a Glossy if there ever was one." Gran' had coined the term *Glossy* as a sarcastic loose acronym for Gracious Ladies of the South. "I notice that Jim Harper isn't with her. Too bad. That's one man who could use a little church-bred humility. But no, as usual, God has to play second fiddle to Jim's 'busy schedule.'"

"That's not very Christian of you," Maggie teased her grandmother.

"We're not Christians, we're Catholics, and we can say whatever we want because we get to confess. Now, let's find your parents, I'm ready to go."

Maggie and Gran' located Ninette and Tug next to the punch bowl, where they were being peppered with questions from locals eager for gossip about the recent deaths at Crozat.

"Honestly, that's all we know right now," Tug told the group, which dispersed disappointed at the lack of news.

Ninette downed her glass of punch. "I've never wished this was hard punch more than I do today," she said as she dabbed the slight sheen on her face with a tissue.

"I happen to know where there's a full bar," Gran' said. "Home again, home again, jiggity jig." She blew an air kiss to Maggie and led the others to their car.

Maggie snacked a bit more and then made her way to the Falcon, where she was less than thrilled to find Ru Durand, dressed in uniform, waiting.

"Hey, Ru. I didn't see you at Mass."

"I couldn't make it. The Lord chose to make it a work day for me instead."

Jan and the Cuties, who were heading for their van, interrupted the perfunctory conversation. "I swear, every time I think I've had the best meal in Louisiana, I have another one," Angela said.

"Oh, that is so true," Suzy echoed.

"Suze, see if you can pry Kyle away from that pretty baker," Jan instructed. "We need to get going."

"Where y'all off to?" Ru asked affably.

"Plantation tour," Jan responded gruffly. Maggie liked Jan all the more for her obvious dislike of Rufus.

"They got some beauties in Natchez, but I wouldn't advise crossing the state line into Mississippi."

"Why not?" Debbie asked, confused.

"Because you're all suspects in a murder investigation," Ru responded, his tone suddenly harsh.

The others stared at him in shock. Maggie felt her stomach start to roil and prayed she wouldn't throw up.

"The Clabbers were murdered?" Ninette gasped.

"Not both of them," Rufus said. "Mr. Clabber died of natural causes—a stroke. But Mrs. Clabber was poisoned."

Chapter Six

"Mrs. Clabber was poisoned?" Maggie repeated. "That makes no sense. He was the jerk, not her."

"Yes, she seemed lovely," Debbie interjected. "I don't think I ever saw her without a big smile on her face."

"Well, even people who smile a lot get offed," Ru shrugged and then faced Maggie. "Two people dying at the same time pushes a button for us law enforcement folk, and the coroner agreed to rush the autopsies so we could rule out any funny business. Well, what do you know, we found funny business. My men are on the way to your place to take statements and collect evidence. And thanks to you Crozats, since it's Sunday, I gotta pay overtime."

"What do you mean, 'thanks to us Crozats'?" Maggie snapped. "Trust me, Rufus, when you're running a B and B, having guests murdered pretty much falls last on the list of 'fun local activities.'" Maggie took in a calming breath; she'd been taking a lot of those lately. "Would it be okay if you interviewed us Crozats first, plus anyone who's at the house, so that these folks could see a plantation or two before they're interrogated?" Maggie asked in her most conciliatory voice as she gestured to the Cuties and Kyle who, sensing something was wrong, had joined the group.

"Well, my goodness, I wouldn't want to let a gruesome death interfere with a day of sightseeing," Rufus said, his mock concern showing the glimmer of acting ability that had won him a lead or two in Pelican Players Community Theatre productions.

"If the ladies and I consent to have our rooms searched while we're gone, maybe you could send one of your men in the van with us to take our statements," Kyle offered.

"And while he's there, maybe he can take some group shots of y'all in front of Oak Alley that you can post online." Rufus shook his head. "The answer is nope. And if you got any complaints about the change in today's—or this week's—schedule, I suggest you take it up with management." Rufus gestured to Maggie. The universe had unexpectedly gifted him with an opportunity to make life miserable for the Crozats, and he seemed determined to take advantage of it.

"Look, Rufus, it's really not fair to drag our guests into whatever issues you have with my family. None of them even knew the Clabbers."

"Well, someone at Crozat knew 'em well enough to murder one of 'em."

"That's just an assumption. Anyone who knew the Clabbers were staying with us could've snuck in and planted the poison."

"Doesn't say much for your security, does it?" Rufus turned to the Cuties. "I'd lock up my valuables while I was staying at Crozat if I was you." Rufus turned back to Maggie. "And I should point out that you were the one who handed Mrs. Clabber the pills that probably killed her. You're lucky I know you well enough to know that you don't have the clankers to murder someone."

"I'm both insulted and relieved."

"Sorry, Maggie, but until my men prove someone isn't a suspect, everyone is a suspect."

Maggie couldn't bring herself to admit that Rufus had a point, so she didn't say anything. Rufus doffed his hat. "See you at Crozat." Then Rufus got into his police car and gunned it, spraying the minivan with dirt and pebbles as he peeled out of the parking lot.

"Your police chief may be a giant pain, but he's right about all of us being suspects," Jan said through pursed lips as her Cutie cohorts exchanged nervous looks.

"I know," Maggie said. "I just hate letting him know that."

"Well, there's one bright spot," Kyle said. "At least he won't be taking our statements. It's not his job. That's up to the department detectives."

Maggie brightened. "You're right. And in Pelican, it's department detective, singular—Henry 'Buster' Belloise. As skeevy as Rufus is, that's how decent Buster is. We'll be okay."

The Cuties hoisted themselves into the minivan. Kyle gave a longing look to Lia, who was busy replenishing dishes that had been emptied of her treats, and then he got behind the wheel. Maggie followed the minivan out of the parking lot. She was relieved to know the case was in the steady hands of Buster Belloise, so relieved that she could afford to feel magnanimous toward Ru. He was right—this was hardly the time to negotiate a sightseeing tour.

*

Maggie arrived at Crozat to find it a buzz of police activity. The department's mobile evidence van sat at the end of the driveway close to the house. Maggie couldn't remember when she'd seen it used for anything besides hauling a float in the town's yearly Mardi Gras parade.

She bounded up the steps into the house, where the front parlor and the Clabbers' bedroom were closed off with police tape. It would take a while to comb through the plantation for evidence since the Pelican police department was small, and usually the most serious crime it handled was the occasional domestic disturbance. The department could use some outside help for the Clabber case to speed up the process, but Maggie knew that was a fantasy given the reality of budgetary restrictions coupled with Rufus Durand's ego and how much he relished seeing the Crozats twist in the wind.

Maggie found Gran' in the kitchen plying Buster Belloise with snacks and sweets. The large belly hanging over Buster's policy duty belt was testament to some good Cajun living.

"Oh, there you are, darlin'," Gran' greeted Maggie. "You want some sweet tea?"

"Thanks, Gran', I'm okay."

"What about you, Buster? You want a refill?" Gran' posed the question with a hint of flirtation. Gran' could Glossy it up with the best of them when she wanted to, and Maggie was relieved to see that she was bringing her Southern belle A game to the conversation with Buster.

"Oh, you know I can't turn down a refill of your sweet tea, ma'am." Buster offered his glass, and Gran' filled it with one hand while adding some petit fours to his plate with the other.

"So Buster can't tell us too much about the investigation," Gran' said.

"Can't compromise it, ma'am."

"My dear man, we wouldn't want you to. But he did very kindly share the means by which poor Mrs. Clabber met her unpleasant end."

"Arsenic," Buster said, or at least that's what Maggie thought he said, since he'd stuffed his mouth with petit fours before speaking. "I can't reveal how it was administered, but the coroner was able to determine that it was of an old variety not readily available these days. We've got a couple of our men searching the plantation, looking for a possible source."

"Arsenic," Maggie repeated. The word jogged a memory, but she couldn't zero in on it.

"Buster's also been taking statements, and he couldn't have been more pleasant given what a terribly difficult position he's in, as a friend of the family." Gran' graced the officer with one of her best grand dame smiles, and he blushed with pride. The Belloise family was and always had been working to lower class, and nineteenth century as it seemed, being treated as an equal by a local aristocrat like Gran' meant something to Buster. Which, of course, Gran' knew and played to.

Maggie helped herself to a chocolate croissant from the large assortment of desserts. "Boy, Buster, I can't tell you how glad we are that you're taking the lead on this case."

"Wish I were, ma'am, but I'm not."

Maggie stopped midbite. "What? You're not? Why not?"

"I'm retiring at the end of the week."

"*Retiring?*" Maggie put down the croissant. She'd lost her appetite.

"Really, Buster? Why, we had no idea, no idea at all. How wonderful for you. Isn't that wonderful, Maggie? Just wonderful." Gran' was doing her best to cover her surprise with effusive charm, but she was as thrown by the news as Maggie.

"Yeah, I'm just here because Rufus asked me to take the lead until they could rush in my replacement from Shreveport. The guy is due here any minute. Wasn't expecting to start on a Sunday. Could I bother you for some more tea?"

"Why, it's no bother, no bother at all," Gran' was beginning to sound a bit like a parrot. "Now, tell us all about your plans for retirement."

As Buster chatted away, Maggie evaluated the family's options. With Buster off the case, they were at the mercy of his replacement. But maybe the change would be a good thing. Whoever he was, being new to the area, it was possible that he wouldn't come with old grudges. He could provide some much-needed objectivity and impartiality. For the first time since the Clabbers had died, Maggie felt she could relax.

"Maggie, Buster and Marnie are thinking about taking a retirement trip up north to New York."

"Really? Have you ever been?"

"No, ma'am. I'd love any recommendations you have. The wife wants a show, I want a ballgame."

"Maybe you'll be lucky and they'll revive *Damn Yankees*, which was a show *about* a ballgame," Gran' quipped, and the three laughed.

"Excuse me."

Maggie, Gran', and Buster looked up to see a tall, slim man leaning against the doorframe. His pale skin provided an unusual contrast to his dark hair and coal-dark eyes. Bedroom eyes, Gran' would call them—a little hooded and sleepy looking. But sexy—definitely sexy. His coloring was unique for a man, but it worked on him. And he *was* a man. There was nothing boy-child about him, the curse of so many guys Maggie had hooked up with back in New York. Where she could imagine all those old boyfriends pushing her aside to escape a burning building, this was someone she could see running in, throwing her over his shoulder, and then casually flipping off the fire on his way out. The image was a definite turn-on.

The man looked vaguely familiar to Maggie. *Probably because he resembles some movie star*, she thought, *but which one?*

"I'm sorry to interrupt," the man continued, "but I'm looking for Captain Durand."

Buster stood and walked toward the man. "You're close. I'm Detective Belloise. Can I help you?"

The man pulled out a badge, flashed it, and then extended his hand. "Paul Durand, but everyone calls me Bo. I believe I'm your replacement."

"Well, hey, welcome to Pelican," Buster gave Bo's hand a hearty shake. He eyed the newcomer. "I feel like I know you. We must've met before at some law enforcement function."

Bo smiled a lazy grin, and Maggie couldn't help noticing that his teeth were as perfect as a male model's. "We may have," Bo acknowledged, his voice deep yet mellifluous, his accent showing the twang that came with living close to the Texas border. "But I'm guessing I look familiar because I remind you of Rufus. I'm his first cousin."

Chapter Seven

When Maggie was eight, Grand-père Crozat shared an age-old joke with her: What's worse than finding a worm in your apple? Finding *half* a worm. He told it because she had just lived the joke. After taking a huge bite of a crispy, sweet apple, she noticed only half a worm in its flesh. She never thought she'd feel as horrified and sickened in her life again.

Then Maggie discovered that the handsome newcomer, the man who instantly made her body feel things that it hadn't felt in way too long a time, was related to Rufus Durand, and she felt worse. But the news was also the slap in the face she needed. It was like falling in love with a gorgeous dress but then seeing its ridiculously expensive price tag and instantly falling out of love. The price on Bo Durand was way too high.

She forced herself to check back into the conversation.

"We've got a couple of guys bagging and tagging evidence and taking statements and prints," Buster was telling Bo.

Bo nodded and then gestured to Gran' and Maggie. "Have we gotten prints or statements from these ladies yet?"

Buster flushed with embarrassment. The tea and snack repast had registered with Bo. It was obvious to Maggie that under the man's relaxed charm was one sharp detective.

"Uh, no, not yet, I was easing into that," Buster said.

"I know we can be tight-asses up in Shreveport, but we're not big on 'easing' into a murder investigation. Get what we need from these ladies—"

"Excuse me, we are not 'these ladies.' We have names, sir," Gran' said in a tone that had brought better men than Bo Durand to their knees. "I am Charlotte LeBlanc Crozat—Mrs. Crozat to you—and this is my granddaughter, Magnolia Marie Crozat."

Gran' glared at Bo, who smiled his lazy smile, completely unfazed. "Nice to meet y'all. Please cooperate with Detective Belloise and answer all of his questions to the best of your ability." With that, Bo turned and left.

"Really, has there ever been a Durand who had anything resembling manners?" Gran' took a bottle of bourbon off the kitchen counter, poured a shot into her sweet tea, and then offered the bottle to Buster, who hesitated. "We won't tell," Gran' cooed.

That's all Buster needed to hear. He gratefully took the bottle, spiked his own drink, and then took out a pad and pen. "Well . . . I guess we best get started."

Maggie and Gran' spent half an hour being printed and giving statements, and then Gran' retreated to recover in her room while Maggie went to check on her parents. As she passed the front parlor, she saw that investigators were using a photo from Georgia One's cell phone of the Clabbers lying dead on the room's priceless rug to recreate an outline of Hal and Beverly. Georgia One had scored; when he posted the picture on a social media website, he could brag about how important it was to a murder investigation.

She found Ninette and Tug outside by the generator gas line with Bo, who was examining it. Buster had made his way there too and was hovering over the new detective.

Bo shined a flashlight on the line. "Yeah, I'd say this was tampered with."

"Sure looks like it to me," Buster echoed.

Bo turned to him. "Make sure the evidence techs dust for prints and get pictures of this. Of the fuse box, too. And have them bag the fuses."

"Yes, sir." Buster's tone was so officious that Maggie thought he might actually salute Bo, but instead he scurried off to make himself useful.

"It's lunchtime and I'm sure everyone's starving," Ninette said. "Would it be all right if I fixed something for my guests? And your people, too, of course."

"Normally I'd have my people fend for themselves," Bo said. "But being that it's my first day on the job, I'll go with making a good first impression, so sure."

"Thank you." Ninette, who found great comfort in cooking, gave the hint of a smile. It was all she could muster, given the circumstances. Maggie was worried by how wan her mother looked. The fine lines on her faced seemed to have deepened, and she'd dropped weight from her already too-slim frame.

"I'll help, chère." Tug put a protective arm around his wife's shoulder and led her back to the house. Maggie was about to follow when Gopher wobbled up to Bo and gave a deep, territorial bark.

"Gopher, quiet," she scolded him.

"It's okay. Hey, buddy." Bo gave the old dog a pet. He kneeled down, took a long Basset ear in each hand, and rubbed them. "How about some ear love, huh?" Gopher gave up his alpha dog act and moaned with pleasure. Then he fell on his back, paws straight up in the air, begging for a belly scratch. Bo obliged with a brisk rub.

"You don't have to do that," Maggie said. "Once you start, he won't let you stop. He's going to follow you around the rest of the day."

"Not a problem," Bo said. "I had a Basset. My wife got him in the divorce. It was okay, my son's pretty attached to Beignet. But I miss him. The dog. And my son. Of course I miss my son."

"Beignet? That's a great name for a dog."

"When he was a pup, he got into a bag of 'em." Bo finished Gopher's tummy rub and stood up. "So I hear you're to blame for my marriage breaking up."

Maggie stared at him. "I'm sorry—what?"

"The curse your family put on us, damning all of our relationships."

There it was. The curse that turned the Durands and the Crozats into the Louisiana version of the Hatfields and McCoys.

The Crozats managed to reinvent themselves after the Civil War and, if not prosper, at least survive reasonably comfortably. The Durands, however, degenerated into low-rent victims who blamed hard luck on everyone but themselves. And they especially blamed it on the Crozats—because the swinish former fiancé of Magnolia Marie Crozat, the man she was rumored to have put a curse on in the mid-1800s, was none other than Henri Durand, the great-great-great-grandfather of Rufus. And Bo.

Bo smiled slightly. Was he making fun of the curse? Was he serious? Maggie didn't know him well enough to tell.

"I'm sorry about your divorce," she said, "but I really don't think you can hold some nineteenth-century hocus pocus responsible for whatever happened."

Gopher started barking again, this time with genuine anger. The target of his wrath, Rufus Durand, came around the corner of the house. It was a steamy day, the kind that made sweat pour off some people, and Ru was one of those people. He glared at Gopher, who barked even louder.

"Gopher, shush," Maggie said, reaching to pet and calm him.

"I'm looking forward to the day when I find that mutt loose and can ship him off to the pound," Ru said. "Hey, Coz, glad you made it okay. I'm guessing you met the Crozat clan by now. If they give you any trouble, just let me know."

"So far they've been very helpful," Bo said as he shook Ru's hand. "Thanks again for working out my transfer. I owe you."

"I'll remember that. What's the line from that movie, *The Godfather*? 'Someday I may ask you to do me a favor.' Or something like that." Ru turned to Maggie. "Bo's ex remarried and the guy got a job on one of the rigs, so they moved down this way with his son, Xander. I got Bo Buster's job so he could be closer to his boy."

"That was really nice of you," she said with genuine sincerity.

"Family is number one, as I'm sure you Crozats know." Rufus gave Bo a poke in the ribs. "So remember the family that brought you here . . . and the family that brought your marriage down in the first place."

Rufus gestured for Bo to follow him back into the house. As soon as they left, Maggie groaned and threw herself on the grass next to Gopher. "Can you believe that idiot, Goph? If there was ever an excuse for a poisoning by arsenic—"

She bolted up from the ground, her memory jogged. She knew where she'd seen arsenic before. She sauntered slowly away from the main house, and then as soon as she was out of anyone's eye line, broke into a run.

Maggie was out of breath by the time she reached the plantation store. She was about to go in when she realized that she didn't have the key. "Dammit," she said, giving the door a frustrated pound. She almost fell into the store when the door unexpectedly swung open. She checked the door handle and lock. It didn't take a law enforcement expert to see scratches on the metal where someone had jimmied it open, something that wouldn't be too hard to do on an old door that was half off its hinges.

She stepped into the room and studied all the shelves until she found what she was looking for. There were a few cleaning products left on a shelf once dedicated to them, all covered with dust. But there was also a clean, empty rectangle. Clean because someone had taken the product that had been sitting there untouched for eighty years—a box of rat poison with a skull-and-crossbones insignia and, in large letters, the words, "DANGER—ARSENIC."

Chapter Eight

Maggie stared at the empty spot on the shelf. All of Crozat's guests except for the Clabbers had accompanied her on the plantation tour. Any one of them—including the Ryker kids—could have easily slipped back into the old store and taken the poison. Then again, so could anyone who lived in Pelican—or who knew the area. It was like looking at one of those online maps that started in tight on a location and then widened out to Planet Earth.

A bead of sweat dripped from Maggie's forehead into her eye, stinging it. The room's air was so oppressive that it had actual weight, and she needed to escape. As she closed the door, Maggie checked to make sure no one had seen her and then headed into the woods. She kept walking until she came to an old tree stump, where she rested and contemplated her next move.

Maggie knew that she was bound by law to share this information with Bo. But he owed his job to Rufus, who could use the discovery against the Crozats. The store *was* on their

property, and the Clabbers were incredibly annoying guests—
Hal in action, Beverly by association. She could just see Ru
trying to twist that into a motivation for murder, painting it
as a crazy, last-ditch effort on the family's part to get rid of
an unwanted guest. On the other hand, there was something
about Bo that read, "I'm my own man." Maybe she should trust
him and avoid the possibility of going to jail for withholding
evidence. She'd seen enough television lawyers use this threat
against suspects to assume it happened in real life.

Maggie groaned. She desperately needed to get advice from
someone. Her parents would insist on following the proper
procedure, as would Lia. Why was she surrounded by such
decent people? Maggie got up from the stump and made her
way out of the woods. She needed someone who was comfortable occasionally making a dodgy moral choice.

*

"Hmmm," Gran' said after Maggie finished filling her in a half
hour later. The two sat in the shotgun's living room, where
a ceiling fan above them whirred at top speed, decapitating
any hapless mosquito that wandered into its blades. "Hmmm,"
Gran' said again.

"What do I do, Gran'? Do I tell, don't I tell? What do you
think?"

"I think we need to clear out our minds and give space for
the answer."

Gran' closed her eyes, as did Maggie. Both sat quietly as
the fan's hum provided a lulling white noise. While no Crozat
or Doucet ever claimed to be clairvoyant, the family did boast

well-developed intuition, a sort of sixth sense that they could tap into, given some intense focus.

After a moment, both women opened their eyes. Gran' spoke first. "I believe we can trust Bo."

"I got the same sense."

"I believe he will share the information with Rufus because he has to. But I think he's clever and fair and won't be swayed by personal obligations. If he feels he owes Ru, he can pay off the debt with a case of cheap beer. But that does not mean he'll do us any favors, especially since at the end of the day, Ru is still family and we are not."

"Yes," said Maggie. She hesitated. "My intuition is telling me that Beverly Clabber's murderer isn't some stranger who snuck in off the road."

Gran' nodded. "Mine is telling me the exact same thing. Someone at this plantation or in this town knew that woman well enough to want her dead."

"Exactly. But who? And why? She seemed like a harmless old lady."

"Well, you know, the thing about us 'old ladies,' dear, is that we've put in a lot of miles on this God-given ground, and there are sometimes events in our past that we hope time will render a distant memory at worst, or at best, erase completely. Unfortunately, there are times when that simply doesn't happen."

"We need to know more about Beverly Clabber. And you know what that means."

"Indeed I do," Gran' said gleefully. She got up, walked over to a small rococo desk, and pulled her iPad out of a drawer. "An Internet search."

"Exactly," Maggie said, pulling her own tablet out of a tote bag.

The two sat in silence, conducting separate searches for any and all information pertaining to Beverly Clabber. "I've come up with plenty of references to Harold Clabber, Conway professor, but only one mentions his wife, Beverly," Maggie said.

"That stands to reason; they were newlyweds, after all. What we need is her maiden name."

"I'll search for 'Beverly Clabber, the former . . .'" Maggie typed it into her tablet. "A post or two on a couple of social media sites and that's it. This woman had a low online profile."

"By choice or not? That's the question."

"She didn't seem the type to put effort into cleansing her Internet presence. We need her maiden name."

"And other married names," Gran' added. "Mrs. Clabber also didn't seem the type who'd stay single for eighty years. I doubt Hal was the first man to put a ring on it."

Maggie laughed. "Gran', listen to you."

"I've got a radio in my car," Gran' said. "I've heard that Beyoncé. She's good. I keep up with the kids."

"I haven't found anything remotely useful, have you?"

"I'm afraid not. I wonder if Mrs. Clabber left any clues in the Rose Room," Gran' mused.

"The police went through it pretty carefully."

Gran' waved her hand dismissively. "That would be Cal Vichet and Buster's son, Artie Belloise. And I believe the last time they CSI'd a murder scene would be never. Now if we were looking for a lost pet or someone to supervise a crew completing their court-ordered community service, they'd be our go-to fellows."

Gran' was right. Pelican PD was the kind of small-town department where all the officers did a little bit of everything, calling to mind the phrase, "Jack of all trades, master of none." It didn't help that Chief Rufus set the bar low when it came to overachieving. An enthusiastic rookie was more likely to be chastised for making his fellow officers look bad than lauded for putting in extra effort. Given their inexperience with murder scenes and the culture of indolence endemic to PPD, there was a strong possibility that Cal and Artie had missed a vital clue.

"Plus," Gran' pointed out, "neither of those boys knows how to think like an old lady."

"And how would an old lady think? Hypothetically speaking."

Gran' leaned back in her chair, iPad on her lap. "I will do my best to tap into the mind-set of a female senior citizen."

"I know it's hard, Gran', but I have faith in you."

"If that was sarcasm, it was not appreciated. Now, when a senior woman travels, it's pretty much a given that she unpacks her belongings. We are not a people who live out of our suitcase like some grad student at a youth hostel. A senior woman also tends to bring her valuables with her, not trusting them to be left at home. This can be jewels, papers, meaningful mementos. Anything important to her."

"If she decides to hide these valuables somewhere in her hotel—or B and B—room, what would she consider a great hiding place?"

"Oh, that's easy," Gran' said. "Her 'unmentionables' drawer."

"Okay, Gran', this *is* the twenty-first century, not the nineteenth—which may be the last time anyone referred to bras and underwear as 'unmentionables.'"

"Still, I would guess Beverly would consider that drawer inviolate. And I would also guess that neither Cal nor Artie would feel particularly comfortable pawing through her undergarments during their search, so they might speed through that particular task."

"Interesting."

"I'd love to see if my theory is right."

"Of course, there's no way of telling without taking a look at the room. Which is locked and off limits."

"True," Gran' stretched, then put her iPad on the desk and stood up. "I could use a little air. Why don't you keep me company? But you might want to change out of your church clothes."

Maggie went into her bedroom and changed from her skirt and clingy top into shorts and a T-shirt sporting the colorful Cooper Union logo. Then she followed Gran' outside and onto the wraparound ground-floor veranda of the main house. The older woman stopped at the French doors that allowed access into the Rose Room from the outside. Gran' glanced around to make sure she and Maggie were alone and then jiggled the door handle. It was locked, but after a few hard jiggles, the ancient latch popped open.

"Rufus wasn't wrong when he mentioned we have terrible security," Maggie said. "I think some upgrades may be in order."

"Put them on the list."

"That list is a study in deferred maintenance." Maggie pulled the doors open a few inches and peeked inside the room, which showed no sign of being a crime scene. "I wish I could take a look in those drawers. I wonder when the police will allow us to go back in."

"Why wait?" Gran' said. She gave her granddaughter a hard shove, and Maggie tumbled into the Rose Room.

"Gran', what are you doing?"

"You're in now, and if anyone asks, you can blame it on me," Gran' stage-whispered into the room, making sure to look in the opposite direction. "If you work quickly, no one will even know. I'll make myself comfortable here on the veranda so that it looks like I'm just relaxing, but I'll be on guard for you. Remember how I used to love bird watching? It made me quite good at keeping an eye out."

"But what if someone uses the inside entrance to the room instead of this one?"

Gran' gestured toward Crozat's front lawn. "I saw the police all head into that mobile van of theirs, probably for some kind of confab. I can see it from here, so if I notice anyone head into the house, I'll give you a sign. I know—I'll say, 'Go away, you awful mosquitoes.' Oh my goodness, that works on two levels, because mosquitoes are annoying and these police officers are as annoying as mosquitoes. Quite clever by accident, if I do say so—"

"Excuse me, but I've just broken into a crime scene. Can we move this along?"

"Fine. Go spy."

Maggie was dubious about following a plan concocted by a woman whose only knowledge of detection work came from 1960s *Pink Panther* movies. But given that she was already in the room, she decided to grab the chance to take a pass at it.

A quick glance around showed Cal and Art had been respectful during their search. Everything was in order and the only evidence of their presence was dust from where they'd lifted fingerprints.

Well aware of how squeaky Crozat's old floors were, Maggie tiptoed over to the room's beautifully carved walnut chest of drawers and slowly opened the top one. Since all the Clabbers' personal items had been removed as potential evidence, the drawer was empty and its lining lay flat against the bottom. She felt safe in assuming that like most women, Beverly would only have used one of the top two drawers for her undergarments. She ran her hand along the bottom of the drawer but felt nothing unusual. She closed it and opened the second drawer, which was also empty. Maggie ran her hand along its bottom and felt a slight, almost undetectable rise in the back right corner. She lifted up the lining and found a thin envelope taped to the bottom of it.

Maggie removed the envelope but resisted the urge to tear it open, knowing that her time was better spent searching the room for other clues. She didn't debate long where to look next. Maggie knew from past guests that seniors often still naïvely believed there was no better hiding place than under the bed.

She got on the floor and shimmied her way under the heavily canopied nineteenth-century bed whose intricate design matched the room's chest of drawers. She was relieved to find the area spotless. *If we survive this nightmare and ever have any extra income, Marie and Bud are getting a bonus*, she thought as she ran her hands along the ancient springs that held up the mattress, feeling for anything unusual.

"Hello."

Maggie froze, heart in her mouth. The voice was male and she knew exactly who it belonged to. She hid the envelope in the back pocket of her shorts and pulled her shirt down to cover it. Then she slowly wiggled out from under the bed and found herself staring up at Bo Durand, who was standing in the inside doorway. Maggie wondered how he'd escaped Gran's professed skill at sentry duty.

"Oh, hey," she responded as casually as possible for a woman caught on the floor of a room where she'd just conducted an illegal search. "I'm glad you're here, I was looking for you."

"Really. I don't know whether to be flattered or insulted that you thought I could fit under there."

"Well, I mean, I was *going* to look for you."

"After you finished unlawfully entering this room?"

Maggie bounced up to her feet. "Look, Mr. Big Shreveport Detective, you don't know anything about us or how this town works. Cal and Art are great guys and decent police officers, but in addition to the fact they've never actually searched a murder scene before, they, like all of Rufus's hires, are good old boys who couldn't be less interested in trying to think how a woman thinks and letting that steer their search. So I was actually trying to help you."

"Which is why you entered this room without first requesting permission."

"My grandma made me," Maggie said a little sullenly as she resorted to her last defense. This elicited a burst of laughter from Bo. "It's true."

"Oh, I don't doubt that at all. I met your grandma."

"I did find out something. Not here, but in the plantation store."

Maggie filled Bo in on her memory of where she'd seen arsenic and the empty space where it no longer sat.

"Good lead."

"Uh, you're welcome," Maggie said. She decided to dial back the sarcasm and be honest with Bo. "I know your cousin would love to see us fail with Crozat, but it's not just our home and our business—which my family desperately needs to survive, by the way—it's also a landmark, something for Pelican to be proud of. Between hurricanes and oil spills and a crappy economy, this state and this town have had such a rough time, and Crozat's survival is a tiny triumph. When we make visitors happy, they go home and tell their friends, and then more visitors come, which is good for everyone. I'm not naïve enough to ask you to help us. All I'm asking, I guess, is that you not hurt us."

Bo looked at her thoughtfully. As she waited for his response, Maggie's mind drifted to wondering how she'd blend colors to create the rich, dark-chocolate hue of his eyes. Then, annoyed at herself, she forced her attention back to the moment at hand.

"Go out the way you came in," Bo said. "I'll pretend this didn't happen. But if I ever catch you contaminating a crime scene again, I will instantly haul your ass to jail."

Bo's harsh words wiped out her dreamy reverie. She left without a word through the room's French doors, glad that she hadn't shared the envelope from the chest of drawers with him—or the gold-and-diamond ring that she'd found hidden under the bed between the mattress and the spring coils.

Chapter Nine

Later, back at the shotgun house, Maggie sat on her bed and pondered the brochures in her lap. After Bo booted her out of the Rose Room, she'd stepped onto the veranda and found Gran' fast asleep. *So much for standing guard,* Maggie thought. She didn't have the heart to wake her grandmother, so she returned home alone, put on a pair of gloves, and carefully opened the envelope she'd found in Beverly Clabber's drawer.

Unfortunately, the only gloves available were Gran's elbow-length black evening gloves, which were warm on a ninety-degrees-plus day. But the last thing Maggie needed was to be busted for tampering with evidence, so damp hands were a small price to pay if it meant she wouldn't leave fingerprints on anything. Her plan was to make copies of both the envelope's contents and the ring, and then replace everything once the Rose Room was reopened, trusting that the Shexnayders would uncover the items during one of their meticulous cleaning rounds and turn them over to the police.

The envelope contained two brochures. One was for McDonough Castle in Perthshire, Scotland, and the other was for a quasi castle—technically a "country home," the brochure explained—in the Gloucestershire county of England. Both had been kitted out as luxury hotels. *Nice life where you can afford these places,* Maggie thought, a little envious. But "life" was the operative word, and both Clabbers' lives had been snuffed out, one by nature, the other by design. There was the possibility that they'd visited the sumptuous establishments before coming to Doucet, but the brochures had a crisp sheen that spoke of being brand new rather than carted across an ocean and through Great Britain.

She put down the brochures and picked up the ring. Designed for a woman, the diamonds on its flat front spelled out an ornate monogram—a small *b* sandwiched between two large *D*s. Except for the small *b*, the initials didn't resemble Beverly Clabber's. Were they from a previous marriage? Did the ring even belong to her? What if a previous guest had left it behind? Maggie could match the initials to archived reservations, but she assumed someone who'd forgotten a ring this valuable would have contacted Crozat the minute they realized that it was missing. Besides, Marie Shexnayder's near-OCD level of maid service could be counted on to unearth anything forgotten by past visitors.

Given that she felt safe assuming that the ring and brochures belonged to Beverly, what did it all mean? Were they connected, or had the woman just found separate hiding places for things she valued? And why exactly were the brochures so important to her? Maggie could see keeping them in a safe place so they'd stay in pristine condition, but hiding them like they were blue chip stock certificates made no sense. Yet that's exactly what Beverly Clabber had done.

Maggie closed her eyes, placed her hands on the brochures and ring, and cleared her mind, just the way Gran' had taught her. After a few meditative breaths, her intuition kicked into high gear, sending the powerful feeling that the answer to why Beverly Clabber was murdered somehow lay in the three items resting under her hands. If she could figure out how the ring and brochures were tied to Beverly's death, it would help lead the police to who did it.

She turned on the color printer that she'd treated herself to when she moved back home and carefully made copies of the brochures and ring. Then she hid the originals under a pile of papers she kept in the bottom drawer of the heirloom desk where generations of Doucets had sat paying plantation bills, keeping diaries, and penning the occasional lovesick note to a potential suitor or mate they were crushing on. She searched for a clean manila folder and couldn't find one, so she stuck the copies of the brochures and the ring in an old folder labeled "Receipts."

Maggie locked the drawer and tugged at it to make sure this was the rare Crozat lock that did its job. Satisfied, she hid the key under the liner in her underwear drawer—it had worked for Bev Clabber—and then pulled off Gran's evening gloves. This took some effort, since her calloused painter paws were larger than Gran's delicate hands. She finally peeled off the gloves and headed to the main house to help her father find accommodations for any guests who wanted to bolt after their police interviews.

She found Tug hunched over his computer in the B and B office. "How's it going?" she asked.

Tug crinkled his forehead and pinched the bridge of his nose as if trying to relieve a headache. "Bad," he said. "Pelican is sold out because of Fet Let. There are three conventions in New Orleans right now, so you can't even find a place to stay on airbnb-dot-com. LSU starts this week, so the Baton Rouge area's a no-go. I found a Motel 6 in Metairie and a few iffy choices everywhere else. Not sure I want to take responsibility for steering our guests toward the Chateau des Femmes Motel on Airline Highway. Especially since I think it's partly a half-way house."

"They could go north, or west to Lafayette."

"For one thing, that's a whole different vacation. And for another, Rufus would probably make a stink about it. He doesn't want to go chasing all over the place if he needs one of them. Too much work."

"We'll give everyone suggestions and let them make their own decisions. Look at the upside: the more guests who leave, the less of them we have to float."

Tug gave his daughter a half smile. "Ouch. You are *cold.*"

"And here I am thinking I'm being an optimist." Maggie put an arm around her dad's shoulder. "We'll present all the options during what might turn into a very unhappy happy hour."

"Just keep the liquor flowing, darlin'."

Which was exactly what Maggie did an hour later as Tug distributed a handout of lodging alternatives to each guest. The only ones missing were the Ryker kids, who were sheltered in their room, and Kyle Bruner. The Texan had told the family in private that he had no intention of bailing on them. Whether this declaration was motivated by pure human decency or the fact he was seriously crushing on Lia didn't matter. He would remain a guest, and a paying one at that.

"These suck," Georgia Two griped as he glanced at the list. "We've stayed in nicer places during spring break, and last year the motel had bedbugs."

"We didn't come to Cajun Country to stay in a Motel 6," Jan declared.

"We also didn't come here to stay where somebody was murdered," Angela countered.

"More wine, Angela?" Maggie made the question rhetorical by filling the Cutie's glass as she spoke. It was Angela's third refill. The flush of gentle inebriation was starting to bloom on her cheeks, as well as those of a few other guests.

"I think we need a family meeting," Lachlan Ryker said to his wife, who nodded. "Let's go talk to the kids."

The Rykers excused themselves. There was grim silence as the remaining guests pondered their choices. Maggie discreetly topped off a couple of glasses. Finally, Cutie president Jan spoke. "You know what? When I look around this room, I don't see a killer anywhere. Do you?" The others exchanged uncomfortable glances. "Well, do you?" Jan pressed. A few glanced around and muttered no.

Encouraged, Jan continued. "You know what I *do* see? People from all different parts of the country who came here to experience the culture and beauty of Cajun Country and of Crozat itself. Nice people, good people whose adventure shouldn't be derailed by a nutjob off the streets or someone who had a vendetta against Mrs. Clabber—who none of us even knew before this week."

The others, gaining confidence, chorused agreement. "I never even thought of that," Emily Butler said. "The poison could have been planted months ago. We all saw how many pills she had. Someone could have stuck poison in one of them and just waited until she got around to taking it."

Maggie debated what she could and couldn't reveal about the box of arsenic found in the Crozat plantation store. "Evidence may be produced that shows a local poison was used," she said, proud of how police procedural she sounded. Or legal procedural. She wasn't sure which but still felt good about it.

"Has anything been proven?" Jan demanded.

"Well, no, but—"

"Then it's just a theory. Besides, lightning doesn't strike twice."

"Unless it's a serial killer," Georgia Three pointed out. "They always strike a bunch of times. That's kind of their job."

Jan flicked a dismissive hand at the student. "I doubt that out of all the places in the world, a serial killer would choose an old lady in a remote area to start his spree. I think Emily's scenario makes the most sense. In which case, this whole crazy nightmare is over." Jan motioned to the other Cuties. She was on a roll now. "I think I speak for all in my group when I say that we're not going to let some psycho ruin our vacation. Evil can go straight to hell where it belongs, because we're going to stay at Crozat and show our support for the wonderful family that has fought through terrible times to keep a small piece of American history alive so that they could share it with the rest of us. Yes, we Peli*can!* Right, ladies?"

Angela nodded a little reluctantly, Suzy with trepidation. Debbie beamed. She leaned over to Maggie and whispered, "That's why she's our leader." Maggie smiled weakly. She was torn between being touched by Jan's support and resenting its price tag. Since the other guests seemed a beat away from giving Jan a standing ovation, it was obvious they shared her commitment to not bailing on Crozat. Maggie's last hope was the Rykers, who hadn't been around to hear Jan's rallying cry.

"The kids want to stay," Lachlan told Maggie when she tracked the couple down after the rest of the guests had dispersed to ready themselves for dinner.

"And," Carrie added with a helpless shrug, "we could hardly say no, could we?"

Maggie, who had heard "no" quite a bit from her own parents while growing up, thought that was exactly what parents were supposed to say when the situation called for it, but this wasn't the time to debate parenting styles. "We're so glad you'll be with us for the rest of the week, and we'll do everything we can to make sure you leave Crozat with wonderful memories," she told the Rykers with the forced enthusiasm of a cruise director before retreating to the kitchen to give Ninette a hand preparing dinner.

Later, as Maggie served the guests, she studied everyone at the table while they made small talk. Kyle, the Cuties, the Butlers, the Rykers, the Georgia boys—did one of them have a connection to the Clabbers that led to murder? She wished that she had Jan's confidence in the innocence of Crozat's guests, but something was bothering her. Why had they all chosen to stick around? She had a sense that it went beyond the understandable lure of a free ride. But a sense was all that she had. Since Rufus would provide nothing but obstacles, Maggie realized it was up to her to ferret out whatever secrets the group might have.

*

That night, long after everyone at Crozat had gone to sleep, Maggie sat in bed typing away on her tablet. She'd decided to research alphabetically, starting with the Butlers. Both Emily and Shane had a heavy presence on social media, which wasn't a shock. So did Maggie. In fact, she was surprised that she'd never crossed iPaths with either of them.

The only revelation, found in a gossipy *New York Post* Page Six blurb about their engagement, was that Emily Butler, née Fuller, came from a Boston Brahmin family while Shane was the first member of his blue-collar Long Island family to attend college. Emily had "married down," as society mavens liked to cluck. She was the only child of divorced parents, and ancestors on both sides could be found on the Mayflower manifest. But when the upper class crashed, it crashed hard. Emily's mother was a model and drug addict who ran off with the lead singer of an eighties hair band. She had died eight years earlier when her heart stopped in the middle of breast lift surgery. Emily's father passed away the month before Emily's wedding of "liver disease"—which Maggie immediately recognized as alcoholism. Maggie imagined that the poor girl welcomed the chance to join the Butler clan, which the *Post* painted in a boring but much more grounded light. Maggie gazed at the wedding party photo that accompanied the story. Emily, in an exquisite 1920s-style beaded wedding gown, was flanked by four women of varying ages who all bore a resemblance to Shane and looked uncomfortable in their elegant ice-blue drapey satin brides-maids' dresses. If the only members of her bridal party were, as she guessed, Shane's sisters, then poor Emily lacked friends as well as family.

Having read all she could find about the Butlers, Maggie moved on to the Cuties. Angela DiPietro seemed to lead the typical life of a suburban empty nester. *Why does every couple feel the need to go on an Alaskan cruise the minute their kids move out of the house?* Maggie wondered as she paged through pictures of Angela and her husband mugging next to totem poles and a series of what she assumed were supposed to be artsy photos of pine trees that instead looked like someone kept dropping the camera.

Maggie yawned and debated powering down but opted to check out one more guest. She typed in an image search for "Debra Stern" and the screen filled with a variety of Debra Sterns from coast to coast. Maggie found a photo that looked vaguely similar to the Cajun Cutie—if the Cajun Cutie had been a female executive who preferred power suits to ill-fitting leggings. Maggie stared at the picture, wondering if she'd made a mistake. She scrolled through a dozen more images for Debra Stern but returned to the original one that caught her eye. She was sure the woman in the navy wool blazer with the confident smile was the Crozat's anemic guest.

The caption under the photo read, "Debra Stern, CEO, SPI." Maggie typed this into her search taskbar and was rewarded with a long list of sites that revealed Debbie had founded Stern Partners International, a headhunting firm with offices around the globe, which she'd sold five years prior for a small fortune. Debra Stern, CEO, was successful and ambitious—the polar opposite of the dim bulb she now appeared to be.

Maggie turned off her tablet and snuggled under the cool cotton duvet cover. But she was too excited to sleep. She'd finally found someone with a secret—perhaps a secret that somehow led to Beverly Clabber's murder.

Chapter Ten

As Maggie drove to her tour guide shift across the river at Doucet Plantation, she pondered the best way to bring up the dichotomy of Debbie to Cuties leader Jan, who might hesitate to talk behind a member's back. She slowed down as she passed through Pelican's infamous speed trap, the brainchild of a very proud Rufus. While Pelican PD usually spared locals, they showed no mercy for people trying to make time between New Orleans and Baton Rouge when I-10 backed up, and Maggie grudgingly gave Rufus credit for gifting Pelican with a steady stream of much-needed speeding ticket income.

The morning went by quickly as bus after bus unloaded vacationers taking advantage of summer's last week. Maggie, suited up in her fake plantation garb, gave back-to-back tours where she patiently answered the same questions over and over again; no, it wasn't hard to be a hired hand at the estate that her mother's family once called home, and yes, she'd pose with visitors for selfies next to the portrait of Magnolia Marie, the ancestor she'd been named after.

By lunchtime, Maggie was ready for a break. She took her sandwich and joined a few of her fellow guides at their private rest area behind the overseer's cottage. "You are Doucet's queen of selfies," Gaynell Bourgeois, a nineteen-year-old coworker, teased her.

"I know, right?" Maggie said as she fanned herself. "If I had a dollar for every one I posed for, I wouldn't need this job." She took off her banana-curled wig, pulled a travel-sized antiperspirant out of her bra, and swiped it across her underarms to avoid the dry-cleaning fee that would come out of her salary if she got sweat stains on her flouncy costume. She was getting to know and like some of the other women working at Doucet, like Gaynell, who seemed sweet and ingenuous. There was only one coworker Maggie wasn't crazy about.

Vanessa Fleer was a tall, zaftig woman teetering on the edge of obese and had the arrogance that sometimes accompanies ignorance. A trend follower who considered herself Pelican's foremost trendsetter, she'd recently tried the ombré look on her bleached blonde perm. The at-home dye job resulted in an erratic patchwork of yellow and orange, giving her hair the look of melting sherbet punch. As if Vanessa weren't unlikeable enough on her own merits, she was dating Rufus Durand.

"Lord, it's a hot one," Vanessa said. She motioned to Maggie's deodorant stick. "Can I borrow that?" Without waiting for an answer, she pulled the deodorant out of Maggie's hand, pushed aside the frilly sleeves of her plantation gown, and swabbed her underarms.

"I had two busloads of Japanese tourists," Gaynell, Maggie's Doucet bestie, shared eagerly. She sat cross-legged on a towel, the edge of her pantaloons sticking out under her knee-length plaid dress. Gaynell, who barely grazed five feet and weighed under a hundred pounds, often got drafted to play a plantation child since she was the only guide who fit into the costume. "I love the Japanese group tours. They take so many pictures with me, I feel famous. And they gave me some real nice tips."

"Japanese don't usually tip, it's against their culture," Vanessa informed Gaynell in her usual superior tone. She tossed the deodorant back to Maggie, who pointedly dropped it into a nearby trashcan. Vanessa didn't seem to notice. She was too busy devouring a diet cookie from her latest weight-loss plan. "The men were probably hoping you'd run off with them and be their geisha."

"God, Vanessa, that's so racist," Maggie said, disgusted. Vanessa rolled her eyes and sat down on a bench. Her hoop skirt popped up like a spring, covering her face and revealing a too-tight pair of Daisy Dukes. The other women roared with laughter.

"Shut up!"

"I'm sorry," Gaynell said as she wiped tears from her eyes, "but it's funny every time."

"Yeah, well, when I marry Rufus Durand and we turn Grove Hall into a showplace, I'm gonna invent a hoop skirt that's way easier to sit in."

Grove Hall, the decrepit plantation home with beautiful bones that Maggie had immortalized in her Save Our Structures series, was the Durand family home. Descendants had been trying to unload the place for years but couldn't without Rufus agreeing to the sale. And Rufus constantly refused, preferring to live in a trailer on the property and get pleasure from how much Grove Hall's decay bothered upstanding Pelican citizens like the Crozats.

"What about the curse?" Gaynell teased Vanessa. "You know all Ru's relationships are supposed to fail. My mom told me he's already been married three times."

"So?" Vanessa adjusted her skirt, which continued to fight back. "That's only one more 'n me. Besides, my relationship with Ru is stronger than any stupid curse. I can't believe your great-great was so mean, Maggie. Then again, she *was* the only River belle who married one a' them Yankees."

It never took long for Vanessa to get on Maggie's nerves. "'One a' them Yankees?' You know, Vanessa, just because you're wearing a hoop skirt doesn't mean it's actually 1860. Besides, Magnolia Marie's 'Yankee' didn't live very long, poor guy. He went in one of the yellow fever epidemics."

Vanessa pounced on this. "Speaking of not living long, ohmuhgawd, that murder at Crozat is so terrible for y'all. People must be canceling their reservations like crazy."

Vanessa was right, but Maggie would never give her that satisfaction, so she kept quiet.

"Their loss," Gaynell declared. "Crozat is awesome."

"Still, Maggie, I feel for you," Vanessa said, doing a bad imitation of somebody who actually felt emotions like sympathy. "I know it can't be fun giving tours here at Doucet when your family used to own it. If y'all lose Crozat, it'd be pain on top of pain."

Maggie drew in a deep breath, quelling the urge to give Vanessa a swift kick in the hoop skirt. "As I've told you a million times, I *do* have fun working here. And while I know us losing Crozat is Rufus Durand's wet dream, it's not going to happen."

Vanessa stood up and held her hands together as if she were praying. She wasn't; instead, she was doing some old-fashioned isometric exercise that claimed to firm up sagging breasts. "I heard—and I can't say from who—that the lady who died wants to be buried here. Someone I know heard from the lawyers for the estate and it turns out she used to live here. Can you believe it?"

Maggie couldn't. Beverly Clabber had lived in Pelican? When? Where? This widened the pool of suspects considerably. Maybe the murderer wasn't a Crozat guest. Maybe it was someone from the woman's past settling an old grudge.

"You and Rufus sure have some interesting pillow talk," Gaynell said, shaking her head, her soft blonde curls floating back and forth as she did.

"I didn't *say* I heard it from Ru Ru, I just said I *heard* it," Vanessa protested lamely. Maggie gagged at the nickname but filed it away as a future tool with which to annoy Ru. Right now, she needed to focus on the new information she'd picked up from the "Loch Nessa Monster," as Vanessa's coworkers secretly called her.

Maggie vowed to run this development by Gran', who wasn't much younger than Beverly and might remember her from the past, given enough clues. "Wow, Vanessa, that's so weird," Maggie said, hoping to stimulate more gossip. "Mrs. Clabber never said a word about it. Did the lawyer say anything else?"

Vanessa shrugged and continued her exercises. "That was all Ru Ru said. And then we got busy, if ya know what I mean."

The women, who knew exactly what Vanessa meant, exchanged a look and managed not to recoil at the image emblazoned on their brains.

*

After finishing her shift at Doucet, Maggie clocked out and drove to Fais Dough Dough, where Briana and Clinton Poche were helping Lia restock the store shelves with gift items. "Your mugs are selling great," Lia told her. "And you know what else are? The mouse pads. I guess people like a little history with their hi-tech devices."

"Can we talk?" Maggie asked her cousin sotto voce.

"Sure. Briana, honey, you're in charge of the register."

"Yes, ma'am," Briana said, thrilled with her newfound authority. "You hear that, Clinton?" she called to her brother. "I'm in charge."

"Of the register, not my life," her brother retorted. He followed this observation with a loud belch in his sister's face.

"Okay, you two, that's enough," Lia said. "Briana, don't make me sorry I asked you, and Clinton, you need to come up with a new party trick."

Armed with chicory coffee and plates of Lia's latest culinary inspiration, Bourbon Pecan Croissant Bread Pudding, she and Maggie retreated to a small café table in the building's back garden. Maggie didn't know which smelled more delicious, the pudding or the border of heliotrope sparkling with drops left by a late-afternoon rain.

"Big news," she told Lia. "Beverly Clabber used to live in Pelican."

"What?!"

"Yes. Total shocker." She related Vanessa's bombshell to Lia, who was as stunned by the news as Maggie had been.

"Do they know anything else, like what her maiden name was?"

"Vanessa and Rufus 'got busy' before she got any more gossip out of him."

"Ugh."

"I know." Maggie finished the last spoonful of her bread pudding. She was one step away from licking the bowl but managed to control herself. Instead she ran her finger along the inside of it. "So . . . anything new between you and that tall drink of Texas water, as Gran' would say?"

Lia laughed. "I think we like each other."

"Want to share something not so blatantly obvious to everyone in the world?"

"We're getting to know each other slowly and carefully."

"How does that work when Kyle has a vacation clock on him?"

"He creates software programs, so he can work anywhere, really."

"So, are you saying he may stick around for a while?"

"Yes. He may. I hope so."

Lia finished the last sip of coffee in her cup and swirled the grounds absentmindedly.

"Let's see what message your coffee sends," Maggie said. "I'll read the grinds."

Lia looked at her skeptically. "You can do that?"

"When my life was imploding in New York, I visited this Iranian psychic a friend recommended. She read my grinds and taught me a little about coffee fortune telling."

"Was she any good?"

"She foretold the death of my relationship," Maggie said in an arch, sonorous tone, and Lia laughed. Maggie took her cousin's cup, placed the saucer over it, and turned the cup upside down. She then righted the cup and looked inside. She grinned at Lia. "I see a shamrock. That means your wish will come true."

Maggie left Fais Dough Dough with a tray of the bread pudding. Ninette, inspired by a rave review Maggie called in, had decided to serve it as the Crozat evening dessert. Maggie kept the Falcon's top up for a change so the car could fill with the sweet, spicy aroma. As she pulled into the driveway behind the plantation's main house, she noticed a nondescript silver sedan parked in her usual spot. A parking decal from the Shreveport PD tagged the car as Bo's. Annoyed, Maggie pulled in next to it a little too close, making sure to ding Bo's car when she opened her door. She grabbed the bread pudding tin and marched into the house. Her stomach fluttered with nerves when she found the detective in the front parlor with Gran'. He had his notebook out and was obviously interviewing her, a grim expression on his face.

Chapter Eleven

Gran' gave Maggie a cheery little wave. She might as well have been welcoming her to a tea party. "Hello, darlin'. Have you heard the latest gossip? Beverly Clabber used to live in Pelican. Years and years ago, when we were both girls. She wasn't Beverly Clabber then, she was Francine Prepoire. Where 'Beverly' came from, I'll never know, you'd think she'd have stuck with Francine. But anyhoo, Bo here—you don't mind if I call you Bo, do you? I feel like we've reached a point where informality is acceptable."

"Bo is fine, ma'am," Bo responded politely. He was too tall for the delicate Victorian side chair he was sitting on, and as he adjusted his position, Maggie caught a glimpse of a gun under his blazer.

"Where was I?" Gran' said, pressing an index finger to the side of her temple. "Oh, yes. Maggie, you remember my dear old friend, Yvonne Rousseau, don't you? Well, in a piece of impressive detecting work on Bo's part, he discovered that during Francine-slash-Mrs. Clabber's brief time in Pelican, she paid

Yvonne a visit. Yvonne may be in a home with Parkinson's, but her mind is still sharp, so Bo was able to interview her about their conversation. He of course can't reveal much of what transpired, but he did share that Yvonne remembered Francine stole my first love from me, Ignace Roubideaux. Isn't that funny? An ancient Pelican soap opera revisited after all these years."

In what was becoming an unpleasantly familiar sensation, Maggie felt the urge to throw up. "Gran', that makes you a murder suspect," she said as she pointed to Bo. "That's why he's here."

"I know. Isn't that exciting?"

"No," Maggie practically shouted as she lost patience with her grandmother. "It's not exciting at all, it's horrible." She glared at Bo. "Does my grand-mère need a lawyer? Because we'll get her one, a great one, the best in Louisiana, the best in the country, and if you've done anything inappropriate here, he or she will have your ass on a plate."

"Magnolia Marie Crozat," Gran' said sharply. "That was incredibly rude. You apologize to Bo this instant."

"It's all right, ma'am, no apology necessary," Bo's tone was quiet but authoritative. Bo turned to Maggie. She noticed that he had well-defined cheekbones and wondered if there was some Houma Indian in his ancestry. "Mrs. Crozat and I—"

"Please, call me Charlotte."

"I prefer Mrs. Crozat."

"All right, fine," Gran' said, a little annoyed.

"Mrs. Crozat and I," Bo continued, "are just trying to see what she remembers from the past about Francine Prepoire Clabber, Ignace Roubideaux, or anyone who knew them."

"And *I* was telling Bo that Francine did me the biggest favor of my life by stealing Ignace from me. I found comfort and love in the arms of your Grand-père Crozat, the most wonderful man I've ever known. Francine and Ignace barely lasted a month or more, then she left town—forever, I thought, until today. Ignace moved to Baton Rouge, where he died many years ago after plowing his car into a tree while drunk. So you see, I'm not a murder suspect at all, am I, Bo?"

Maggie didn't like the way Bo only responded with a slight smile. Gran', however, was oblivious. She gave Bo a friendly pat on the knee. "My, you must have worked up an appetite with all this talking. Why don't you stay for dinner?"

"Thanks very much, ma'am, but that wouldn't be appropriate." Bo glanced at the tin in Maggie's hands a bit wistfully. "Although whatever you have there smells pretty good."

"Well, if you won't stay, we'll just make you a plate to go, right, Maggie?"

"No, really," Bo said. "As an officer of the law, it's improper for me to accept gifts of any kind. That includes free food and beverage."

"Oh, please," Maggie snorted. "Ru's closets are probably full of stuff he 'confiscated,' or got as 'thank-yous.' But," she hastened to add, realizing she might be encouraging Bo to join them for a meal, "I respect your ethics."

Bo acknowledged this with a nod and another of his slight smiles. She couldn't be sure, but this one seemed a little less enigmatic—it bordered on being a genuine smile and created a crease on the right side of his mouth that in other circumstances she would have called sexy.

Bo stood up to go. He wore his blue sport coat over a finely checkered tan button-down shirt and jeans, and she tried to ignore how the casual work look somehow seemed sexy on him. "Thank you both for your time. My men got called away to an accident on I-10, but they'll be back later to finish searching for that box of poison you remembered seeing, Miss Crozat."

As soon as Maggie was sure Bo was out of earshot, she turned to her grandmother. "Gran', you need to remember that until they catch whoever killed Beverly or Francine or whatever her real name is, we are all suspects. *All* of us. Everyone in this house and now pretty much everyone in Pelican."

Gran' waved her hand dismissively. "Save your lecture, dear. The new addition to Pelican PD is as smart as he is handsome. He's an astute enough judge of character to be able to see that I had absolutely nothing to do with Francine's death. I'm sure the genuine shock on my face when he told me who she was quickly ruled me out as a suspect. I wonder if I have any pictures of her. I must dig up my yearbook. Oooh, maybe a picture in it will help lead Detective Dreamboat to the real murderer."

Gran' took off to search her past for evidence of Beverly/Francine. While it didn't seem to bother Gran' much, Maggie hated that Durand was eyeing her grandmother as a potential murderer. *I have to deflect his attention from her to someone else,* she thought as she walked down the hall into the kitchen, where her mother was preparing dinner. Maggie put the bread pudding down on the counter; her arms ached from carrying the sweet carbo load for so long.

"Hey, chère," Ninette said without taking her eyes off the beef she was seasoning in a large cast iron pan. She was cooking up a large batch of grits and grillades, a meal usually served at breakfast or lunch. But since Crozat's guests found the dish too heavy for breakfast and were rarely around for midday meals, Ninette enjoyed making it the centerpiece of a dinner menu. "Is that detective done giving Gran' the third degree?"

"I'm not sure who was messing with whom there," Maggie said.

Ninette let out a deep sigh. "I just want this whole horrible business *over*," she said.

"I know, Mama. Me too." Maggie noticed perspiration doing a slow drip down the side of her mother's face. She took a paper towel and gently wiped it away and then kissed Ninette on the cheek. "You feel warm," Maggie said, concerned.

Ninette laughed. "For goodness' sake, why wouldn't I be warm? I'm cooking."

Tug came in through the kitchen back door, laden with groceries. "Here you go," he said to Ninette as he put down the bags. He gave his wife an affectionate pat on her bottom. "Everything for your fete crawfish."

"Ohmygod, I totally forgot about the fete," Maggie said with a groan as she helped her mother unload groceries into the cupboards and refrigerator.

Ninette checked the crisper drawers. "I need okra and red pepper from the garden."

"I'll get it," Maggie said.

"Next year I'm not going to all this trouble. I'm just gonna make a big pot of franks and beans."

"Yeah right, Mom," Maggie laughed. Fet Let participants claimed bragging rights to certain dishes, and Ninette was famous for her Crawfish Crozat, a delicious pasta dish. Her mother threatened not to make it every year, but Maggie knew Ninette relished the moans of gustatory delight she got from her long line of customers. Fet cooks competed to see who'd run out of food first, but mostly they fought over second place because Ninette always nailed the top spot.

Maggie went out to the garden, where she picked enough okra and red pepper to fill a large basket. She was about to take it inside when she saw Cuties Debbie and Jan walking through Crozat's parterre. The formal garden, whose design dated back to Crozat's earliest days, featured immaculately clipped bushes and gravel paths laid out in a symmetrical pattern; maintaining it was a labor of love for Tug.

Jan's sturdy frame and height of close to six feet meant that she dwarfed Debbie. But Maggie noticed there was nothing intimidating about her presence at the moment; in fact, she seemed parental with her compatriot. When Debbie yawned and said something to Jan, the Cutie board president nodded and patted her sympathetically on the shoulder. Debbie then headed toward the coach house, most likely to nap before dinner. Jan gave her a little wave good-bye and continued her stroll through the parterre, stopping now and then to admire the flowering plants that the trim bushes encircled.

This was Maggie's chance to get the Cutie president alone and do a little digging about Debbie and her alter ego, Debra Stern. She put her basket in the shade and made her way over to Jan, who seemed pleased to see her.

"This garden is fantastic," Jan said. "It's very calming."

"I know. It sure seemed to have that effect on Debbie— almost like it made her sleepy."

"She's a little tired from all of our sightseeing."

"Is Debbie okay?" Maggie asked, concern coloring her voice.

"Oh yes, she's fine. Just needs some rest."

"It seems like something's wrong. Is she unhappy with her stay here? I would totally understand, given the crazy circumstances."

"No, she's not at all unhappy here. She loves Crozat. We all know that what happened had nothing to do with your family."

"What a relief. I can't tell you how much we appreciate y'all's support." Maggie hoped a little charm and flattery might open Jan up, but the woman's lack of response proved that Gran' had not passed on the Glossy gene to her granddaughter.

As Maggie walked with the Cutie president, she debated the best way to draw the woman out. If she boldly asked what the deal was with Debbie, she'd reveal herself as a snoop, which would put Jan off. "A friend said she recognized Debbie from articles on the Internet," she said, mixing a white lie with the truth. "My friend says she's this incredibly successful business-woman. I told her she must be wrong, because, no offense to Debbie or anything, but she doesn't seem like that kind of person."

Jan's paced slowed. "Actually . . . your friend is right."

"Really?" Maggie played up the surprise in her voice. She hoped she wasn't milking it too much. "Wow, I don't see that at all."

"Well . . . she *was* a successful businesswoman. She's not pursuing that anymore."

"Why not?" Maggie adopted an innocent tone, grateful that she still remembered a few tricks from a high school drama elective.

"It's just . . ." Jan hesitated. She glanced toward the coach house. There was no sign of Debbie or any other Cutie, for that matter.

"You're not gossiping if you're trying to help someone understand a friend," Maggie gently prompted her, hoping that Jan wouldn't wonder why she should feel compelled to help an innkeeper's daughter "understand" a fellow Cutie. Luckily, Jan took the bait.

"You're right," Jan said. She hesitated again, and then launched into her story. "A few years ago, Debbie went through a horrible experience that almost destroyed her. Before she joined the Cuties, she was one of the country's top female entrepreneurs. She'd started her own headhunting company and expanded it all over the world. Then one of those venture capital types mounted a hostile takeover. The only way Debbie could keep the company away from him was to sell it. Stern Partners International was her life. She never married or had kids or even a pet. When SPI was gone, she had a total nervous breakdown. She wound up in a psychiatric facility and underwent ECT—electroconvulsive therapy."

"Electroshock? God, that's so old school."

"It's made a comeback. Her psychiatrist assured us that ECT has changed a lot over the last few decades, and it's the most effective treatment available for severe depression. But it wiped out months of memory. Between that and the huge doses of antidepressants she's on, Debbie's a completely different woman now. I've been with her when we run into people from SPI, and they don't even recognize her at first." Jan shook her head sadly. "The Cuties have become her family, her whole world. We look after her. When she wanted to serve on the board, Suzy insisted that she be given the job of secretary, even though she was a gimme for treasurer. But Suzy was adamant about how it would be too stressful for Debbie and even offered to serve as treasurer herself. That's how much we all care about Debbie and look after her."

Maggie clucked a few appropriately sympathetic remarks, but Suzy's alleged altruism set off an alarm bell, and she replaced Debbie as a potential suspect in Maggie's mind. Maybe this Cutie had a personal agenda for steering Debbie away from managing the organization's finances and taking on the task herself. State and federal prisons were peppered with white-collar criminals doing time for embezzlement, and Maggie wondered if Cutie Suzy had succumbed to the temptation of tampering with the Cajun Cuties' books. If this was so, and Beverly Clabber had accidentally stumbled upon information that would have exposed Suzy, Beverly's death might just be a deadly case of "follow the money."

Chapter Twelve

Maggie slept on her theory about Suzy and in the morning decided that it would behoove her to do some digging into the woman's past before sharing it with anyone. Besides, the Clabbers' service loomed.

While the Clabbers' lawyer provided Pelican PD with detailed instructions regarding Mrs. C's postmortem journey, the couple's will had no stipulations about what to do with Mr. C, who apparently considered himself immortal. The entire town was surprised to learn that Francine/Beverly owned an ornate tomb in the local cemetery where she was to be laid to rest. According to Vanessa Fleer, who was becoming a font of information, when Rufus cracked a joke about just tossing Hal into the tomb with Beverly/Francine, the late couple's lawyer said, "Sounds like a plan."

The day dawned gloriously. Sunny, but not too humid, made comfortable by a light breeze off the river. It was the perfect day for a fete—and a funeral. PPD officers Cal and Artie had finally shown up and were devouring plates of biscuits and gravy before embarking on their search for the missing box of arsenic. Unlike Bo, they had no problem accepting free food, and as much of it as they could ingest without exploding their stomachs. It never seemed to affect Cal's long, skinny frame. But even though Artie was only in his late twenties, he had inherited his father's build, and his gut was already expanding with what locals called a "Pelican pouch." He'd also inherited Buster's sandy tight curls that tended toward thinning, and Maggie noticed an embryonic bald spot on his crown.

The Crozats and Crozat guests slowly assembled on the veranda. Everyone had dressed as appropriately as they could, given that the guests hadn't figured a funeral into their vacation plans. The hipster Butlers, of course, had plenty of black in their wardrobe. Shane even lent a couple of tees to Georgias Two and Three, who may have been half a head taller than the compact New Yorker but managed to squeeze themselves into apparel from a trendy Manhattan men's store. The general mood was one of awkward solemnity. Since everyone had only known the Clabbers an unpleasant day or two, there was little genuine emotion, just a general feeling that respect was owed to the late couple.

"It's so strange that Mrs. Clabber never told anyone she had a crypt here," Cutie Jan mused.

"I know," Shane said. "Not even Mr. C."

"Some people are just way weird," Georgia One said solemnly. He yawned and stretched. It was a little early in the day for a frat boy on summer break. "This is an awesome shirt. It really moves with you, ya know?"

"You can have it," Shane said. "I've got a ton of black shirts."

Georgia One's face lit up. "Seriously? Thanks, man. You rock."

The group caravanned over to Pelican's Assumption of Mary Memorial Park, where both Clabbers would now spend eternity together in the missus's tomb. And what a tomb it was. Like its neighbors, the tomb was raised off the ground due to South Louisiana's high water table. But unlike the others, which were modest in decoration, Beverly/Francine's boasted ornate carvings and was topped by two statues of angels holding hands as they gazed upward to what they assumed was a welcoming heaven. Their cherubic faces bothered Maggie, but she couldn't figure out why.

"I always wondered whose tomb this was," Tug said as the group awaited the arrival of Father Prit, who had kindly agreed to lead the funeral service even though he'd never laid eyes on the Clabbers. "There was no name, no information on it. It was just sitting here . . . waiting."

"I wonder why Mrs. Clabber didn't tell us she'd lived here," Ninette said. "That's usually the first thing that guests who've moved away do. 'I grew up on Richard Street, near the elementary school.' It's odd that she never said anything."

"Maybe she was waiting, for some reason," Maggie theorized. "She wanted to find just the right time to share that, but she died before she could."

Ninette shuddered, and Tug put a protective arm around her shoulder. "You got a chill?"

Ninette shook her head no. "Just the shudders."

"Well, if you're gonna get them anywhere, you're gonna get 'em here," Gran' said, gazing around the cemetery with distaste. "That's why I'm considering that thing where they float your head in space for a century or two after you kick the bucket."

"Or," Maggie teased her grandmother, "we could just have you stuffed, mounted, and put on display in the Cabildo down in New Orleans."

"Oh, honey, that's goin' in my will."

"Stop it, you two, you're being ghoulish," Ninette admonished them. "Good, Father Prit is here. Now we can get things moving. I want to get home; I have Crawfish Crozat to prepare."

The group clustered around Father Prit as he led a brief service. "From I Corinthians 15:51 through 58," he intoned in his thick Indian accent. "'Behold, I tell you a mystery. We shall all indeed rise again: but we shall not all be changed. In a moment, in the twinkling of an eye, at the last trumpet: for the trumpet shall sound and the dead shall rise again incorruptible. And we shall be changed.'"

As the priest continued with the reading, Maggie's attention wandered back to the angels on the tomb. She gasped and then covered her mouth, but not before Gran' jabbed a warning elbow in her ribs.

"Sorry," Maggie whispered, "but I just got why those statues bother me so much. They have the same grins on their faces as Mrs. Clabber always had."

Gran' looked at the statues and also gasped. Ninette shot her mother-in-law a look. "Charlotte, please."

"Sorry," Gran' said and then leaned toward Maggie. "You're absolutely right."

Maggie bit her lip to keep from giggling, as did Gran', but a couple of chuckles sneaked out. Ninette glared at them. "You two need to walk over to another tomb until you get yourselves under control," she whispered.

"Sorry, Mom, we'll behave."

Gran' turned her attention back to the service, but Maggie's mind was elsewhere. Ninette had a point when she questioned why Mrs. Clabber hadn't brought up her past in Pelican. Was she killed to prevent her from revealing something? But what? She sighed in frustration. Debbie Stern, who was standing next to her, gave Maggie a sympathetic smile, mistaking the sigh for sadness.

"Death is so hard, isn't it?" Debbie whispered. "No matter who the departed is or what our relationship with them was, it reminds us of our own mortality."

Maggie nodded but didn't speak, not wanting to risk another scolding from her mother. She focused on evaluating the differences between Debbie and Suzy. Suzy was by far the most stylish of the Cutie foursome. Her silver hair was cut in a perfect shoulder-length bob, and while the liver spots on her hands hinted that she was at least in her sixties, her face possessed only a smattering of lines. She'd obviously had some work done, but it was discreet and high end, as were her black linen slacks and top. If someone made Maggie sum up Suzy in one word, it would be "immaculate." Which would be the last word she'd use to describe Debbie.

Debbie had yet to stray from her uniform of leggings and slightly worn oversized shirts that did a desultory job of hiding the weight that had settled in her middle. Everything from her limp, dry hair to her makeup-free face sighed, "I give up." If the dull look in Debbie's eyes indicated her mental state, Suzy's insistence on giving her a light volunteer load was not unreasonable. But at least Suzy offered the possibility of another suspect besides Gran'.

Father Prit finally launched into the Lord's Prayer and concluded the service. The Crozat guests all took off in various directions dictated by their sightseeing plans for the day, and the family returned to the plantation to prepare for Fet Let. They were greeted by the now-familiar sight of Bo's bland silver sedan parked in front of the main house. Its appearance was always a harbinger of some ominous development.

"Now what?" Maggie muttered.

"Maybe it's nothing," Ninette said, trying to sound as if she actually believed that. "I'm sure the detective is just here to supervise. If you don't mind, sweetie, pull into the back so I can go straight into the kitchen. I'd rather not be distracted from my dish by the officers."

Maggie parked the Falcon in the back motor court. Gran' went off to the shotgun house to rest before the fete while Maggie, Tug, and Ninette headed for the kitchen, hoping to bypass any law enforcement representatives. But when they got there, they found it closed off with police tape. Cal and Artie, under Bo's tutelage, were dusting one of the upper kitchen cabinets for fingerprints.

"Oh no," Ninette murmured. "No, no, no."

"What's going on here?" Tug asked. "Why can't we get into our kitchen?"

"We found the box of arsenic," Bo said. He pointed to where Cal and Artie were toiling. "On the top shelf of that cabinet."

Maggie, Ninette, and Tug stared at where Bo was pointing. It was the shelf equivalent of a junk drawer, packed with old pots and broken but not completely useless bowls and cups. And there, tucked between a chipped vase and dented saucepan, lay the dusty yet still lethal box of arsenic.

Chapter Thirteen

"But . . . I don't understand," Tug said. "We would never have arsenic, or any poison, in the kitchen. How did it get here?"

"It's obvious, Dad," Maggie said, trying to control the anger she felt welling up inside. "Whoever murdered Mrs. Clabber thought it would be a great place to hide the 'weapon.' It works on a couple of levels—it's a shelf that hardly ever sees action, and if anyone does go up there and finds the arsenic, it incriminates our family. Am I right, Detective?"

"Ms. Crozat, can you identify this as the arsenic you saw in the plantation store?" Bo asked, ignoring Maggie's combative tone. He motioned to Artie, who carefully removed the box with gloved hands and showed it to Maggie, who nodded curtly. Artie bagged the box and handed it to Bo.

"Okay, you've got what you need. Now can you get out of our kitchen so we can get into it?" she asked.

"Sorry, but we're not done," Bo said.

"Well, when *will* you be done?"

"Can't say for sure, but I wouldn't count on getting in here until at least tomorrow."

Ninette gave a small groan of despair. "No. My dish. How am I gonna make my dish?" She put a hand over her eyes and began to weep. Ninette, fragile ever since her bout with cancer, had shown unexpected strength during this stressful time, despite the worries of her family. It took the threat of no Crawfish Crozat to put her over the edge. And her mother's tears worked Maggie's last nerve.

"Look what you've done to my mother," she yelled at Bo. "I've had it, with you, with all of this. Let us into our kitchen right now."

She tried to shove Bo out of the way, breaking the police tape. Bo stumbled back a few steps and then regained his balance. He put out his hands and held her back. For a moment, she flailed helplessly like a cartoon character trying to battle a muscled bully, and then Tug pulled her off.

"Maggie! Enough."

"They're ruining our lives." Maggie struggled to get out of her father's grasp. Cal and Artie exchanged uncomfortable glances, while even the preternaturally nerveless Bo seemed thrown by her outburst.

"Um . . . should we arrest her?" Cal asked Bo, with a marked lack of commitment to the idea.

"No," Bo said. "Not necessary."

Ninette placed a hand on her daughter's arm and the gentle gesture sent a message to Maggie, who forced herself to calm down. "It's my fault," Ninette said. "I was just upset about not making my dish for the fete. But I was being selfish. I'm sorry if we caused you any trouble, Detective Durand."

"It's all right, ma'am. I wish things could be different."

Tug glared at his daughter. "I think someone here needs to throw around a few 'I'm sorrys.'"

As much as she hated to admit it, Maggie knew her father was right. She was embarrassed by her own behavior. She opened her mouth, but before she could get a word out, Bo held up his hand to stop her. "This is a very difficult situation for everyone. If someone made my mother cry, no telling what I'd do."

This time Bo's smile was real and warm, prompting Maggie to fight a sudden tickle of attraction, which felt highly unbefitting to the circumstances. Luckily for her, Cal chose that moment to join the conversation.

"You know, sir," he said to Bo. "Ninette's dish is pretty famous around here."

"He's right," Artie chimed in. "People wait all year for it. When it comes to the Fet, there's a real lack if there's no Crawfish Crozat."

"Nicely put, you almost got it to rhyme," Cal congratulated his partner, who beamed. "We did finish the refrigerator and pantry areas," Cal pointed out to Bo. "Maybe you could see your way to the Crozats at least retrieving their ingredients."

"That would be great," Maggie jumped in. "We could help you cook everything in the shotgun kitchen, Mom. It's not big, but it's functional."

"That's a very nice idea, but it's up to the detective." Ninette looked at Bo, eyes filled with hope. Bo turned to Cal and Artie.

"Give the Crozats what they need," he directed.

"Thank you," Maggie said, so grateful that she found herself tearing up. "We'll get out of your way fast."

Cal and Artie helped the Crozats cart ingredients, pots, and other essentials over to the shotgun. "I can't tell you how much we appreciate this," Ninette told the officers once the last of the necessary items had made the trek.

"The Fet ain't where it's at without Crawfish Crozat," Artie said, adding a few beat box sounds for effect.

"Hah, look who's a rapper." Cal slapped his partner on the back. "We gotta give you a rapper name now."

"His name is Artie so . . . how about R2DCool?" Maggie offered, happy to do anything, however inane, that would keep the cops on the Crozats' good side. Cal and Artie both loudly approved the new moniker, and the atmosphere became close to pleasant.

"We gotta work a double shift tonight, Mrs. C.," Artie told Ninette, "so if you could save us a couple'a bowls, that'd be great."

"We'll save you your own pot of it," Tug assured the officers, who then headed back to the main house to complete their investigation. The Crozats got to work chopping, sautéing, and boiling. Gran' wandered in, fresh from a nap, and Tug filled her in on what had happened. Gran' turned to Maggie.

"You know what you have to do, Magnolia Marie."

"Yes, ma'am."

Maggie slunk into the parlor, sat down at the rococo desk, and opened an elegant gray box. Inside lay note cards,

100 percent cotton and embossed with a monogram of her initials. The Brooklyn hipster in her bowed to the Southern manners ingrained since birth—which, she thought, may have been when Gran' first gifted her with genteel personalized stationery. Civilization may have been two decades into a new millennium, but among Southern Louisiana gentry, a behavioral cow patty like the one she had just dropped still required a written note of apology. "All I'm missing is a quill pen," Maggie muttered, annoyed that she felt obliged to follow social protocol. But she did, so she hunted around the desk, dug up a pen that sported the logo from Gout's Beef Palace, and started writing a note to Bo Durand.

It began as a simple apology for her angry eruption. But for some reason Maggie couldn't explain, she kept writing. She admitted that it wouldn't be fair to blame her blow-up on the fallout from the Clabbers' deaths. Her frustration had been building since her return to Pelican six months ago. She filled the inside of the card as she tried to explain how alien she often felt in her own hometown—only matched by how alien she'd sometimes felt in New York City, where her friends would respond with patronizing amusement whenever the Southerner in her slipped out.

Maggie turned the card over and continued on the back. She wrote about the heartbreak that still haunted her. She had given her longtime love, Chris, space to decide whether he was ready for marriage. He was—but not to her. After six years with Maggie, Chris met and married another woman within six months, and the couple now shared the home and business that he and Maggie had created together.

She then wrote about her fear that she would never achieve her dream of creating exceptional, evocative art—and if she didn't do that, what was her future? Who would she be? She shared her worry that the strain of a murder investigation would cause her mother's cancer to return. And finally, she revealed her deepest shame: there was a part of her that dreaded the possible loss of Ninette beyond the grief it would bring. Maggie knew that if her mother died, she would step into Ninette's place as Crozat's chatelaine, trading her own dreams for her parents' because she loved them so dearly.

She signed her name in the only tiny blank space left on the card and then placed it in an envelope and addressed it to Bo. She thought for a moment and put the card next to a pile of books on the desk, knowing in her heart that it was something that you write but never send. Then she checked her phone. It was time to get ready for Fet Let. She'd reread the card later that night for her own catharsis and then tear it up and write the simple note to Bo that she intended to write in the first place.

*

The streets around Pelican's town green were closed to traffic for the evening, so the Crozats parked behind Fais Dough Dough and shuttled tables and supplies to their spot next to Lia's in front of her shops. The Butlers and the Georgia boys pitched in to help. All of Crozat's guests were excited to be part of the town's festival. It was a welcome distraction from the deaths of Crozat's elderly duo. "I'm really starting to feel at home in Pelican," Emily told Maggie as the two transported a large table to the Crozats' site. "Who knows, Shane and I may never leave."

Maggie smiled. "That would be nice. I could use some new friends. Most of the ones I went to high school with are married and going on their second or even third kid, so they don't have much time to get together. Or much interest, to be honest."

"Ugh." Emily made a face. "Can you imagine being around thirty and already having three kids? It seems so old-timey."

"I know. But there's a part of me that envies them. I wish I could want that. I mean, I know I want it someday, but I wish I wanted it now. I feel like it would make my life so much simpler."

"That's funny, thinking having kids would make your life simpler," Emily said. "My parents always said that their lives were so much easier before I came along." Emily tried to make this sound like a joke but couldn't hide the hurt underneath.

Maggie felt for her. "What a crappy thing for parents to say. I'm sorry." She hugged Emily, who brightened.

"I'm going to look for Shane. If you need us, text me."

"Will do."

Emily went to find her husband, and Maggie focused on setting up her family's table. She waved to Lia and Kyle, who were bringing out baked goods and candies from Bon Bon and Fais Dough Dough for Lia's Fet Let booth. Kyle waved back and Lia blew her a kiss. Maggie was happy to see Lia's playful side reemerge after a long period of mourning.

An hour later, Fet Let was in full swing. Bunting in green, gold, and purple decorated the lacy iron balconies of Pelican's historic town center. A Cajun band followed a Zydeco group on the bandstand, and revelers two-stepped to the classic tunes. But traffic at the Crozat stand was surprisingly light. The band took a break and the dancers dispersed. Yet for the first time in the history of Ninette's Crawfish Crozat, no long line of hungry patrons formed. A few out-of-towners browsed but didn't buy. It was as if some kind of subliminal message had gone out to all Fet attendees. Maggie had heard actor and comedian friends in New York talk about "flop sweat," the panic they felt when an audience wasn't responding to their material. She was beginning to know how it felt. She smiled and tried making eye contact with some festivalgoers, friends and neighbors she'd known for years, but they looked away. She was horrified to realize that they were actively avoiding her.

The one person she had no interest in seeing, Rufus Durand, finished planting a sloppy kiss on girlfriend Vanessa and then wandered over to the Crozat table. His belly strained the buttons of the shirt he wore to the Fet every year, a purple polyester button-down with a pattern of yellow cocktail shakers.

"Hey there, Crozats."

Ninette and Tug greeted Rufus politely, but Maggie chose to pass on the pleasantries. "Any updates for us, Ru? Did you get anything useful off the poison box, like prints or something?"

"I wish I had some news, but I'm afraid I don't. These complex investigations take time, sorry to say."

Maggie wanted to yell at Rufus that she knew he was dragging his feet because the sooner the case was solved, the sooner the Crozats' lives could get back to normal, and that's the last thing he wanted. He was having way too much fun watching the family twist in the humid Louisiana wind. Instead, she dished out a bowl of crawfish and offered it to Ru with a smile. "Here you go. On the house."

"That's real generous," Rufus said, "but I'll pass. I know y'all are up to code and real thorough about everything. But still . . . we did find a box of poison in your kitchen today."

Rufus strode off, and Maggie's face flushed with humiliation. He had nailed the reason Ninette's dish had no takers. People were afraid to eat it. She assumed local gossip had progressed to the point of pegging one of the Crozats as the murderer, but the locals actually fearing her family was a low that she hadn't foreseen. Maggie debated how to break the news to her parents, but she didn't have to. They'd overheard her conversation with Rufus.

"I've never been so embarrassed," Ninette said, her voice quavering.

"I'm sure people are just being . . . you know . . . careful maybe . . . or busy." Maggie hated how lame she sounded. She noticed that Ninette was stirring her pot as if she had a weird tic, tightly clutching the large wooden spoon and whipping it around the pot in repetitive circles. "Mom, let me do that. Please take a break, the stress isn't good for you."

She reached for the spoon, but Ninette refused to let go. "It's my dish and my job."

Tug, furious, balled his hands into fists and pounded them together, a substitute for actually pounding someone. "We've known these sonuvabitches all our lives," he muttered. "Now I never want to see 'em or speak to any of 'em again. Ever."

Emily and Shane bounded over, holding hands. They'd been dancing and both were damp with perspiration. "I'm starving," Shane said. "Tell me you still have food left. I know how popular your dish is."

"Oh, that's so not a problem today." Maggie filled the Butlers in on the crawfish debacle. The couple was incensed on the Crozats' behalf.

"Unbelievable. Em, come with me."

Shane marched off with his wife, and Maggie wondered what he might up to. She found out a few moments later when he returned with every Crozat guest—the Cuties, the Georgia boys, Kyle, even the Ryker family. They formed a line at the stand.

"I hear this is the best dish at Fet Let," Shane announced loudly, for the benefit of passersby.

"As a guest of Crozat Plantation, I know what care they put into their delicious food and what fresh ingredients they use," Jan said. She couldn't have sounded more stilted, and Maggie couldn't have been more grateful. Ninette and Tug happily dished out hearty bowls to all their guests, whose pleasure didn't have to be faked.

"Oh my God, this is amazing," Carrie Ryker said as she dug into her pasta.

"It's beyond amazing." Lachlan Ryker held out his bowl, which he'd quickly emptied. "I must have some more."

As the guests devoured their portions, Cal and Artie sauntered over, still in uniform. "We just got off," Cal said. "Now where's that pot of Crawfish Crozat you promised, Tug?"

"If the Pelican PD, the guys who searched our kitchen, are eating here, you should too," Maggie, emboldened, called to the crowds of festivalgoers. And slowly customers trickled up to the stand until a line finally formed. Ninette's dish might sell out after all.

The Crozat guests dismissed the family's thanks. "Uh, excuse me, we're doing ourselves a favor eating this," Georgia One said as he tucked into his third helping.

"That is the truth, my friend," Artie agreed. "It's okay to get fat if it's on Crawfish Crozat."

"Hah, that's my partner, Rapmaster R2DCool." Cal guffawed and then coughed as he choked on a crawfish. Shane Butler gave him a swat on the back and the fish went down Cal's gullet. "Thanks, buddy. Almost saw my maker. But what a way to go."

"The police here are so much nicer than in New York," Emily Butler whispered to Maggie. "I once saw a cop screaming at a homeless man trying to wash car windows outside the entrance of the Lincoln Tunnel. I felt so bad for the guy that I gave him two dollars, even though we don't even own a car." Maggie recalled the time she'd seen Rufus sock a local driver whose brakes went out at a stop sign but chose not to share the story with the guests. Better to have them retain an image of Pelican as a Cajun Brigadoon, which it was living up to at the moment.

"Maggie, hon, would you mind picking up a couple of beers for your mom and me at the beverage tent?" Tug asked. Her father's face was reddened by the large crawfish pot's steam and his shirt pocked with sweat stains, but Tug was in his element tending to the growing line of customers.

"Sure, Dad. Be right back."

She headed to the beverage tent, which was being manned by the Crozat support staff, Marie and Bud Shexnayder.

"Glad to see business is finally picking up at the stand," Bud said.

"Yeah, it was iffy for a while."

Marie made a face. "That idiot Rufus Durand came by and was giving us grief about working at 'the scene of the crime.' Even implying that we might want to quit, especially since he don't know if they'll ever solve the murder."

"More like he don't want to," Bud grumbled.

"You know it, Bud," Maggie said. She got the beers, delivered them to her parents, and then sat on bench under one of the giant oak trees that encircled the green. Bud was right. Ru would throw up every roadblock he could to the investigation. Maggie realized that the only option was to circumvent him. She hurried back over to the Shexnayders.

"You guys have been so wonderful during this horrible time," she told them. "I don't know how we'll ever thank you, but we can start by giving you the rest of the week off. Paid, of course."

"Oh, Maggie, that's sweet, but it's not necessary," Marie said.

"Yes it is. Do something fun, like go down to New Orleans."

"You got a pretty full house," Bud said. "Who's gonna do all that cleaning?"

Maggie waved off the question. "Not your problem, but don't worry, we'll make sure it gets done."

Bud hesitated. "I don't know. I feel like we should be there for you."

"You have been, Bud. That's why we want to do something special for you. Really, we insist."

Marie hesitated. "It has been a while."

"I hear they fixed up Broussard's," her husband said. "I'd love to see that. And now that I'm thinking New Orleans, I'm craving a Mother's Oyster Po'boy. Dressed, with extra everything, lettuce, tomato, mayo . . . mmmm."

Marie smiled at her husband. "Now you got me craving one, too. If you really think it's okay, Maggie, then I guess we're going to New Orleans for a getaway weekend."

"Excellent. And bring me back one of those po'boys, you hear?"

Maggie bought a beer from the Shexnayders and left them eagerly planning their trip. She checked on her parents, who were dishing out the last of Ninette's Crawfish Crozat, which was once again the hit of the Fet. She scraped herself a bowl from the bottom of the pot and then found a square of empty grass on the crowded green to enjoy her meal.

She gave herself a mental pat on the back for coming up with the idea to take over the Shexnayders' housekeeping and maintenance duties. Both jobs offered great opportunities for snooping. The fact that Beverly Clabber had once lived in Pelican certainly widened the pool of suspects beyond Crozat's boundaries, but the B and B at least offered a convenient starting point for Maggie's informal investigation. While she hated to think that any of Crozat's guests might be responsible for Beverly Clabber's death, Rufus Durand's call to inaction for the PPD meant that someone had to either rule them out as suspects or reveal one of them to be a murderer. And it looked like that someone would be Maggie.

Chapter Fourteen

Early the next morning, an unhappy Maggie surveyed the mass of cleaning products jammed into the Crozat housekeeping closet. Tending to each guest room in the B and B now seemed like an enormous task, and she had no idea where to begin, having sent the Shexnayders off on their minivacation without asking for any guidance.

"I really didn't think this through," she muttered. For a moment, she was tempted to hire a cleaning crew. But she reminded herself that housekeeping provided the perfect cover for investigating the plantation's guests.

Maggie noticed what appeared to be a schedule slipped into a plastic holder taped to the wall and pulled the paper from its holder. She nudged an upright vacuum cleaner out of its snug space and then leaned against it and perused the schedule. She was relieved to see that Bud and Marie had carefully notated how and when to attend to each guest room. She was equally relieved to find that each guest had opted for the politically correct choice of alternate-day sheet-and-towel washing, which would save the environment a little wear and tear and Maggie a bundle of time. Still, she'd have to hustle if she was to service each room every day that the Shexnayders were gone. Maggie's roommates in New York would have appreciated the irony of a "primo, number one slob," as one redundantly called her, being tasked with maintaining Crozat's pristine cleanliness.

She wheeled out the housekeeping cart, checked to make sure it was stocked with supplies, and then pushed it down the hall. As she pushed, she laid down some ground rules for herself. Initially, at least, she'd limit her investigating to whatever was in plain sight, only peeking in drawers or suitcases if nothing was obvious. For one thing, blatantly going through her guests' belongings made her uncomfortable. For another, if she was to meet the cleaning demands of the day, she'd have to work within a tight time frame that would limit the opportunity to poke through people's private possessions. She'd keep the possibility as a backup plan, but Maggie hoped it wouldn't come to that.

She reached the end of the long hallway and parked the cart. The Georgia boys were bunking together in one of the upstairs bedrooms. Another housed Kyle—when he was there. Maggie was thrilled to note that the gentleman from Texas spent less and less of his time at Crozat and more and more of it at Lia's.

I'll have to fit a gossipy update into my agenda, she thought as she trudged up the stairs laden with buckets holding cleaning supplies.

She unlocked the Georgia boys' room, opened the door, and was assaulted by the mess and stench one would expect from three twenty-year-old frat brothers sharing a single room. Her eyes stung with tears engendered by both the locker-room-meets-old-food smell and the thought of having to plow through the piles of clutter. But Maggie would do what had to be done, so she drew in a deep breath—which she instantly regretted because it filled her nostrils with the scent of unwashed gym socks—and went to work.

After an hour of shallow breathing through her mouth, she'd finished most of the cleaning. She checked the Shexnayder schedule and was depressed to see that she'd taken three times as long as the allotted time per room. The Georgias were given the same twenty minutes of attention that the rest of the guests got. Apparently a triple threat of messy frat boys didn't faze Bud and Marie.

Aside from a selection of graphic novels featuring buxom, borderline pornographic heroines, Maggie had yet to uncover anything of interest. She cleaned the bathroom, made the bed, gave the room's dresser bureau a quick dusting, and straightened out a few piles of papers. Then she picked up the room's trashcan and dumped its contents into a large plastic bag. A few items missed the transfer and fell to the floor. She picked up one, a brochure for a costume rental company, and noticed that someone had circled a Confederate Army uniform. Typical, she thought with disgust. Southern frat boys still romanticized the brutal and devastating Civil War one hundred fifty years after it ended. At least the Georgia boys' car didn't sport the bumper sticker, "Hell no, the war ain't over," like she'd recently seen on a local's pickup truck.

She tossed the brochure into her trash bag and retrieved a crumpled piece of loose-leaf paper from the floor. She uncrumpled the paper and read the words scribbled on it: "Slaves? How much? A chase—fun!!"

Maggie sat on the edge of the room's double bed, being careful not to disturb the hospital corners she'd almost thrown out her back making. There was something ominous in the papers she'd discovered. What exactly were the Georgia boys up to? Was it illegal or just horribly offensive? And if it was illegal, had Beverly Clabber somehow stumbled on a plan that led to her needing to be silenced? That seemed a stretch, but Maggie decided she could no longer view the trio as three harmless goofballs. She'd have to keep an eye on them. She'd also learned an invaluable lesson, something every Hollywood tabloid reporter already knew: if you wanted to dig up garbage on people, dig through their garbage.

*

Maggie spent the rest of the day tending to all the rooms. She flipped the schedule around, based on who liked to hang out their "Do Not Disturb" sign until noon (the Butlers) and who bolted early for sightseeing adventures (the Rykers and Cuties). Since this was her first day on the job and she'd already used up too much time dealing with the Georgia boys' slobbery, she put sleuthing second to her housekeeping duties, knowing that familiarizing herself with the routine meant she'd be able to power through it faster.

By early evening she was drained, but she dragged herself to the kitchen where Tug and Ninette were preparing dinner. Maggie noticed that her dad was making a treat he'd invented that combined unsweetened chocolate, raisins, a dash of salt, and honey, which gave the candy a hard-taffy consistency. Tug had proudly named his concoction "Chulanes" as an homage to his alma mater, Tulane University. Maggie knew that putting up a batch of Chulanes relaxed her father. It was his way of dealing with tension.

"Oh, honey, you look beat," Ninette said, casting one eye on her daughter and one on the bowl of fresh shrimp she was dumping into a pot of gumbo. "It was sweet of you to give the Shexnayders a break, but I wish you'd checked with us first. We could have timed it so we could bring in someone else to do the cleaning."

"Unless you dug up Lafitte's treasure, there's no way we can pay for that," Maggie said as she spooned a shrimp from the gumbo pot. "Especially considering that we're not generating any income from our guests right now."

"That's for certain," Tug said as he finished filling a tray with Chulanes. He put it in the freezer to harden and then turned to his daughter. "But if you need a hand, you let me know. And you be careful, okay?"

"Okay, Dad." The look in her dad's eyes told Maggie that he knew she was up to something. Giving his tacit approval didn't mean he wouldn't worry about her. "Why are you using the small pot for the gumbo, Mom?" she asked, trying to change the subject.

"Looks like it's just us for dinner tonight. Everyone else made other plans. Even Gran's off playing bingo at the assisted living."

"Yay! Not that I don't love our guests, but still . . . yay." Maggie collapsed onto a chair at the kitchen table and put her feet up on another, relieved for a break in the 24/7 B and B hosting duties. "To celebrate, I'm not going to shower or put on makeup before dinner. Tonight, what you see is what you get, people."

Tug poured each of them a glass of wine while Ninette dished up big bowls of gumbo and set them on the table. Maggie roused herself to cut hunks of fresh bread and then dropped one on each soup bowl, where they floated like tasty little rafts.

The family was just about to eat when Bo Durand appeared in the doorway.

"Sorry, I didn't mean to interrupt your dinner. I had a bit of good news and thought I'd share it in person. It's just a bit, like I said, but still."

"A bit is better than nothing and you're not interrupting anything," Ninette jumped up and gestured to a chair. "Why don't you join us?"

"That's kind of you, but I brought company."

Bo stepped back and gently nudged a slight boy about seven in front of him. "This is my son, Xander."

"Hey there, Xander," Maggie smiled and waved from her seat, as did Tug. Gopher raised himself from his canine stupor, galumphed over to Xander, gave him one sniff, and then parked himself next to the boy. Xander was slight, with features that were delicate for a boy. He had his father's thick, straight hair but it was blonde instead of black, and his eyes were green, not Bo's deep, dark brown.

Ninette bent down so she was eye level with Xander. "Nice to meet you. Can I talk you into some gumbo?" Xander, his expression serious, shook his head no. "Then how about a hot dog?" With the same serious expression, Xander nodded yes. "Okay, then. You and your daddy join us at the table while I get your dinner. Maggie, get Bo a bowl, please."

"Bet you're sorry you skimped on the showering and makeup now, ain't ya?" Tug teased her in a whisper.

"Shut up," she whispered back and then stood up and fixed Bo a bowl of gumbo. He took the bowl and thanked her with a grin that to Maggie's surprise seemed a little shy. A surge of warmth coursed through her body, and she quickly looked away from him. Her eyes caught her dad's. Tug winked at her, and the warmth turned into a flush of embarrassment. "So, Detective, we're still waiting for the good news," she said, her tone as businesslike as she could manage.

"There are no fingerprints from any members of your family on the arsenic box. In fact, there are no prints at all on it. The theory is that someone planted the box either to implicate or cause trouble for your family."

"You mean, exactly like I told you when you found the box?"

"Maggie," Ninette said in a singsongy warning tone. "Manners." Ninette fished Xander's hot dog off the range grill, placed it on a bun and dressed it with ketchup and mustard. "There you go, sweetie," she said as she handed it to him.

Xander looked at the hot dog and his serious expression morphed into panic. He began shaking his head fiercely and flapping his arms. Then he began to sob. Gopher, who seemed to have appointed himself Xander's guardian, barked in concern.

"It's okay, buddy," his father reassured Xander while Maggie and her parents stared, confused. "I'm real sorry. It's just . . . he doesn't like it when different colors and flavors touch each other." There was a look of anguish in Bo's eyes, as if he were begging them to understand.

Ninette quickly removed the hot dog, and Xander calmed down. "It's my fault," she said. "I should have asked before I dressed it. Xander, I am so very, very sorry. I'll make you a new hot dog and let you put whatever you want on it yourself. Would that be okay?"

Xander stopped flapping and shaking. He nodded yes, his demeanor no longer anxiety ridden but once again serious.

"Thank you, ma'am," Bo said. "We should probably wash up first. Be right back."

Bo took his son's hand and led him out of the kitchen to the restroom. As soon as he was gone, Maggie turned to her parents. "What was *that* about?"

"For goodness sake, Magnolia, show some sensitivity." Ninette had never snapped at her that way before, and Maggie felt ashamed of her flip comment. "That poor child obviously has some serious issues. I remember when we hosted that end-of-year lunch for the Pelican Elementary teachers, I heard them talking about how so many kids today are 'on the spectrum.' I think that could be the case with Xander. I'm guessing he's either autistic or has Asperger syndrome."

Tug sighed. "When I was a kid, we just called boys like him weirdoes and treated them that way. I hate to think how they suffered because we just didn't know any better."

"Well, nowadays we do know better." Ninette glared at her daughter. "And we need to show that with our behavior."

"You're right, Mama," Maggie said, abashed.

Ninette finished grilling a second hot dog for Xander just as Bo returned with his son. She looked to Xander before placing the hot dog in a bun, and he solemnly nodded his approval.

"Condiments are over here, sweetie," Ninette said, pointing to the kitchen table. Xander stared at them thoughtfully and then carefully squirted a thin line of ketchup on his frank. He eyeballed the line, and then squirted a fine thread of mustard so thin that it paralleled the ketchup almost exactly. Maggie was impressed by his precision. The boy sat down to eat his hot dog. After getting a refill of gumbo, she took a seat next to him. The others joined them at the table. While Bo, Ninette, and Tug chatted about Fet Let, Maggie focused her attention on Xander.

"Is it good?" she asked. Xander nodded yes as he slowly ate his hot dog. Maggie noticed that he was counting each bite before he swallowed. "You know," she continued. "I'm an artist and I hate when certain colors get mixed together, too. I can show you, but I'd have to mix the ketchup and mustard." She turned to Bo. "Do you think it would be okay? I don't want to upset him again."

Bo laid a hand on his son's shoulder. "Xander, would you like to see that, if she does it on her own plate and not yours?"

Xander pondered the question for a minute and then, a little wary, nodded yes. Maggie took the ketchup and mustard and squirted both into her now-empty bowl. She took a spoon and mixed the two together until they formed a muddy paste.

Xander watched, both repulsed and fascinated. She showed the homely result to Xander.

"Ugh, ugly. I don't like this at all. Do you?"

Xander shook his head no. He looked at her expectantly, waiting for what might come next. Maggie panicked for a moment, but then she had a brainstorm. "Would you like to come over tomorrow and mix pretty colors with me?" she asked the boy. Xander nodded and this time, for a brief second, there was a flicker of a smile in his eyes. Maggie turned to Bo. "I mean, if it's all right with you."

"Uh, yeah. It's great. Absolutely."

The meal finished without incident and Maggie gathered up the dirty dishes. "I'll clean up," she told her parents.

"Xander and I'll help," Bo said.

"Actually," Ninette said, "I was thinking Tug and I might show Xander our new chicken yard. It's pretty big because we want to produce free-range eggs for the plantation."

"That sounds like way more fun than washing and drying dishes, doesn't it, son?" Bo winked at his son, who responded with his de facto solemn nod. Ninette and Tug each offered the boy a hand. He stared thoughtfully and then took them. The trio headed for the chicken yard, with Gopher on the seven-year-old's heels.

"Dogs know, don't they?" Bo said as he watched them go.

"Know what?" Maggie asked.

"When someone . . . when a kid . . . is special."

"Xander *is* special, Bo. And in the best way that word can mean."

133

Bo began gathering plates and placing them in sink. "Thanks. He liked you."

"Really?" she said as she began rinsing dinnerware and placing it in the dishwasher. "How could you tell?"

"Eye contact. He looked you in the eye. He hardly ever does that. So it means something."

"Wow. That's great." Maggie was surprised by how good this made her feel and then slightly depressed that the approval of a seven-year-old would mean so much. *The bar's been lowered since the days when it took Julian Schnabel remembering my name to get me excited,* she thought. Maggie handed Bo a towel. "Why don't you dry the stuff that has to be hand-washed?"

"Yes, ma'am."

The two washed and dried in a silence that felt surprisingly comfortable to her. When they finished, they worked together to put everything in its proper place. Bo wrinkled his nose. "I keep smelling some kind of chemical. I wonder if there's a leak at one of the plants. Maybe I should call headquarters."

"No, don't bother," The lingering scent of disinfectant on Maggie's clothes had disrupted their camaraderie, and she found herself annoyed as well as mortified. "It's me. I gave the Shexnayders some time off and I've been doing the cleaning."

"That was nice of you. Although . . . interesting timing."

"How so?" Her face flushed bright red, contradicting her innocent tone.

"It would've made a lot more sense to wait until after the case is solved to give your help a break. I wouldn't think you'd want to take on the extra work right now. Of course, never know what you'll find in other people's rooms."

"Boy, you detective types sure are suspicious," she responded with what she hoped was a casual shrug. *If this investigation is going to drag on, maybe I should invest in some acting lessons,* she mused. Maggie had never been very good at disguising her "tells," as old poker buddies, flush with winnings they'd taken off her, would attest to. She steeled herself for a scolding from Bo—"Don't meddle, it's not safe, you're interfering with police business." But instead, Bo asked, "Where does this big bowl go?"

"Oh. Bottom shelf."

Bo had chosen to let the subject slide and she was relieved but still on guard. Years of run-ins with Bo's slippery cousin Rufus had taught her that it was best to watch one's back when dealing with a Durand.

"So," said Bo as he put away the bowl. "I got your note."

"What note? I didn't—" Maggie was puzzled, and then it hit her. Gran' must have found and mailed the apology note that Maggie meant to throw out. She couldn't blame her grandmother; it was her own fault for not tearing it up.

"Thanks for sharing all that," Bo continued.

"Glad you liked it." Maggie kept her response neutral but inwardly panicked as she tried to remember exactly how much she'd bared her soul in that note to this virtual stranger.

"It actually made me feel better about a lot of stuff."

Hearing Bo's positive reaction, she relaxed. "My life is such a mess that yours looks good in comparison now?"

Bo laughed. "No. More like—we're going through a lot of the same things. Feeling unsettled. Not sure if we're making the right or wrong choices with our lives."

"And you're a dad, so that makes things even more complicated."

"Yes. Exactly."

Bo's face lit up, and for a split second, Maggie felt dizzy. She shook it off and focused on putting away leftovers. "It's weird how you can have a life that feels like an appearance of a life. Do you know what I mean?"

"Yes. That's what my marriage was—an appearance of a marriage."

"How long were you married?"

"Nine years. Got married right out of college. Yes, I went to college, don't look so surprised. You can't be an idiot and be a detective."

"But I guess you can be an idiot and be a police chief, at least in Pelican." Maggie winced. "Gah, I've got such a big mouth. Sorry, I know Ru is family."

"Doesn't mean I have to agree with him. Or even like him."

"I have to be honest, it's hard to believe you two are related. You're the total opposite of each other. He's such a dumbass good ol' boy. And you're so not."

"That's my mom's doing. She was one of those old-fashioned types who wanted her kids to have a better life than she did, so she made sure we had manners, and spoke well, and got a good education."

"You said 'was.'"

"Died of a brain tumor when I was sixteen."

Maggie, who had spent her entire life terrified that Ninette's cancer would return and claim her, felt for Bo. "I'm so sorry."

"Thanks."

Noticing that Bo's mood had darkened, she changed the subject. "You seem to have a good relationship with your ex. What broke you guys up?"

"Whitney and I just realized we're different people. Different needs, different interests, different dreams . . . things you don't give much thought to when you're twenty-two and just hot for each other. Scientists say that the brain doesn't fully form until we're twenty-five. I believe that and as far as I'm concerned, there'd be a whole lot less divorces if people weren't allowed to get married until they were over twenty-five. Whitney's a good person and the mother of my son, but we both heaved a pretty big sigh of relief when we agreed to divorce. And it's not the easiest thing being married to a detective. I spend a lot of time in my head."

"So do artists."

"See? Something else we have in common."

Bo flashed his sexy grin, and once again Maggie felt dizzy. She downed the last drop of wine from a bottle and then tossed it into the recycle container. "I didn't know we had anything in common."

"We both think Ru's an idiot."

She had to laugh. "You have no idea how much I enjoy hearing you say that."

"More than an idiot. He's a right bastard. Whitney remarried a guy who works out on a rig, Zach Evans, so they moved down here to be closer for his work. I wanted to be near Xander, so Ru got me a job with PPD, and I owe him for that. Except that . . . There's a school in Baton Rouge for kids like Xander. It's an amazing place, but it's real expensive. I'd have the money if the Durand family sold Grove Hall, but thanks to the Napoleonic Code, we can't do that unless we all agree to the sale."

"And Rufus won't."

"What, Rufus give this town the satisfaction of seeing Grove Hall beautifully restored and cared for? Not gonna happen. As long as it's a wreck, it's his flipping the bird to Pelican."

"Oh, that stinks on every level," Maggie said. Bo nodded grimly. She closed the fridge door and looked straight at Bo. "Am I wrong in thinking that Ru's personal flipping the bird to us Crozats is stonewalling Bev Clabber's murder investigation?"

"I can't reveal anything. All I can say is, trust your instincts."

She appreciated Bo's subtle honesty. It encouraged her to share what she'd learned about the Cajun Cuties. "I found out something you should know," she said, and filled him in on the executive board shuffle that put Suzy at the financial helm of the nonprofit.

"That's a very interesting angle," Bo said when she was done. "I'll get in touch with the IRS and see if they've sniffed out any improprieties with the organization's returns or 501C3 status." Bo grinned. "Nice work. Maybe we should put you on the force as a reserve."

Maggie shook her head vigorously and waved her arms no. "Nuh-uh, this is all about survival for me and my family. Although," she giggled, "it would be hilarious to see Ru's reaction if he saw me behind a station desk."

"What the heck are you thinking, bringing a Crozat in here, Coz?" Bo said in a spot-on imitation of his cousin. "The curse, man, the curse!"

Maggie and Bo were still entertaining themselves with this unlikely scenario when Tug and Ninette returned with Xander, who was clutching a bouquet of lettuce varieties that he handed to his father. "Cool," Bo said as he admired the collection of greens. "Did you pick this yourself?" Xander nodded yes. "Well, I can't wait to eat them. Now we better get you home to bed. It's a school night."

Maggie bent down and looked Xander in the eye. The young boy held her glance. "I'll see you after school for that art lesson," she told him, and Xander responded with one of his solemn nods. Bo thanked the Crozats for their hospitality and then took his son's hand and led him out of the house to their car.

After they left, Maggie poured herself a glass of wine and took it with her onto the veranda. She sat in one of her family's heirloom rocking chairs, handed down through generations of Crozats, and contemplated the evening. She knew Bo was right about trusting her instincts. But those instincts weren't helping her answer one very important question: could she trust Bo? She feared her nascent attraction to him might be coloring her judgment.

She closed her eyes, trying to release the stress nipping at her mind and tensing her body. And as she relaxed, Maggie realized something.

Xander hadn't said a single word the entire night.

Chapter Fifteen

When she woke up at dawn, Maggie ached in muscles she never knew she had. But she soldiered on with Crozat maintenance, picking up the pace as she grew more familiar with the routine. While her cleaning skills grew, her detecting ability seemed to have leveled out. Aside from discovering that Cutie Debbie was hoarding mini shampoo bottles, she didn't dig up incriminating dirt on any of the guests.

She finished folding towels in the Rykers' bathroom and then pushed the cleaning cart back to its home in the supply closet and locked it up, done for the day. As she strode back to the shotgun, now focused on organizing art supplies that would appeal to Xander, her frustration dissolved. Maggie walked into her bedroom, lay on the floor, and reached under the bed. She pulled out an old box of acrylic paints and threw out the few that had dried up. She checked her supply of canvases, choosing an 8' × 10" for her young charge. She was surprised to notice that her heart was racing. *I'm a little too excited about this art lesson*, she thought, and took a few breaths to calm herself.

She remembered that she'd never confirmed a time with Bo, so she pulled her cell out of her back jeans pocket and sent him a text. Then, mindful of his reaction to the scent of cleaning fluid that permeated her being after a day of housecleaning, she jumped in the shower. An internal debate about what outfit to wear followed, as well as a light but effective application of makeup. Maggie, in slim jeans and a purple fitted T-shirt that subtly enhanced her figure, was completely ready for the arrival of father and fils when Bo texted that he and Xander wouldn't be able to make it: "Sorry. Bad day. Xander bullied. Rain check."

Her excitement turned to grievous disappointment, which she also noted as a disproportionate reaction to a seven-year-old's art lesson. When Gran' sauntered into the shotgun carrying two Sazeracs, Maggie grabbed one and took a large gulp.

"I hate bullies. They're the worst," she said, her tone bitter. She followed the pronouncement with a big swig of her drink.

"Hmm," Gran' said, as she eyed her granddaughter thoughtfully. "Not a particularly erudite observation, but I'd have to agree." Gran' took a dainty sip of her cocktail while Maggie drained her glass. "In fact, Yvonne Rousseau and I were talking about that very thing last night at the seniors' bingo game. We both agreed that Francine-slash-Beverly was a terrible bully when she lived here."

Maggie took in this revelation. "Really? I never would have guessed that from meeting Mrs. Clabber. How was she a bully?"

Ellen Byron

"Honestly, darlin', I couldn't say. I guess I just blocked it out. Yvonne remembers it pretty well, though. You might want to speak with her."

"I will. Do you think now would be a good time to visit?" Maggie knew that a few of Gran's friends suffered from Sundowning Syndrome. They might be alert and coherent in the morning, but as the day progressed, their faculties faded and dementia increased.

"Oh, Yvonne is all there mentally. It's her poor body that's failing her, what with that horrid rheumatoid arthritis. She'd love to see you. I'd hop on over there right now."

"I will." Maggie gave her grandmother a soft kiss on the cheek. "Thanks for the intel. I'll clean up these supplies and take off."

By the time Maggie got to the Camellia Park Senior Village, it was 4:30 p.m., and before she even entered the faux plantation building, she could hear the china clatter as residents took advantage of the dining room's first seating. Yvonne was delighted to hear from Maggie and had given detailed instructions on how to find her one-bedroom apartment in the assisted living section of the complex. Maggie still managed to get lost in the collection of identical corridors, which seemed designed to taunt hapless seniors who were already teetering on the edge of dementia. She hoped no poor soul had ever been carted off to the Alzheimer's wing of the facility because they were found wandering the halls in a legitimately confused daze.

"Magnolia, down here, honey!"

She was relieved to see Yvonne waving a gnarled hand from her wheelchair in front of one of the interchangeable doors. Her

142

silver hair was styled, and she wore an ancient Chanel suit. It touched Maggie to see that Yvonne had dressed up for their meeting. She hurried to the older woman, kissed her on both cheeks as she handed her a bouquet of flowers, and followed her into a compact apartment. The décor theme seemed to be "extended-stay motel," but Yvonne had added some personal touches via artwork and photographs. A small, sleek Art Deco cabinet was the only piece of furniture that Maggie vaguely recognized from Yvonne's elegant former home on the outskirts of Pelican.

"Isn't this place wonderful?" Yvonne said with genuine enthusiasm. "My kids thought I'd miss all my space and my stuff, but I don't, not for a minute. I don't have to think about anything here except what's going on in the activity room and when the next meal is. It's like being on a cruise ship but without the seasickness."

"I'm glad you're happy, Mrs. Rousseau. It makes sense only keeping things that you feel sentimental about, like that gorgeous cabinet."

Yvonne looked puzzled, and then she burst out laughing. "There's nothing sentimental about that old thing." She rolled over to the piece and gave the front of it a hard thump. The top sprang open and a full bar popped up, as if the cabinet were a booze-filled jack-in-the-box. "It's five o'clock somewhere, and that somewhere is *here,*" Yvonne declared. "What can I do you for?"

"A gin and tonic, thanks."

"You got it."

Yvonne went to work, her crippled hands no obstacle when it came to mixing drinks. She rolled to a small table near the kitchen area and motioned for Maggie to join her. Maggie raised the glass Yvonne handed her and toasted the older woman. "*A votre santé.* To your health."

"Oh honey, my health is in the rearview mirror. Let's drink to your health and happiness. *Laissez les bons temps rouler.* 'Cuz it'd be nice for something to roll around here besides me, and it might as well be good times."

"*Eh bien. Laissez les bons temps rouler.*"

The women toasted and drank. It occurred to Maggie that she was doing way more drinking with Pelican's eightysomethings than she'd ever done with New York's twentysomethings.

"Now," Yvonne said, "let's get down to business. You want to know about that and-it-rhymes-with-witch Francine."

"Gran' said that you recalled Francine was something of a bully."

"No 'something' about it. It was the late forties when we were all in high school together, right after the war ended. Many of the boys we knew lied about their age and went off to fight. And so many didn't come back."

Yvonne paused. Her eyes, faded by age to a pale gray-blue, watered. "I lost both my older brothers, you know. Papa and Ma'mere were never the same after that. In those days, a daughter didn't count for much. Much like the Chinese girl baby these days. The Chinese have finally realized they were wrong about that. I don't believe my parents ever did."

Maggie gently laid her hand on Yvonne's, and the older woman's swollen, bent fingers gripped hers. "Thank you, dear. Listen to me, going off track like that. What I was trying to get at was that between the loss of so many, and the ones who came home just to go off to college on the GI Bill, there was a serious lack of young men in Pelican. I'm afraid all of us gals became somewhat competitive over who was left. In other circumstances, Ignace would hardly have been considered a catch, what with his sense of superiority and fondness for brown liquids, if you know what I mean. The man never met a bottle of bourbon he didn't like. But he was good looking enough and very much knew how to turn on the charm, so he became your Gran's first boyfriend. And you know how intense that can be."

"Oh, yes," Maggie said. She felt a stab of emotional pain as she recalled the initial passion that she and Chris shared. She had never lost that feeling; when did he? Maggie found herself slipping into depression and forced herself back into the moment. She wasn't there to moan about her sorry love life to Yvonne.

"Francine had burned through many of the other local boys, either by her choice or theirs," Yvonne continued. "So she turned her sights on Ignace. She'd assembled a clique of girls who were terrified of retribution if they didn't follow her lead, so when she put them to the task of spreading vile rumors about your grandmother, they jumped on it like the Wicked Witch of the West's flying monkeys. They knew if they didn't do Francine's bidding, they'd be turned from aggressors to victims."

"What kind of rumors did they spread?"

"At first it was silly stuff, like she dyed her hair and stuffed her bra. But it wasn't enough for Francine to steal Charlotte's boyfriend; she had to bring her down completely. So she spread the worst rumor of all." Yvonne leaned in and whispered to

Maggie, as if the rumor still had the power to destroy. "She had her minions let it be known that your grandmother and Ignace had . . . relations."

"What?"

"I know. You see, Francine was always what we used to call a tart. But when she started that rumor, she managed to reverse roles and paint your Gran' as the one with loose morals. Oh my goodness, that led to such a scene. Charlotte demanding that Francine retract this horrible lie, Francine refusing. And Charlotte screaming, 'If you don't, I swear, I will kill you.'"

Maggie felt her stomach drop to the floor. "Gran' said that?"

"Oh yes, to Francine, to us. Of course, when Francine ran off with Ignace to get married, everything went back as it was. Your Gran's reputation was restored and Francine's was back in the gutter, especially when Ignace abandoned her only weeks after their quickie wedding. From what I heard, Francine was so humiliated about the damage done to her character that she couldn't face returning to Pelican. But my, did that trollop lord it over Charlotte while she could. She was from a very white trash family and was just sick with jealousy over Charlotte's pedigree and beautiful breeding. You know what they say, there's new money, old money, and no money. And around here, if you have no money, you better have class. Francine had neither. Eventually she managed to marry some money, hence that fancy crypt at Assumption of Mary Memorial Park. She wasn't able to buy class, so she buried herself next to it. I'm guessing you didn't notice that Francine's crypt is right between both sets of your great-grandparents."

Maggie tried to quell the panic coursing through her body. "Mrs. Rousseau, there's a chance a detective may want to interview you."

"Oh, you mean, that young Detective Durand? Who knew that family could ever produce someone so handsome? I give complete credit to the genes on his mother's side."

The fact that Yvonne Rousseau knew Bo was not good news. "So you've already been interviewed by him," Maggie said, her voice heavy.

"Yes, but don't you worry, dear. I didn't say a word about your Gran's threats when I told the detective about Francine's visit to me last week. For heaven's sake, that was over sixty years ago. I can't imagine it would mean anything now."

Maggie stared at the old woman. "Francine visited you?"

"Oh yes. Just showed up here without even a call or a box of chocolates. And I wouldn't call it a visit. She wanted to show off. That's when she told me about the crypt, boasting about it in a very unladylike way. I guess she never lost her grudge against your Gran'. Francine told me she was going to reveal some huge piece of news that would offer the final role reversal for her and Charlotte. She bragged that she was going to wind up on top after all."

Yvonne rubbed her forehead and Maggie sensed the old woman was tired. "Thank you so much, Mrs. Rousseau, for sharing this all with me. And a big thank-you for being so selective about what you shared with the detective."

"Chère, I've known your Gran' since we were both born and I sincerely doubt she'd ever kill anyone."

Maggie bid Yvonne good-bye and managed to find her way back to the parking lot. She sat in the car and stared in the distance as the sun began setting over Mississippi, but the beauty of the moment was lost on her. All she could focus on was Yvonne's statement that she "doubted" Gran' could kill anyone. Yvonne didn't say she was "sure." She "doubted." After their conversation, Maggie was filled with her own doubts. Had Gran' really not recognized Francine, or was she lying? Could Gran' have been carrying a grudge against Francine that flared back to life when the woman unexpectedly showed up?

Could her beloved Gran' have killed Francine Prepoire?

Chapter Sixteen

Maggie wasn't ready to go home and face Gran'. Instead, she drove into town and parked in back of Lia's shops, which were keeping late summer hours. Lia's teen employees greeted her with shy smiles as they packed online orders for shipping. Kyle was hunched over the computer, pulling orders off Lia's website and distributing them to the kids. He'd obviously made himself an integral part of the Bon Bon/Fais Dough Dough operation.

"Oh hey, Maggie," he said, greeting her with a smile. "Lia's tending to customers. I installed a search engine optimization program I wrote, and online sales have exploded, so I'm handling things back here."

She thanked him and walked into Bon Bon, where Lia was ringing up a sale for a chubby middle-aged couple in identical T-shirts that sported a drunk leaning against a lamppost above the words, "I Left My Lunch in New Orleans." Lia wore a flowing cotton multicolored dress, and her thick mane of black curls was piled in a bun that was held in place by two pencils. Watching her, Maggie understood what her mother meant when she once said of a happy friend: "She was positively glowing." Lia radiated a serene happiness that Maggie had never seen before, not even during her years with Degas, who, not to speak ill of the dead, Maggie had always found to be a bit prickly.

"Enjoy your candy and mugs," Lia told the tourist couple. Before handing them their bag, she dropped in a few chocolate coins. "That's what we call a lagniappe. A little something extra for you."

The tourists, thrilled with their freebie and the new word they'd show off to their friends when they returned home, headed out, and Lia came around the counter to give Maggie a hug. "I feel like I haven't seen you in forever. Blame the end-of-summer rush. Is everything okay at the house?"

Maggie hesitated. She couldn't bear tarnishing her cousin's glow with her fears about Gran'. Lia deserved whatever joy Kyle brought into her life, so Maggie would keep her worries to herself. "As good as it can be with a murder investigation going on. Which, by the way, doesn't seem to be bothering our comped guests one bit anymore. Never underestimate the power of a freebie."

Lia nodded. "Something every good businessperson knows. I can't tell you how often my gift of a little chocolate lagniappe generates repeat customers and five-star reviews online."

"Hey, Lia, what's Le Grand Plantation Estates like?" Kyle called from the back room.

"Trailer park."

"Oh. Well, forget that."

Maggie gave her cousin a quizzical look. "Anything you want to tell me?"

"I was waiting to say something," Lia blushed. "But Kyle is looking for a house here."

"Lia, that's amazing!"

"I know. He can work from anywhere, really. And I guess he wants that anywhere to be here."

"Uh, I wonder why." Maggie grinned and hugged her cousin tightly.

"Hey, we're going to grab a bite at Crawdaddy's in a short while," Lia said. "Come with us. You won't be a third wheel, I promise. It'll just be three friends hanging out."

"Thanks, but I'll take a rain check. You guys go. Have fun. Oh, Li, I'm so, so happy for you."

Maggie promised to join Lia for lunch sometime during the week and wandered out of the store and down the street, strolling aimlessly as she tried to stave off a case of the blues. Twilight had faded into night. Pelican was far enough away from a big city for the stars to fill the sky, so Maggie tried to distract herself from troubling thoughts by identifying constellations. She gave up after finding the Big Dipper and Orion's Belt, the only two she recognized.

Maggie was about to climb into her car when she heard C. J. Chenier and the Red Hot Louisiana Band coming from a jukebox and the murmur of muffled laughter. She looked across the square to Junie's Oyster Bar and Dance Hall, Pelican's favorite watering hole. Junie was long gone, but her son, known to all as JJ for Junie Junior, despite his given name of Philippe-Jean, had inherited the family business. He ran the place under the watchful ashes of Junie, whose urn held a place of honor next to Clinton, the stuffed alligator that rested atop the hangout's turn-of-the-century bar. Clinton had wandered out of the swamps and onto Junie's porch one day and hung around for the next twenty years. He'd passed away the night of Junie's funeral, so JJ honored the odd couple by making sure they spent immortality side by side.

Maggie walked across the square and into Junie's. She breathed in a collision of scents—beer, gumbo, and a hint of mildew from the hundred-plus-year-old walls.

"There she is, there's my Magnolia Marie," JJ called from behind the bar, where he was filling a pitcher with Bayou Teche Biere Pale. Tonight the fifty-five-year-old had squeezed his three hundred forty pounds into one of his late mother's evening caftans. The sequins and seed beads sparkled every time they hit the light, as did those on JJ's matching turban. On someone else, the outfit would have been Norman Bates-y, but JJ's charm and exuberance dispelled all creepiness. It also helped that he and Mama Junie often clothes-swapped when she was alive.

JJ maneuvered his way around the bar and gave Maggie a bear hug that almost cracked a few ribs. "Ya hungry? I got crawfish boudin."

"Sounds great. I'll take one, with a side of dirty rice."

"Bien, coming right up."

JJ sashayed into the kitchen and Maggie sat down at a small table. The place was dimly lit, the better to hide how worn everything was, but the beer was cold, the atmosphere warm, and the entertainment exceptional. Unfortunately for Pelican, Junie's had been discovered by the New Orleans cognoscenti, so it was packed on most weekends, but the crowd was light and local this Thursday evening, even with it being the week of Fet Let. A band was setting up on stage. Maggie was happy to see a rubboard, which indicated the music would be Zydeco. A slim blonde woman, her back to the patrons, did a nimble run on the heavy accordion around her neck. She turned around and Maggie saw it was Gaynell. Maggie waved to her friend from Doucet, and Gaynell squinted into the bright stage light. She smiled when she saw Maggie and then took off her accordion, hopped off the stage, and headed over to the table.

"Hey," Gaynell said as she hugged her. "Thanks for coming tonight. I really appreciate the support."

"Anytime," Maggie said, covering the fact that she'd completely forgotten about the flyer announcing the first-ever performance by Gaynell and the Gator Girls that she'd stuffed into her glove compartment. "How are you feeling?"

"Nervous but excited." Gaynell eyed Maggie. "Are you okay? You look kinda upset about something."

"No, I'm fine. It's nothing."

Gaynell plopped down in a seat across from Maggie. "I got an hour to kill that I'd love to spend not worrying about my set. Talk to me."

Normally, Maggie would think twice about confiding in someone she barely knew that a family member might be a murder suspect. But Gaynell radiated sensitivity and intelligence, so much so that Maggie was ashamed of herself for dismissing the nineteen-year-old as just another Pelicanette who'd wind up married and pregnant by twenty. Maggie poured out every detail of her conversation with Yvonne as Gaynell listened intently. "What do you think? Could my Gran' have actually . . ." Maggie couldn't finish the sentence.

"This may sound awful dark, but I think every one of us has the potential to kill someone. A lot of murderers are psychopaths, but a lot are just people like you and me who get pushed too far and snap. Do I think your Gran' wanted to kill Francine? Probably, when it all went down. I bet pretty much everyone's fantasized at least once about taking out someone they're really mad at. I only met your Gran' once or twice, but you can't live in Pelican without hearing everything there is to hear about the Crozats, and from what I heard, she and your grand-père loved each other something fierce. So, do I think that she'd hold a grudge for sixty or more years against some slutty chick who stole her loser boyfriend? No, I do not."

Maggie was relieved by Gaynell's blunt words. "How'd you get so smart?"

Gaynell threw up her hands. "Dumb luck."

"Thanks," Maggie said with a laugh. "I feel much better. You have no idea how happy I am that I came tonight."

"Here's hoping you still feel that way after our set." Gaynell crossed her fingers and then returned to the stage and started tuning up various instruments.

JJ brought over Maggie's food, which she devoured, her appetite having been restored. The restaurant slowly filled up, and Maggie was less than thrilled to see Ru Durand and Vanessa in the crowd. It struck her that everything Vanessa had on was tight, from her sequined fuchsia tank top to her consciously ripped white jeans. Even her rhinestone-encrusted sandals were too snug; the fleshy tops of her feet were so constricted that Maggie feared for her coworker's circulation.

Vanessa leaned against rotund Rufus with her hip jutting out like Maggie assumed she'd seen actresses and models do in magazines. But Vanessa looked less like a celebrity than like the handle to Ru's teapot. *Lucky for Ru,* Maggie thought to herself, *that in Louisiana, a family's pedigree still offered a level of influence found in few parts of the country.* Ru happily used the fact that his family was descended from pre–Louisiana Purchase French colonists to socially intimidate the locals. So while others at the police academy had outpaced him at every challenge, he would probably retire someday still Pelican's chief of police.

Ru retrieved drinks from Old Shari, Junie's ancient bartender, and handed one to Vanessa, who rewarded him with a slobbery, open-mouthed kiss. A man standing next to them pulled away in disgust, and Maggie's heart flip-flopped when she saw it was Bo. She quickly focused on her dinner plate, pretending to dig up scraps from its empty surface. It was too late—Bo saw her and walked over.

"Don't think you're gonna find much there. If you're up for some company, I'll order us popcorn shrimp."

"Sure," she said, giving up her fake foraging.

Bo placed the order with JJ and joined her at the table. Gaynell and the Gator Girls spared them having to make awkward small talk by taking the stage and launching into the Zydeco classic, "P'Tit Fille O'Paradis." Junie's dance floor filled up and stayed filled as the band delivered one great song after another. Gaynell was an enormous talent, playing the accordion, rubboard, and guitar with equal panache. Maggie forgot her discomfort. She and Bo hooted and hollered with the rest of the appreciative crowd. When Maggie heard the opening notes of her all-time favorite song, "Jambalaya," she leapt to her feet and pulled Bo up with her. He responded by whipping her around the room in a wicked Cajun two-step, and the two sang as they danced, like the other couples on the floor. They joined in the explosion of applause that greeted the end of the song.

Gaynell followed the foot-stomper with the much gentler strains of the Cajun waltz, "Jolie Blon." Bo didn't give Maggie the option of returning to her table. He pulled her close and they danced together gracefully, their bodies perfectly in tune.

"You have great eyes, you know," Bo said as he stared into them with his own chocolate orbs. "They're green, but they have that circle of orange in them. A ring of fire. Like the Johnny Cash song."

"I like that song."

"Me too."

The two shared a smile and then broke apart to applaud as Gaynell finished "Jolie Blon." She announced that the band would take a break, and Bo led Maggie back to their table where a big bowl of popcorn shrimp awaited them, steam rising off the crustaceans' crusty coating. "So," Bo said, "I've got some information on Suzy."

"Really?" Maggie said. "I can't wait to hear."

"Don't get too excited," Bo cautioned. "Her husband's a successful divorce attorney, so they've got plenty of money.

The IRS has nothing on the Cajun Cuties. Their tax return is simple and straightforward—money in, money out, with no hint of impropriety. It's a tiny nonprofit and they run a lean, clean operation, so it's pretty hard to imagine what Suzy would get out of stealing their coin."

"Oh," she said, deflated. "But you never know about people. Look at how many kleptomaniacs have plenty of money and just steal for the thrill of it. Maybe Suzy's like that."

"Could be." Bo picked up their drained beer glasses. "I'll get us refills."

As Maggie watched him walk away, she was overwhelmed with guilt for withholding what she'd learned from Yvonne about Gran'. He was clearly the one good apple on his low-class family tree.

Bo returned with the beers. The shrimp had cooled off enough to eat, so Maggie gave them a good dousing with Tabasco sauce and Bo dug in. She picked up a shrimp and toyed with it. Nerves had dampened her appetite. "Bo," she said. "I discovered something that I need to tell you." She took a deep breath and then related her conversation with Yvonne, not leaving out a single damaging detail. When she finished, much to her surprise, Bo simply shrugged. "Yeah, Yvonne told me all that already."

"What?" Maggie yelped. "She told me she never breathed a word of it to you."

Bo shook his head at her naïveté. "She's an eighty-year-old lady who doesn't get many visitors and then finds herself in the middle of this town's most exciting drama in years. You think she's gonna keep her mouth shut?"

"Oh, I am so mad at her. Look, Bo, even if what she said is true, I'm begging you to give Gran' the benefit of the doubt. I just can't bring myself to believe that she'd ever do something this horrible."

Bo popped a shrimp in his mouth and crunched it. "Me neither."

She stared at him. "Really?"

"Really. Two facts we know for sure: the murder weapon was that old box of rat poison, and it was planted in your kitchen to frame someone in your family. There's no way on earth you could convince me that your Gran' would do that. I may not be a Louisiana aristocrat, but you can't function in this state if you don't understand how they operate. And they would be ruthless about protecting their own; they'd never betray them."

Maggie was overcome with a sense of relief. "I was so worried I didn't even think about that. Thanks for figuring out what should've been totally obvious to me. God, I'm starving now."

She grabbed a handful of shrimp and popped them into her mouth. Bo laughed. "Glad to see I gave you back your appetite. But we're supposed to be sharing those." He reached for a shrimp and she playfully pulled the bowl toward her. As they tussled over it, they didn't see Ru approach the table.

"Well, look at you two."

Maggie and Bo let go of the bowl. Ru's appearance had ruined both their appetites. "Cavorting with the enemy," Ru said, shaking his head. "Nice, Coz."

"It's consorting, not cavorting," Maggie shot back before Bo could respond. "And he's not. He's just being polite and keeping me company because I was here alone."

"Never could hold on to a boyfriend, could ya, Magnolia?"

"Hey, that's enough, Rufus." Bo stood up, towering over his cousin by a good head. "My personal life is none of your business."

"Relax, I was just kidding around," Ru said. "But you know what is my business, Bo? Your job, which won't be yours much longer if you keep company with the Crozats. It's not exactly the way to repay me, is it now?"

Bo's face reflected his fury, and Maggie was afraid that he might strike Rufus. "We were talking business," she said, trying to cover. "I was telling him something important about the murder."

Rufus and Bo both stared at her, Ru with skepticism, Bo with confusion. Maggie froze. She didn't dare say anything about Gran' to the police chief to make his dream of jailing a family member come true. She wracked her brain, and then remembered something. "Footsteps. The night before Mrs. Clabber died, I went into the woods by the bayou to paint and I heard footsteps. They spooked me so much that I just grabbed everything and ran back to the house."

"You're just remembering this now?" Ru's tone oozed distrust.

"I know I should have remembered sooner, but with all the craziness going on, I didn't put it together that it happened the night before she died. That's what Bo and I were just talking about."

"Funny how a couple of turns around the dance floor jogged your memory." Ru turned to Bo. "Check it out in the morning. And it better not be bull or you'll be reloading whatever you unloaded from your pickup truck and looking at Pelican in your rearview mirror." Having delivered this ultimatum, Ru headed back to Vanessa.

"I'm not lying," Maggie insisted to Bo. "I did hear footsteps and they did scare me."

"I believe you." Bo looked toward Ru, his expression grim. "But it'll be a whole lot better if we find something to prove that."

Chapter Seventeen

"I have a newfound respect for your job," Maggie said late the next morning as she and Bo crawled through the forest thicket trying to find any clue that would prove someone had been in the woods the night she'd come to paint. It was one of the summer's steamiest days, and bits of leaves and twigs had found a home in her hair, which tended to expand with humidity.

"Yup, it's a lot of grunt work," Bo said as he scanned the ground and examined the branches of trees to see if any fiber from a shirt or pant leg might have gotten caught. He'd left his blazer in the car and stripped down to his T-shirt, which clung to his cut, sweat-soaked body. It was a good look for him. But then, thought Maggie, pretty much anything seemed to be a good look for Bo. And for a moment, she felt her body go weak.

Bo noticed Maggie falter and reached out to her, but she brushed him off. "You know, once when I was walking through Central Park in New York, some detectives stopped me and showed me a picture and asked if I knew the girl," she said, trying to defuse the moment with mindless chatter. "They were canvassing everyone. Turned out she was killed by her boyfriend. But I remember thinking, wow, those detectives have to do that all day, how sad and bor-*ahhhh*!"

She suddenly lost her balance and tumbled into a hole that had been clumsily covered with a canopy of twigs and leaves. Bo raced over, reached down, and pulled her out. "Are you okay?"

Bo gently examined her, and still stunned by the fall, she let him. "Ow," she said. "That fall really hurt. I feel like every bone in my body got a shake."

"You're banged up, but I don't see any serious damage. More like you were in a fender bender than a big wreck."

"What the hell?" Maggie rubbed her head where it ached from colliding with a wall of the hole. "What is that? I mean, I know what it is, but what is it doing here?"

Bo kneeled at the edge of the hole and examined it closely. "This is recent. Any guess why someone would be digging on your property?"

"Yes. It used to happen sometimes when I was growing up, but not since I've been home, so I forgot about it. The other night Gran' was telling stories, and one of them was the legend about pirates burying treasure in our woods. It sometimes gets people to thinking they should go on a treasure hunt. I did it a few times myself with friends when I was a kid. I bet one of our guests has been doing some prospecting."

"Any guess who?"

"No. I haven't seen any shovels or metal detectors when I've cleaned, but I haven't been looking for any. I'll look tomorrow when I clean again. They might be keeping them in their car, so I'll peek into those too."

Maggie stood up. She felt stiff and sore. "Do you think this could have anything to do with Beverly's murder?"

"Maybe. If someone actually found something and Bev caught them. She could have been killed to keep her quiet."

"Which once again rules out Gran'. She was born and raised here. No way she'd search for buried treasure unless she had a sudden attack of the seniles." Maggie checked her phone. "I need to go. I'm due at Doucet for my shift in an hour, and I need to shower first." She took a step and felt aches in a variety of body parts.

"You should find someone to cover for you for a few days. That was a bad fall. They'd understand."

"Yeah, but my bank account wouldn't. I'll be fine. Walk it off. Isn't that what sports types say?"

Bo laughed. "Yeah, the 'sports types' do say that, Miss Artist. Speaking of which, I do want to get Xander together with you to paint. Maybe next time I have him."

"I'd like that. And let me know if you find anything. I'll do the same."

Maggie headed out of the woods, trying to disguise the pain from her bumps and bruises. She knew Bo would have jumped to help her, but for a reason she couldn't define, she didn't want to display any weakness. It was her way of protecting herself, but from what, she wasn't sure.

*

Doucet was packed with tourists getting in some last-minute plantation oohing and aahing before summer ended, and Maggie led four full tours before getting a break. By the time she sat down to rest and eat a yogurt, she was exhausted. The lack of answers for the minimysteries surrounding the bigger mystery of Beverly/Francine's death was also getting to the artist. What was the big news B/F planned on throwing in Gran's face? What exactly were the Georgia boys up to? And who was digging holes in the family property? Was it somehow related to the Georgia boys' scheme? Was it a different guest? Maybe it wasn't a guest at all. She groaned and dropped her head into her hands.

"Well, somebody looks like the last dog at the pound."

Maggie looked up to see Gaynell, who flashed a sympathetic smile and then took a seat next to her. "It's just . . . stuff," Maggie said with a shrug.

"Wanna talk about it?"

"You know what, right now I'd actually like to take a break from talking or thinking about it."

"You got it."

"Thank you. Hey, I never told you how good you were last night."

"Thanks. We're working on a set we can submit for JazzFest. Playing there would be the dream of all dreams."

"Well, if I can help in any way, let me know." The two women ate lunch in companionable silence, and Maggie enjoyed letting her mind wander aimlessly for a change. It landed on a moment with Bo from the night before. "Gaynell, do you happen to know the lyrics to the song 'Ring of Fire'? At least some of them? All I know is the 'down, down, down' part."

"Sure," Gaynell said. She began singing the plaintive tune in her rich alto. Gaynell filled each note with emotion, bringing to life the song's pathos and longing. Maggie, who had a sweet voice of her own, joined in, and the two women harmonized on the chorus. As they wrapped up, a couple of Asian tourists applauded and snapped their picture with smart phones. Maggie and Gaynell laughed.

"Looks like I got myself a backup singer," Gaynell teased.

"Yeah, right. If you only do one song."

"It's a good one, though. Hot. Super sexy."

"Yes. It really is."

"June Carter cowrote the song about how she was falling in love with Johnny Cash, even though I think they were both married to other people." Gaynell raised an eyebrow. "Anything you wanna tell me, Maggie?"

"No, relax, it's nothing like that. Marriages aren't the only thing that can make liking someone complicated."

"Ain't that the truth."

"Not that I like someone," Maggie backtracked.

"Right." Gaynell stood up and picked a piece of lettuce off of her antebellum ball gown. "I gotta go take a tour group. If you need to talk, I'm around."

"Thanks."

By the time Maggie's shift was over, the injuries from her fall, though minor, caught up with her, and she couldn't wait to get home. The shotgun was empty, so Maggie drew a bath and soaked while listening to a download of vintage the Mamas & the Papas. Feeling much better, she threw on jean shorts and a tomato-red cotton halter top. She noticed the bag of art supplies for Xander on the floor of her closet and had an idea. Rather than wait for their lesson to happen, Maggie would get them to Xander so he could do some art experimenting on his own. She'd drop them off at the police station for Bo later on. But first she needed to check in at the main house to see if she could be of any help.

Maggie found Gran' relaxing in the office chaise longue, ubiquitous iPad on her lap. Gopher snored at her feet. "I tell you, there are some funny if wildly inappropriate videos on YouTube," Gran' said. "If you're looking for your parents, they're both napping. Ninette needs her rest and Tug is worn out from picking up your cleaning shift."

"I feel bad about that."

"Don't, that man needs the exercise. He's got a gumbo pot for a stomach. So, I heard you did get in a visit to Yvonne yesterday."

"Yes, and that woman is one huge gossip."

"Don't begrudge a lonely old lady a bit of entertainment." Gran' put down her iPad and looked Maggie in the eye. "You do know that I had nothing to do with Francine's passing?"

"I know, Gran'."

"Good. I swear, even in death, that tart is causing me trouble. Making me a murder suspect. The nerve of that woman."

Maggie tsk-tsk'd with her grandmother, but something disturbed her. She'd never heard Gran' call anyone such a harsh name before. Protestations to the contrary, Francine/Beverly still got to her.

Gran' yawned and got up. "I'm going to take a bit of a lie-down too." She vigorously shook her head. "I think I have a case of tinnitus. I keep hearing a humming sound."

"I hear it too." Maggie looked around the room and saw the source of the problem. "It's the paper shredder. Someone left it on."

"Oh my, that was me. Cutie Debbie wanted to shred something earlier, so I turned it on for her. I forgot to turn it off. Oh well, blame A-G-E syndrome."

Gran' and her iPad left for their nap, and Maggie turned off the paper shredder. She stared at it a moment. "Hmm. Is it weird that a retiree on vacation would need to shred a document, Goph? Or am I being paranoid?"

Gopher looked up at her, saw she was treat-free, and went back to napping and snoring. She decided to trust her suspicious instincts and opened the shredder. It was a rarely used, decrepit machine that, luckily for her, chunked the pages rather than shredded them. Having studied collage and mixed media at art school, she had no trouble reassembling Debbie's document. Maggie found herself reading a meticulously laid-out business plan for co-opting the nonprofit Cajun Cuties, booting Jan from the presidency, and turning the group into a profit-making venture that Debbie would eventually take public for a generous financial profit.

It appeared that Dim Debbie wasn't so dim after all.

Chapter Eighteen

Maggie figured that she had just enough time before dinner prep to drop off Xander's art supplies and deliver the latest guest bombshell to Bo. But first, she applied some lipstick and just enough eye shadow to bring out the orange in her eyes that Bo had commented on. She then drove to the Pelican PD, where she found Artie Belloise working the front desk, as well as a large fried crab po'boy.

"Hey, Maggie. Anything to eat in there?" He eyed her bag hopefully. "I could use some sides with my sammy."

"Sorry, just art stuff for Bo's kid."

"Oh." Artie didn't try hiding his disappointment. "I'll get it to him."

"Actually, I need to talk to Bo, so can you let him know I'm here?"

"He ain't around right now."

"Oh." It was Maggie's turn to be disappointed. "Well, let him know I came by and have some information."

"Will do." In pretty much any other jurisdiction in America, a law enforcement official would have found this message intriguing enough to pepper Maggie with questions. But Maggie could put money on Artie's lack of interest in anything but his po'boy.

She got back in her car and headed toward Crozat. Her cell rang, and she put in her earbud to answer it. The caller was Tug.

"Hey, Dad. What's up?"

"I'm at the hospital with your mother."

"*What?*" Maggie, her heart racing, pulled over and parked near the Pelican town square. She was too distracted by Tug's news to drive.

"Nothing to panic about. She's been having night sweats and wasn't feeling well this afternoon. We could tell she had a fever, so I brought her here. I didn't want to take any chances."

"No, of course not."

"The doctors want to keep her at least overnight and run some tests in the morning. It's probably nothing."

Or, Maggie thought, *it's a very bad something.* But she kept her attitude upbeat with Tug. "I'm sure you're right, Dad. I want to see her, though. I'll be there as soon as I can."

"All right, sweetie." Tug's voice cracked the tiniest bit. "I love you, bebe."

"I love you too, Daddy."

They ended the call. Maggie sat in the Falcon for a moment and then got out. She needed air. She walked to the bandstand in the middle of the square, leaned against the opening, then slid down to the top step.

When Maggie was going through her brutal breakup with Chris and thought she'd never find love, she'd seen a therapist, who discouraged her from "catastrophic thinking."

"Stop going to worst-possible outcome scenarios," the therapist told her. "It's a waste of time and energy because things rarely get that bad."

Now, as an unsolved murder haunted her family's home and livelihood and her mother faced a potential health crisis, Maggie was tempted to call the therapist and yell that she wanted her money back. Instead, she sat on the steps of the bandstand, overwhelmed with emotions—sadness, frustration, anger at herself for allowing her life to get messed up in such a big way. Then she dropped her face into her hands and began to cry.

"It's okay. Everything's gonna be all right."

A hand rested gently on her shoulder. She lifted her puffy, wet face to see Bo. He sat down next to her on the bandstand steps, keeping his hand on her shoulder. "Thanks for the art supplies. Xander'll love them."

"How did you find me?"

"Uh, excuse me, it's my job to track people down," Bo said, faking indignation. "I saw your car and looked left." Bo grinned and she couldn't help grinning back through her tears. She wiped them away, smearing her carefully applied eye makeup. "What's going on?" Bo asked.

Maggie looked at him. He only had a few years on her, yet he seemed so much wiser and more mature. "Bo . . . was there a moment when it hit you that you had to grow up and be an adult?"

"That's an easy one for me. It was the moment Xander was born. But you need to stop beating yourself up about where you are and give yourself some credit. You're working two jobs, helping your parents, getting your art going. You *are* an adult, Maggie."

"I feel like I've regressed. Like I'm more of an adult-in-training these days."

"Whatever you want to call it, it's something to be proud of."

Bo turned Maggie's head toward him so she could see how sincerely he meant those words. And she saw something she'd never seen in the eyes of any man she'd ever been involved with: kindness.

Their faces were close enough to inhale each other's warm breath. Then instinctively, both pulled away. "I got a message from Artie that you wanted to talk to me," Bo said, making his voice brusque and businesslike.

"Yes, right." She shook off the moment and filled him in on Debbie's secret machinations to oust Jan and turn Cajun Cuties into a moneymaker.

"Interesting," Bo said. "Gives us a new suspect. If Beverly Clabber found out what Debbie was up to, it's a possible motive for murder. What if Clabber felt she needed to tell Jan that one of her Cuties was planning a coup d'état? It would have destroyed everything for Debbie."

"Exactly."

"I'm gonna go do a background check on this Debbie Stern. Rufus is off today, so he's not around to stonewall me. I'll let you know what I come up with."

Maggie and Bo exchanged a little more information and perfunctory good-byes, each choosing to deny the heat between them.

"Hope your mom's okay," Bo said as he started toward his car.

"Thanks," she responded. "I'm heading over to the hospital to check on her."

She forced herself to concentrate on the road as she drove to Francis Xavier Medical Center, the closest hospital to Pelican. Rush hour was just beginning, and cars darted in and out of lanes without warning as they battled the growing clog. Maggie swore to herself that if she ever got a vanity license plate, it would read, "UZ SGNL."

She parked and went into the hospital, where a receptionist directed her to Ninette's room. Maggie gave the door a gentle knock.

"Mom?"

"Come on in, chère."

Maggie walked into the typically antiseptic hospital room, where Ninette lay on a bed that had been raised for her comfort. Tug sat in a chair next to her, holding his wife's hand. Maggie had never seen her mother look more pale or frail. She kissed her father and then sat on the edge of the bed.

"Mama." She reached down and hugged Ninette, hiding her face so the tears slipping down her cheeks wouldn't show.

"My sweet baby." Ninette patted the bed, and Maggie crawled in next to her. "This is just like when you were little."

"I know. I'd use any excuse to get into bed with you and Dad. A storm, a bad dream. Which is what this feels like right now."

"Everyone is overreacting. This is just some little thing."

Tug squeezed Ninette's hand. "I'm sure it is, but we could do with some medical facts to back that up." He awkwardly rose to his feet. "I'm stiff from all this sitting. I need to stretch my legs. I'm gonna take a lap around the floor. Be back in a few."

He left, and the women rested in each other's arms. "I know I've been going back and forth about whether or not I should have come home," Maggie said. "But I'm beyond glad I'm here right now."

"Me, too." Ninette stroked her daughter's hair.

"Oh, Mom, I'm so sorry."

Ninette looked at her daughter. "For what?"

"For everything. For leaving. For being so conflicted about coming back. For being who I am—and never fitting in here."

"You've always fit in, honey," Ninette said. "You just never wanted to. I think you were afraid that would make you the same as everyone else here, and you wanted to be different. But you can be who you are and we'll all still love you."

Maggie pulled her mother closer. "You're amazing. I love you so, so much."

"I love you more."

"Impossible."

"Nuh-uh."

"Uh-huh."

It was a game they'd played since Maggie was a toddler. Ninette usually let her win. Tonight, Maggie gave her mother the victory.

Tug returned to the room. "I need to get back to the house and tend to our guests. Why don't you stay with Mom?"

"I think you should stay with her, Dad." Maggie slid out of her mother's arms and stood up. "I'll take care of every else."

"You sure?" Tug asked. He looked nervous. "There's cooking involved."

"I can handle it. I promise I won't poison our guests." Maggie gasped and put her hand over her mouth. "I can't believe I just said that."

Tug managed a half-smile. "Don't worry about it. Just stick to that promise."

*

After getting her dad's assurances that he'd text her with updates about Ninette's condition, Maggie raced home. She was one of those people who, raised by a great cook, preferred to compliment the chef rather than prepare anything herself. If there were health risks associated with microwave use, she was destined to be Patient Zero. But now she had to feed a houseful of people, none of whom was expecting a nuked Lean Cuisine.

She parked and ran into the shotgun, where she knew Gran' had a few boxes of jambalaya rice. Maggie grabbed them and planned an ad hoc meal in her head as she rushed to the kitchen in the main house. She stopped in the doorway and gawked at the sight before her.

Gran', a butcher's apron over her taupe silk blouse and slacks, was tossing shrimp into a large sauté pan while Alice Ryker chopped celery. The girl's brothers stood next to Gran' holding measuring spoons and spices. "Two bay leaves and a teaspoon of thyme," Gran' ordered. The boy measured and tossed in the spices. "Well done. Now I need the celery." Alice walked over and tossed celery into the pan; it sizzled as it hit butter melting in the pan.

Gran' dumped a bowl of tomatoes into the concoction on the stove. "Hello, chère," she called to Maggie.

"Uh . . . you cook?"

"Of course. Children, cover your ears." The Ryker kids did so. "Back in the day, there was a saying: if you want to get a man, you need to be a maid in the living room, a cook in the kitchen, and a bad girl in the bedroom. Nowadays, I'd take a fist to anyone who said this, but it did motivate me to pick up a few recipes. Why don't you throw together a salad and heat up some dinner rolls while I finish making my Shrimp Creole?"

"Can we uncover our ears?" Sam asked.

"Yes, my apologies, I forgot all about that."

Maggie put together a salad, impressing herself when she jazzed it up with dried cranberries and chopped pecans. Ninette had left a bowl of dough to rise, and she pinched off balls to turn into rolls.

"Your mama's going to be fine," Gran' told her as they worked. "I got a real strong sense of it."

"I hope you're right," Maggie said. "I'm not getting a thing from my sense." She pulled a tray of browned dinner rolls out of the oven, took a picture of them, and sent it to Ninette with the text, "#Success!" Anything to distract her mother from the unspoken fear that they all shared.

The meal that night was a group effort. The Rykers and Butlers served the appetizers that went with the drinks Kyle mixed at the bar. The Georgia boys provided music that was more suited to an electronic dance party than a sedate lodging like Crozat, but at least it was upbeat. Cuties Jan, Angela, and Suzy set the table and took charge of the dessert Lia brought over. The only guest not pitching in was Cutie Debbie, who seemed so believably semicatatonic that Maggie wouldn't be surprised if Bo unearthed some acting lessons in the woman's background.

Maggie looked around the table as everyone dined and chatted. The night felt more akin to a family gathering than a hostess tending to her guests. She had trouble believing that one of these lovely people might be a killer. It would be like finding out that the fun cousin who taught you how to make armpit farts was leading a double life as a violent criminal.

After dinner, she thanked everyone for their help and then shooed Gran' off to bed, taking on cleanup duties herself. She was finding it therapeutic and would have added cleaning to her Crozat duties if she didn't know how much the Shexnayders needed the job. She finished loading the dishwasher and turned it on. Her phone pinged and vibrated with a text, and she eagerly read the message from Tug: "Mom sleeping well. Fingers crossed."

Her emotions vacillated from disappointment that the text wasn't from Bo to relief that her dad seemed optimistic. She sent him heart and fingers-crossed emoticons and then pocketed her phone and headed toward the back door through what the family called the Event Wall Hall of Fame. Every event held at Crozat since its inception as a B and B was commemorated with a framed photo on this wall. Aside from decorating a dull area few guests ever saw, the pictures served as visual reminders of highlights from one successful event that the family could use for another. In this way, the wall served as a large scrapbook of party-planning ideas.

As she walked past them, Maggie realized that she'd missed dusting the tops of the frames. She went back to the kitchen, grabbed a rag, wet it, and returned to the hall. Cynic that she was, she wondered how many of the couples were divorced by now as she dusted a handful of wedding portraits. Her eye landed on one of the older photos, taken about ten years prior. The groom, smiling and elegant in a morning coat, looked familiar. She struggled to place him. Then it hit her, and the realization of who he was made her gasp.

The groom in the photo was Kyle Bruner.

Chapter
Nineteen

Maggie stared at the picture. She knew Kyle had lost his wife
in a car accident. Was she the beautiful bride standing next to
him, or had he been married previously? Either way, why had
he never mentioned that he'd stayed at Crozat before? That
he'd been *married* there?

Kyle was keeping secrets. And in a place where a murder
occurred, secrets could be dangerous.

Maggie knew this was something that she couldn't with-
hold from Bo. But she had to talk to Lia first. She pulled her
cell out of the back pocket of her jeans and texted her cousin
to meet at the bandstand and then ran to the kitchen and
extricated a reusable grocery bag from a pile stashed under the
sink. She returned to the Event Hall of Fame, removed the
photo from the wall, and stuck it in the bag. Then Maggie
raced out of the house and hopped into the Falcon, whose top

was down. As she drove, her heart thumped unpleasantly. She hated to think that Kyle wasn't the sweet, considerate guy that he appeared to be. But every psychopath she'd read about or seen in movies seemed to present a perfectly amenable façade.

As soon as she reached Pelican's historic business district, she parked and jumped out of the car. Lia was already waiting for her at the bandstand. Maggie grabbed the bag with the photo and ran to her cousin.

"Lia, I wish there was an easy way to say this, but there's not," Maggie said. She was out of breath from running, so her words came out in puffs. "Kyle lied to us. Well, technically, he didn't tell us something, but it's the same thing. Anyway, I found something at Crozat and I have to show it to you because I'm scared for you. Here." With that, she pulled out the photo and handed to Lia. Lia gave the picture a cursory glance and handed it back to her.

"I know."

"You *know?* What do you mean, you know?"

"I know about the photo. I know about the wedding at Crozat. I know why Kyle is really here."

Maggie stared at her cousin, annoyed and confused. "Well if you *know* all this, do you mind sharing it with me?"

Lia shook her head. "I can't."

"Oh, come on, Lia—"

"I can't because it's not my place to tell his story. Come."

Lia motioned for Maggie to follow her, and the two women walked through the park across the street to Fais Dough Dough. Lia led Maggie to the back room, where Kyle was alone, once again hunched over the computer as he processed an online order. Lia laid a hand on his shoulder, and he started.

"Maggie knows about your wedding and Crozat," Lia said.

Kyle froze for a moment. The room was silent. Maggie felt her chest contract and realized that she'd been holding her breath. She released it slowly.

Kyle spoke. "It was only a matter of time until someone noticed that picture. We were just playing a waiting game."

"I think you better tell her everything," Lia said.

Kyle nodded, his lips pursed. He turned his back to the computer and faced Maggie. "Beverly Clabber killed my wife."

"But . . . I thought she died in a car accident."

"She did. And Beverly Clabber was behind the wheel of the car that broadsided Sara."

"Oh my God. What happened?"

"Mrs. Clabber ran a stop sign. She claimed it was because the rental car she was driving had an acceleration problem. Not only that, but she sued the rental company, which didn't want the publicity of a lawsuit and settled with her out of court. So she actually made money off my wife's death."

"That is unbelievably horrible. But why did you follow her to Crozat? Actually, how did you even know she was staying with us?"

Kyle smiled grimly. "I wish I could say that I used my expert abilities as a computer programmer to ferret out that information, but Beverly, like a lot of seniors, has a passing interest in social media with no idea how to use it properly. She posted on a couple of sites where she hadn't activated any privacy settings. She and Hal were supposed to spend their honeymoon visiting several Louisiana plantation B and Bs. When I saw Crozat was one of them, I had to come here. I wanted to confront her where Sara and I got married, to make her see and feel what she took from me. I wanted to show her that wedding picture on your wall, and then I was going to show her this."

Kyle took a wallet out of his pants pocket. Maggie noticed that his hands were shaking slightly. He extracted a square of paper and handed it to her. She stared at the blurry black-and-white image.

"It's a sonogram," Kyle said. "Sara was two months pregnant. When I got the strength to go through her purse after the accident, I found it. She was going to surprise me."

"Kyle, I feel for your loss—really I do—but you've been lying to us."

"Not lying," Lia said, jumping to his defense. "Call it a sin of omission. When Beverly was murdered, Kyle told me everything and swore he had nothing to do with her death. I asked him not to go to the police. Knowing Ru, he would have been all over Kyle and done nothing to find the real murderer."

Maggie shrugged. "I'm not surprised Rufus never put you and Beverly together," she said to Kyle, "but I am surprised Bo Durand didn't find the connection."

"She was using her original given name and the surname of one of her husbands, so anything on the Internet about the accident would have listed her as Fran Walker. She hadn't married Hal Clabber yet."

"Man, that woman had more husbands than an old-time movie star."

"I also went on this jag where I cleaned the Internet of everything about the accident," Kyle continued. "I couldn't stand it out there, where anyone could read about it. I didn't want to just wipe it from my memory, I wanted to wipe it from everyone's memory."

Maggie grimaced and rubbed her forehead. She turned to her cousin. "Can I talk to you in private?"

Maggie and Lia walked into the Fais Dough Dough store-front, where Maggie confronted her cousin. "How could you not tell me any of this?"

"I had to protect Kyle."

"Who you've known for what, a week? How do you know he's even telling the truth and not some psychopath? Because let me tell you, his behavior is kind of psychopath-y."

"I just know, Maggie. The way we all know when we clear our minds like Gran' taught us, to give space for the answer and let our instincts take over."

"I'm beginning to see that there's a big difference between intuition and wishful thinking."

"I didn't mean to hurt you or make things any harder on the family," Lia said. She squeezed her hands together and held them in front of her as if begging Maggie to understand. "I didn't know what else to do. I guess I just hoped that the police would find the real murderer, and no one would ever have to know anything about Kyle and his connection to Beverly Clabber. I was afraid if they heard about it, they'd stop looking for anyone else."

Intellectually, Maggie understood Lia's dilemma, but she still felt angry and betrayed by her. "Either Kyle goes to Bo and tells him everything, or I do," she declared. "You may feel the need to protect Kyle, but I sure don't. I feel terrible for his loss, but he is not my family, and I will not risk being accused of obstructing justice for him."

Lia nodded. "I'd never expect you to do that. Now that you know his story, of course Kyle has to tell it to the police. God knows what Rufus will do when he finds out."

"Yeah, well, your instincts were right about that," Maggie said, softening a touch. "Rufus would have slapped the cuffs on him and thrown him in jail and said, 'Case closed.' He'll probably do that now. But if you truly, truly believe he's innocent, at least we have Bo to pursue other suspects behind Ru's back."

"Do you really think he'd do that for us?"

Lia looked so desperately hopeful that Maggie could only say yes and pray that she was right.

"Okay, then," Lia said. "I'll talk to Kyle."

Lia turned out the store's lights and the two women returned to the back room. Kyle was no longer at the computer. "Kyle?" Lia called. "Kyle?" But there was no answer.

Kyle was gone.

Chapter
Twenty

"His car's gone, too," Maggie said, panting after a sprint to the parking lot and back.

"I know he didn't run away," Lia insisted. "That's not who he is."

"Agh!" Maggie groaned in frustration. "Again, Lia, a week. Seven days. If I could multiply seven times twenty-four in my head, I'd tell you how many hours. Okay, now I have to do that just to prove I can." She closed her eyes and did the math. "A hundred and sixty-eight hours. Not much time to 'know who he is.' I'm calling Bo." She took out her cell and dialed the police station. "Hi, Artie, it's Maggie Crozat. I need to talk to Bo, it's urgent . . . Thanks."

Maggie paced while a prerecorded message from the PPD warned her never to leave a purse in the car or her home unlocked. She let out another groan of frustration when the phone went to Bo's voicemail. "Great, he's away from his desk." She tapped her foot impatiently until she could leave a message. "Hey, it's me, Maggie. You need to put out an APB or whatever you call them to stop Kyle Bruner. I have really important information for you. Lia and I are on our way over now."

Maggie ended the call. "Close up the stores and come with me," she told her cousin. Lia nodded and quickly locked up Fais Dough Dough and then did the same to Bon Bon. She turned off the lights as the two women headed out of the store. "We'll take my car," Maggie said. "We can make tracks in it. Thank you, Grand-père Crozat, for springing for the V8 engine."

The two women jumped into the Falcon, Maggie gunned its engine, and they sped off to the Pelican police station. She pulled into the only spot available, hoping that the handicapped would forgive her, and then ran into the building, followed closely by Lia. Artie was on duty again, only this time his food companion was a bag of pork rinds.

"We have to see Bo," Maggie told him.

"Sorry, but he's interrogating a person of interest," Artie said. "I believe it's the guy you've been hanging with, Lia."

"Kyle?" Lia ran to the front door, threw it open, scanned the parking lot, and pointed to a vehicle. "There. That's his car. He turned himself in without us." She turned to Maggie. "I told you I knew him," she said, with a note of triumph that she instantly retreated from. "Wait, no, he's just made himself a suspect."

Lia collapsed on a metal bench. Maggie sat down next to Lia and hugged her. "Kyle knew what he had to do and did it," she said. "He came here on his own. That says something about his character."

"The police don't care about character. They just want a suspect, and right now, Kyle is the only one they have. He's doomed."

Maggie wished that she could argue her cousin's point, but she couldn't. Kyle was the PPD's primary suspect, and Maggie blamed herself. If she'd never seen that picture, if she'd never confronted Kyle about it, she wouldn't be sitting on a cold, hard bench comforting Lia as she was about to lose another love, this time to the brutal Louisiana penal system. "This is all my fault."

"No it's not. Kyle wanted to go to the police right away and share his connection with that woman, but I begged him not to. And now everything just looks worse because he withheld information. It's my fault if he goes to jail."

"If it makes you feel any better, there's a real good chance you could go to jail with him," a male voice said.

The women looked up to see Rufus Durand looming over them. Occasionally, Rufus transformed from a lazy sack of cow manure into a genuinely dark presence. This was one of those times. "You withheld evidence," he told Lia, his tone hard and angry. "That's a crime. A jailable crime."

"There's no such word as 'jailable,'" Maggie blurted without thinking.

"Lock this one up for contempt," Rufus told Artie, who looked confused.

"I'm sorry," Maggie said. "That just came out."

"Cuff her," Rufus ordered Artie, who shrugged and came around the entry desk, cuffs in hand.

"Oh, come on." Maggie gave the officer a look. "Artie, really?"

"You wanna add resisting arrest to the charges?" Rufus asked.

Maggie knew by his tone that Rufus was serious. She shot him a venomous look and placed her hands behind her back. Just as Artie was about to slap handcuffs on her, Bo appeared from the hallway. "What the hell is going on here?"

"Your girlfriend here has been mouthing off to law enforcement," Ru said.

"I'm not his girlfriend, and if I offended law enforcement in any way, I am truly sorry." Keeping her apology generic and not specific to Rufus somehow made the whole nauseating business more bearable for Maggie. She could see in Bo's eyes how much he despised his cousin and admired him for keeping his tone polite when he spoke.

"She apologized, Ru. You really want to waste your time on this? That's giving her the power, man."

Ru contemplated this new angle and then nodded curtly to Artie. "Let her go. But take this as a warning, Magnolia. You better show me and my boys respect every time you see us or you'll be making your home in the cell next to Kyle Bruner."

"He's in jail?" Lia cried out.

"I'm sorry, Lia," Bo said. "Between the strong circumstantial evidence and the fact that he has no alibi, we had enough to charge him with first-degree murder."

Lia grew so pale that Maggie was afraid she might faint. "He needs a lawyer."

"He has one. I recommended Quentin MacIlhoney. He's on his way down from Baton Rouge. He's one of the best in the state."

"Hey, whose side are you on?" Rufus demanded.

"I'm on the side of what's fair, Cousin. That's it."

"Can I see him?" Lia asked. "Please, even just for a minute?"

Bo shook his head. "Look, the most important thing he needs to do right now is to meet with his lawyer. Why don't you two grab some coffee and come back in an hour? MacIlhoney should be here by then."

Maggie held a hand out to Lia. "Coffee nuthin'. We're going to Junie's. Come on."

Lia took Maggie's hand and allowed her cousin to lead her out of the police station. The women climbed into the Falcon and drove to Junie's.

"I was right," Lia said, her voice dull. "The police are going to stop looking for other suspects and just lay this on Kyle."

"I can't argue with you. But what I can say is that they would really need to find some actual evidence to get him convicted of first-degree murder. And if he didn't do it, there won't be any."

"'If.' You said 'if.' Even you think he might have done it."

"You're right. My bad. What we need to do is focus on other suspects. If you have faith in him, I do too. And he certainly scored points by turning himself in."

*

Since it was Friday night, the New Orleans crowd had come upriver for a little local color, and it took longer than usual to find a parking space. Maggie and Lia walked into Junie's just as Gaynell and the Gator Girls were ending a set, and they were jostled by a throng of people abandoning the dance floor for the bar. But when JJ saw them, he shooed away a too-cool-for-school city couple and claimed their stools for the women. JJ was clad in an elegant sleeveless black linen caftan over white slacks. But even with the ceiling fans going full blast, the place was sticky with heat, and JJ's mascara dripped down from the corners of his eyes, giving him the look of a mournful clown.

"What can I get for my two favorite dollies?" he asked Maggie and Lia.

"Two Jim Beams, neat."

JJ eyed them curiously. "It's a hard liquor night, huh? Something must be up. Talk to me."

Before either woman could say anything, Gaynell joined them at the bar. Her Zachary Richard concert T-shirt was so drenched with perspiration that she looked like she'd run through a sprinkler, but she had the afterglow that came with a great performance.

"Hey," she greeted the others, who responded in kind.

"Dolly, I order you to stop being so good," JJ mock-scolded Gaynell as he pulled her a beer from the tap. "I do not want to see you lured away from me to some hot club in New Orleans." He turned to Maggie and Lia. "Now, back to you two."

"Kyle . . ." Lia stopped, too emotional to continue.

"PPD arrested him for Beverly Clabber's murder," Maggie said, stepping in for her cousin. The others reacted with shock.

"We're sure he didn't do it," she continued, emphasizing the "we" for Lia's sake, "but it turns out he did have an incriminating history with Mrs. Clabber."

Maggie brought JJ and Gaynell up to speed on Kyle and then started listing other potential suspects. "Of anyone local, Gran' really had the most reason to kill off Beverly/Francine, but Bo agreed that we can basically rule her out. The Georgia boys are up to something, but I haven't figured out what yet. At first I thought there was something hinky about Suzy, but turns out she's okay. But her fellow board member, Debbie Stern, is planning a coup d' Cutie, so covering that up gives her a motive. Then there are the Butlers, who spend *way* too much time in their room for a couple on a vacation. Nobody has that much sex."

"Except maybe a couple that's hot for each other and is on vacation," Gaynell said with an impish smile. Maggie snorted dismissively.

"Oooh, jealous much?" JJ teased her.

"Uh, noooo." The others cast skeptical looks at Maggie, and she caved. "Okay, fine, a little. Anyway, back to suspects. There's also whoever's been digging for treasure. I'm sure it's one of our guests, but which one I don't know. Could be the Butlers, the Rykers, even the Georgia boys. If they did actually find something, covering *that* up gives them a motive."

"Hmm," JJ said as he dabbed his shiny forehead with a cocktail napkin. "First off, you need to find out what those college kids are doing and who's diggin' up the pea patch."

"Believe me, I've tried. I took over housekeeping to do some snooping, but it's hard, because I actually do have to clean, which eats up a lot of time. Curse my parents for maintaining such a high standard."

"I'll help," Gaynell volunteered, much to Maggie's surprise. "Really?"

"Sure. It'll make cleaning *and* snooping go faster."

"If you're sure . . ."

"I am. I used to help my Gran' clean the Cavalier Motel off I-10, so I pretty much know the drill."

"That makes one of us," Maggie smiled at Gaynell. "Okay then, thanks."

Lia checked her phone. "It's been almost an hour. We should go back. Hopefully the lawyer has gotten there by now."

After confirming a meeting time with Gaynell and arguing with JJ, who refused to accept money for their drinks, Maggie and Lia drove back to the police station. There was a new car in the parking lot—a bright purple Bentley with a vanity plate that read, "LWYR UP."

"I'm guessing Quentin MacIlhoney's here," Maggie said as she eyed the car. "He must be pretty good at his job if he can afford this."

"Maggie . . ." Lia said, then hesitated. Maggie put a comforting hand on her cousin's shoulder. "Can I see the picture again?"

"Sure."

Maggie reached into her grocery bag and pulled out the photo. She handed it to Lia, who stared at it for a moment. There was no gray in Kyle's hair, no sadness in his smile. Sarah, his new bride, had her arm entwined with his and leaned against him slightly, a lock of curled red hair resting on his shoulders.

"She was beautiful," Lia finally said.

Maggie gently extricated the picture from Lia's hands and placed it back in the bag. "Let's go inside," she said softly. "Kyle needs you."

As they walked into the station, they were greeted by an unexpected sound—roars of laughter. A middle-aged man in pressed designer jeans and a yellow sport coat was in the middle of telling a story to a small circle of officers. He was trim and of average height with white hair and a beard that made him look like Father Christmas after a weight-loss program. His sockless feet were clad in soft, expensive-looking Italian loafers, and a top-of-the-line Rolex watch peeked out from under the French cuffs of what looked to Maggie like a bespoke cotton shirt. His gold cufflinks glittered under the florescent lights of the police station lobby, as did a medallion shaped like a Mardi Gras coin that rested on a bed of white chest hairs made visible by the fact that he left open the three top buttons of his shirt.

"So the guy says to his lawyer, 'Lady, that's not what I meant by 'get me off,' but I sure do appreciate it," the man said to another round of laughter from the officers.

Lia stepped forward tentatively. "Excuse me, are you Mr. MacIlhoney?"

"It's Mac, honey, which answers your question. You must be my client's beloved." Quentin "Mac" MacIlhoney gave Lia's hand a hard shake. He turned to Maggie. "And you are?"

"Maggie Crozat, Lia's cousin. My family owns Crozat, where the murder happened, and none of us believe for a minute that Kyle did it."

"Neither do I, dear," Mac said, then gestured to the officers. "We just have to convince these doubters here."

"And a judge and a jury," Artie Belloise, who was food-free for a change, retorted.

"A hundred bucks says it don't even get that far." Mac pulled a bill out of his blazer breast pocket—a hundred dollar bill. "Tell you what: none of you even have to put up the money." Quentin brandished the bill and the officers gaped, as did Maggie. "I lose, this goes to your Boys and Girls Club, along with a crawfish boil on me. If I win . . ." Mac took a sharp pencil out of the same pocket, stuck the bill on it, and then flung the pencil and money up to the ceiling, where it lodged in a soft acoustic tile. "I take back my bill. Deal, boys?"

Impressed, the cops nodded. Mac walked to the door and held it open for Lia and Maggie. "Ladies, if you will," he said with a gallant wave. As they left, he winked at Pelican's men in blue and then followed the women out the door. The minute they cleared the officers' eye line, Mac's demeanor changed. "Your boyfriend is in some serious trouble," he said to Lia tersely. Even the timbre of his voice was different—low and rough. "There are no other viable suspects and enough circumstantial evidence for the DA to build a case. I'll talk to the judge first thing in the morning about posting bail, but around here, it's a tough sell on a murder one charge."

Lia, shocked into silence, simply nodded. But Maggie had to know. "Mr. MacIlhoney—Mac—what was all that?" she said as she gestured toward the police station.

"Law enforcement sees defense attorneys as the enemy," Mac took out a key fob with the initial *M* emblazoned in what Maggie swore were real diamonds. "If I break the ice, pal around with them, it levels the playing field a little. Creates a friendlier atmosphere." Mac pressed the fob and his door unlocked. "And believe me, if your boyfriend wants to beat a possible death sentence, he's gonna need a lot of friends."

Mac got into his car, which started so silently Maggie wasn't sure it was actually on. She and Lia jumped when the car accelerated and pulled out onto the highway with a roar. As Quentin "Mac" MacIlhoney drove away, green-and-gold tracer lights around his vanity plate flashed in the night.

Chapter
Twenty-One

Maggie offered to spend the night at Lia's or have Lia stay over at Crozat. She was worried about her cousin being alone after experiencing one of the worst days of her life. Lia thanked her but said that she'd be okay. "Please don't worry about me. Between what all's going on at Crozat and your mom being sick, you've got enough to deal with. What you can do, though, is come up with other suspects that even Rufus Durand can't ignore."

"I will, I swear."

But Maggie wasn't as confident as she pretended to be, and she had a restless night. There was no evening break from the heat, and when she wasn't having nightmares about Crozat guests dying in horribly gory ways, she was awake listening to the buzz of mosquitoes trying to find an opening in the net around her bed.

She forced herself to get out of bed at six and called her dad before she prepared breakfast for the guests. "The doctors knocked down your mom's fever, so that's the good news," Tug reported. "But the first test they ran was inconclusive, so they want to run a couple more."

"What kind of tests are these, Dad?"

"Who can remember all those medical names? I'm hoping to be home this afternoon. I'll let you know for sure later." Tug ended the call before Maggie could protest. For whatever reason, he didn't want to talk specifics about the tests. Maybe, she thought, it's too painful for him.

Given how preoccupied she was, Maggie's ability to pull together a decent breakfast surprised her. Gran' roused herself early to help out, and the two set out bowls of scrambled eggs, plates of sausage and bacon, and a basket of rolls that Maggie hoped no one would recognize as leftovers from the previous night's dinner.

"I am tired like I done a big ironing," Gran' yawned as she untied her apron. "There's a reason your dad only trots me out to entertain the visiting troops. He knows what I've refused to admit until now: I'm too old to do actual work."

"You've been incredible, Gran'. Why don't you go back to bed?"

"Yes, ma'am. I'm outta here, as the kids say." Gran' tossed her apron over her shoulder and left the kitchen for the shotgun. Maggie popped a roll in her mouth and chased it with a cup of strong chicory coffee. She was worn down to the point where it would take everything short of speed to keep her going.

As promised, Gaynell showed up at Crozat promptly at 8 a.m. dressed to scrub. "Put me to work," she told Maggie. Unfortunately, it was the one day when Crozat's guests seemed primed to laze around the property rather than sight-see, so access to their rooms was nil. Then Maggie had an idea.

"I haven't been able to check out anyone's cars without looking nosy or suspicious," she said. "What if we surprise them all with a free car wash? We'll say that washing off the dirt and dead bugs is Crozat's little gift to them. We won't be able to get into the cars right away, but it gives us a way to look in the windows and see if there's anything interesting."

"I like it," Gaynell said. "After we surprise them with the outside, we can ask if they want us to clean the inside too. If someone says no, it may mean they have something to hide."

Maggie and Gaynell dragged buckets, rags, sponges, car wash detergent, and a hose to the gravel lot where guests parked. They filled the buckets and added soap and then hosed down the first car, which was the Cuties' minivan. The two each took a sponge and a side of the car, and as they washed, peered into the windows. They saw nothing besides the usual tourist ephemera of maps and brochures. The same held true for the Butlers' rented sedan. The inside of the Georgia boys' truck, much like their room, resembled the inside of a trashcan. The floor was inches deep in fast food wrappers, and the stench from rotting food leaked through the closed windows.

"I'm actually hoping that these guys don't want us to clean inside here," Gaynell muttered, turning her face away from the stink.

"I know. But I'd like to dig up a little more info on whatever it is they're doing."

Maggie and Gaynell dried off the truck with rags and moved on to the Rykers' rented SUV. The car floor, like the others, was littered with travel detritus, including receipts and a few toys. As Maggie washed the back window, she noticed a blanket in the storage well of the car. "Hmm. Now why would you need a blanket at summer's end in Louisiana?"

Gaynell stopped washing to ponder the question. "If you had valuables in the car, you could use the blanket to cover them up. Or—"

"Or you use the blanket to hide something. Like maybe a metal detector." Maggie pointed to what looked a small steering wheel poking out from under the blanket. "I did enough treasure hunting as a kid to know one when I see it. Looks like we found our diggers. Too bad. They seemed like a nice family. But sneaking around property looking for something you don't plan on sharing with the owners isn't very nice, is it?"

"No, it is not. Well, we know who won't want us cleaning the inside of their car. Are you gonna bust them?"

"Nope. Not yet. Although this does add them to the suspect list. If Beverly somehow found out they were scavenging for Lafitte's treasure, Carrie or Lachlan might have wanted to shut her up."

"Ugh." Gaynell shuddered. "That would make them super-terrible parents."

"Even without that, they won't win any parenting awards. They're either lying to their kids about what they're doing or making their kids lie to us."

The women finished cleaning the Rykers' car and corralled the cleaning supplies. They stopped at the Crozat laundry facility, threw all the rags into the washing machine, and then walked into the dining room where the guests were finishing the breakfast Maggie had made for them. "'Morning," she said. "This is my good friend, Gaynell. We wanted to let you know that as a special thank-you for your patience during this awful time, the two of us washed all your cars."

There was a smattering of applause and appreciative comments. Maggie noticed Carrie and Lachlan Ryker exchange a nervous look and then plaster on smiles.

"And we'd be happy to clean inside the cars of anyone who's interested," she continued. There was a chorus of enthusiastic "yes," "sure," and "thanks." Gaynell didn't look too happy when the Georgia boys signed on for the cleaning. As predicted, only the Rykers demurred.

"That's so sweet of you," Carrie said. "But we're going to have our kids clean our car."

"Right," Lachlan said. "We believe chores give them a sense of responsibility. In fact, I think it's time to take this lesson a little further and have them clean up our room as well."

The Ryker kids groaned and Carrie shushed them. "Your father's right, and I don't want to hear a single argument from you three." She addressed Maggie. "So you can take our room off your agenda today, thanks so much."

"That's what I like to hear," Jan honked in her thick Noo Yawk accent. "Parents setting their kids right."

Maggie clenched her teeth to keep from blurting out, "If you only knew." Instead she flashed her best hostess smile.

"I'm sure you all have fun things planned"—*Hint, hint,* she thought, *clear out, everyone, so we can get into your rooms*—"so whenever you get back or when it's convenient for you, we'll finish our complimentary car washes."

This engendered chatter about the day's activities. The Georgia boys were meeting up with friends at LSU, while the Rykers were going to Bataria Preserve. "Pirates used to live there," Sam said, excited.

"We're not going because of that, we're going to do a swamp walk," Lachlan said a little too quickly.

The Cuties had scheduled a visit to the Jungle Gardens at Avery Island, but Debbie begged off. "I think I'm going to take it easy today. Maybe get a ride into town and do some souvenir shopping."

"Have fun," Jan said as she hugged her. "Do what you need to take care of yourself so we don't have to worry about you."

Maggie wanted to yell, "Worry, Jan, worry!" But once again, she forced herself to be quiet. Revealing what she knew about Debbie's plans would out her as a snoop.

"We're going into town," Shane offered. "Why don't you come with us?"

Debbie thanked the Butlers and agreed to take them up on the offer. The guests gradually made their way out of the dining room, and Gaynell helped Maggie clear the tables, ignoring protestations that she really didn't need to. "Now for the fun part," Maggie said. "Housekeeping." The two headed off to the supply closet and rolled out the heavy cart.

*

The morning flew by as double the workers cut the cleaning time in half. Rather than split up and take separate rooms, Maggie and Gaynell worked together. They quickly finished the Cuties' rooms, finding nothing that would solidify a case against Debbie or incriminate another one of them. They emptied each Cutie's trash into the large bag attached to the housekeeping cart and then pushed it past the Rykers' suite. Maggie stopped in front of their door and contemplated ignoring Carrie and Lachlan's instructions not to clean it.

"We could say we forgot," she told Gaynell, who shook her head no.

"Sounds lame," Gaynell said. "They'll suspect something, and if there's anything to remotely show they were involved in Beverly's death, you'll never have a chance to find it."

"You're right," Maggie said. She wheeled the cart toward the Georgia boys' room and parked it. "How long can you hold your breath?" she asked Gaynell.

"Not very."

"That's about to be a major problem for you."

Maggie opened the door and the scent that wafted out actually forced Gaynell back a few steps. "Lordy May!" Gaynell exclaimed as she reeled. "Are you sure Beverly's body isn't actually in there?"

"Yes. But you know what's super scary? I'm getting used to the smell."

The women pushed the cart into the room and powered through the cleaning process. "Hey, this is interesting," Gaynell said, holding up a bright blue T-shirt emblazoned with Greek letters that she'd found under a pile of candy bar wrappers. "Your Georgia boys are Pi Pis."

"Say what now?"

"Pi Pi Iota. It's a Southern fraternity. So Southern that it was supposedly founded by some KKK members. There are only a few chapters left. A lot were kicked off college campuses because of some hardcore hazing practices. I know about them because they rushed my brother and he said, 'No thank you.'"

"Really? There has to be a tie-in to what I found." She told Gaynell about the brochure for Confederate uniforms and the "slave" scribbles.

"I'll check with my brother and see what he knows about the Pi Pis," Gaynell said. "He's a Navy lieutenant and his ship is deployed to the Black Sea, so it may take a few days to hear back."

"Thanks. Not to lay on any pressure, but the sooner, the better. I hate to think of poor Kyle stuck in some awful jail cell."

"Do you know if he was able to post bail?"

Maggie shook her head somberly. "Lia hasn't called me, which isn't good. The lawyer didn't sound too optimistic."

The women finished their tasks and moved on to the Butlers' room. Emily and Shane were among the neater of the Crozat guests, so cleaning the place was comparatively easy.

"Anything?" Maggie asked as Gaynell gathered some loose scraps of papers off the floor.

"Just doodles. Take a look and see if they mean something."

Gaynell handed the papers to Maggie, who examined them carefully. "Lots of square boxes—that is such a guy thing—a cartoony-looking face on a knight with a shield," she said.

"You're right, just doodles. Not bad, though. I like the detail on the shield. Whoever drew this isn't much of a visual artist, but they have a talent for animation." Maggie thought for a moment. "I wonder if the knight is from a statue or suit of armor from Emily's home? I did a little research on the Butlers and she comes from one of those WASPy New England families that goes back to the Magna Carta or something. They're 'Brahmins'—you know, Boston high society."

"You mean, like the Crozats are Pelican high society?" Gaynell teased.

Maggie gestured to her sweaty tank top and stained jeans. "Hello, have you smelled me lately?"

Gaynell laughed. "You, lady, are Louisiana royalty on both sides of the family and even a little BO won't let you escape that."

Maggie rolled her eyes and tossed the paper scraps into the bathroom trash bin that Gaynell had carried into the bedroom. As Gaynell emptied the trash, something wrapped in tissue fell out of the bottom of the bin and rattled onto the floor. Maggie bent down to pick it up.

"This is interesting," she said as she unwrapped the tissue. She held up a pregnancy stick.

"Wow. Is it positive?"

Maggie checked. "No."

"Too bad, they're obviously trying." Gaynell made a face. "I feel skeevy now. Like we're getting in people's personal business."

"I know." Maggie carefully rewrapped the stick with the piece of tissue and placed it in the large garbage bag. "It's a little weird, though. This was hidden on the bottom of the bin, all covered up. It's like Emily didn't want Shane to know about it."

"Huh." Gaynell considered this. "Maybe she didn't want to disappoint him. She could be waiting until she has good news to share."

"That's true. Or . . ."

"Or?"

"Maybe she had an affair and is terrified she's pregnant by another man, and Mrs. Clabber found out and was going to tell Shane, so Emily killed her."

Gaynell burst out laughing. "Okay, now we've gone from snooping to telenovelas."

"I know. I clearly need a break. Let's roll this baby out of here. This was the last room, so we're done."

"Except for the inside car cleaning," Gaynell reminded her.

Maggie groaned. "Oh, I really, really hope no one takes us up on that today."

The women put away the cart, and Maggie insisted on fixing Gaynell a bite. It was early afternoon and guests were already trickling back. They passed the Georgia boys, and by their loud voices and slight staggers, Maggie assumed they'd enjoyed a liquid lunch. Jan pulled the Cutie van into the parking lot and called to them. "Have you seen Debbie? We bought her some hot sauce."

Maggie and Gaynell shook their heads no and continued into Crozat's kitchen, where Gran' was enjoying a turkey sandwich and a Brandy Milk Punch. Maggie introduced the two women.

"You're Undine Bourgeois's granddaughter, aren't you?" Gran' said as she scrutinized Gaynell. "You're even prettier than your grandmama. I want you to know that she and *her* mama always carried themselves with an innate grace. You can be proud of your ancestors." Since Gaynell's ancestors were fisherman and farmers, not plantation owners, this put them on a low rung of Pelican's dated but still very much alive social ladder.

"Thank you, ma'am," Gaynell said, more politely than she needed to, thought Maggie, who, much as she loved Gran', found the compliment condescending. She hated to admit it, but Gaynell was right. Even in the twenty-first century, it was hard to escape from the class system that had ruled Louisiana for so long.

"Look who's home."

Tug walked into the kitchen, followed by Ninette, who was instantly enveloped in a hug by her daughter. "Mom, we were so worried about you."

"I'm fine." Ninette kissed Maggie on her cheek. "I have to say, though, being in the hospital was a bit of a vacation. Lots of sleep, meals delivered, press a button and someone's there to look after you. It's like a resort."

"Mama, if being in a hospital felt like a resort, we need to get you on a real vacation."

"Someday, honey. For now, I'm gonna wash up and make lunch."

Maggie and Tug protested, but Ninette waved her hand in the air to dismiss them. "None of this treating me like an invalid. Putting together a meal is all the medicine I need."

Ninette went off to the restroom and Maggie addressed her father. "Did the doctors run the tests?"

Tug nodded. "Yes, but we won't have the results for a couple of days." He sat down and Maggie registered how drawn he looked. "One thing that did concern them . . . her white cell count is up."

Maggie laid a hand on her dad's shoulder. She couldn't find the words to respond.

Ninette returned, and everyone put on a good face. Maggie introduced her parents to Gaynell, and Gran' talked Tug into fixing a pitcher of Milk Punch. "It's got dairy, and the brandy kills germs," she said. "So it's really a health drink."

"Sold," Maggie joked. "Dad, pour me a tall one."

"Lunch is ready," Ninette announced. Before they could sit down to eat, Carrie Ryker appeared.

"Sorry to bother you, but might we get a bag of ice? Lachlan turned his ankle at the preserve and I'd like to treat it."

"I'm on it." Tug filled a bag with ice and handed it to her.

"Perils of treasure hunting, huh?" It came out before Maggie could stop herself.

Carrie gave her a funny look. "We weren't treasure hunting. Lachlan fell getting out of the swamp tour boat."

"Of course," Maggie said quickly, silently cursing her big mouth. "I don't know where that came from."

As soon as Carrie left, the others began eating. They all enjoyed the quiche that Ninette whipped up and served with a side salad of pears, pecans, homegrown lettuce, and a tangy balsamic dressing. The group finished their meal, and Gaynell left with a small bag of Chulanes pressed upon her by Tug.

"Those are rum and pecan," he said. "Watch out, they got a bit of a kick."

"I owe you for today," Maggie told her friend as the two walked to Gaynell's car.

"No you don't," Gaynell. "It was fun. Well, as fun as trying to prevent a man from being wrongfully accused of murder can be."

"I'll let you know the minute I hear anything from Lia."

"That would be great," Gaynell said. She got into her Mini Cooper and began backing out of the gravel lot. "I'll see you tomorrow."

Suddenly there was a loud scream, a woman's scream. Gaynell braked hard and threw her car into park. "What was *that*?"

"I don't know," Maggie said. The scream came again and didn't stop. Maggie took off running toward the sound of it, which came from the parterre. Gaynell jumped out of the car and ran behind her. Maggie reached the parterre at the same time as Tug and Ninette. They all found Emily Butler standing over what appeared to be a bundle of clothes, screaming her head off. Maggie grabbed the girl by the shoulders. "Emily, what is it, what's wrong?"

Emily didn't form words. She just continued to scream as she pointed to the bundle in front of her.

It was then that Maggie realized the bundle was a very dead Debbie Stern.

Chapter
Twenty-Two

What followed the discovery of Debbie's body felt unpleasantly familiar to Maggie: the 911 call, the scream of sirens, Pelican PD descending on Crozat. Once again, the coroner's van carted away a body. Once again, an evidence van decorated the front lawn. And once again, Rufus Durand couldn't keep himself from pointing out the tragedy's potential negative impact on Crozat's fortunes.

Only this time, there was Bo Durand.

Maggie knew that Bo's loyalty to his profession came first, but she finally trusted that he'd be about as fair as she could expect from any PPD law enforcement official. She even let herself hope that he'd be more than fair, that he'd show her family some clandestine partiality.

Bo screeched up to the plantation, the light flashing on top of his unmarked sedan. He walked over to where officers had sealed off the crime scene and was about to say something to Maggie but saw Ru and decided against it. She made eye contact with Bo, and his brow furrowed as if to ask, "Are you okay?" Maggie gave a tiny shrug that he acknowledged with an equally easy-to-miss sympathetic head nod. Then he conferred with the officers, instructed the crime scene investigators, and huddled with Ru, sending the message that whatever had transpired in the past, he was now the consummate team player.

"Everyone who's here is waiting for you in the parlor 'cept for the kids," Rufus told Bo.

"Cause of death?"

"Strangulation."

"Weapon?"

"From the size of the marks, the best guess of our guys is some piece of fabric with a little width to it."

Bo took this in and then started toward the house. Maggie and Gaynell followed. "I can't believe we're going through this again," Maggie said. "Ugh, that sounded really callous. Poor Debbie."

"Fill me in on how the body was discovered."

Maggie gave Bo details of how she and Gaynell heard Emily screaming and, in rushing to her aid, discovered Debbie. Then something dawned on her. "Kyle wasn't here. He couldn't have murdered her. So that proves he's innocent."

"That proves he's innocent regarding *Debbie's* death."

"Are you telling us that you don't think Beverly and Debbie's deaths are connected?" Gaynell asked, her tone skeptical.

"At this point, there's no evidence to support that. Much as I hate to say it, because I do like the guy, there is evidence to support a claim that Kyle held a grudge that could have led to him taking revenge on Beverly. And Maggie herself handed over the evidence that could implicate Jan Robbins, if she knew about Debbie's plot to oust her."

Maggie groaned. In trying to help nail a murder suspect, she had inadvertently put another nail in Kyle's potential coffin, and the first one in Jan's. She was starting to feel like living proof of the old adage "No good deed goes unpunished."

"You haven't talked to Lia, have you?" Bo asked her after a moment of silence as they walked.

"No. Why?" Maggie felt a knot of dread in her stomach.

"The judge denied bail."

"What? Oh, no. I swear, I can't stand it anymore. When will this end?"

Bo instinctively reached out to comfort Maggie and then just as quickly pulled away. When they reached the Crozat front parlor, they found Artie keeping an eye on Tug, Ninette, Gran', and the B and B's guests. As soon as Bo, Maggie, and Gaynell entered, the guests converged on Bo.

"What the hell's going on here?"

"You're not gonna hold us again, are you? We've got classes in a couple of days, man."

"Is there a serial killer on the loose?"

"For God's sake, a woman is dead," Jan yelled at the others. Maggie could see that she, as well as the other Cuties, had been crying. "Get over yourselves and show her some respect. She was a good person."

"A very good person," Angela parroted while Suzy nodded vigorously in agreement. Maggie knew otherwise. She felt sorry for Jan, who was in for a shock as great as the one of her supposed friend's death—that is, if Jan herself wasn't the murderer and faking her grief. *Or was it "murderess" if the killer was a woman?* Maggie wondered but then forced herself to focus.

"You'll be free to go as soon as we verify contact information and conduct a thorough search of the area," Bo told the guests. "Right now, I need to interview you individually, like I did when Mrs. Clabber expired. And to answer another question, no, I don't believe that there's a serial killer targeting Crozat."

"We can't apologize enough to all of you for what's happened here," Tug told the group in somber tones. "We'll make calls and see if any of the nearby B and Bs or inns or motels have rooms available. It may be tough since people who came for Fet Let tend to stick around for a couple of the other local end-of-summer festivals in the area this week. But if we can't find accommodations and you choose to continue your stay with us, we will comp you again."

"Comp" is officially my least-favorite word, Maggie thought. She clutched Ninette's hand and sneaked a look to see how this new disaster was affecting her mother. Ninette seemed stoic. The hospital visit appeared to have done her so much good that Maggie pondered a stay there herself.

She turned her attention back to the conversation. "We're going to post a twenty-four-hour guard to ensure your safety," Bo was saying.

"I'd like to volunteer for the first shift, sir," Artie said, mindful that a Crozat dinner would soon be placed on the table.

"Great, we get Officer Hollow Leg," Maggie muttered to her father, who put his fingers to his lips to shush her.

"I'm going to ask you to wait on the veranda while I conduct my interviews," Bo told everyone. "Please don't talk about Ms. Stern. I don't want you coloring each other's recollections. Artie, stay with them."

"Yessir."

Artie led everyone out except Maggie. "Do you need me to do anything?" she asked Bo.

"Yes. I'm going to interview the Cuties simultaneously. I don't want to give them a chance to communicate among themselves. I could use another pair of eyes to check out their instant reactions to the news about Debbie's planned coup. For all we know, one of them might have been in on it with her. Or found out and killed her to protect Jan."

"Rufus won't be happy if he sees me in here with you."

"Yeah, well, I'll take that chance. It beats whatever lackey of his he'd send in to 'help' me. Plus, you know these women better than any of us, so you're more likely to pick up on anything unusual."

Bo stepped outside to confer with Artie, who showed Jan, Suzy, and Angela back into the room. The women sat as a unit on the parlor's high-backed couch. Their faces were streaked with tears. Maggie studied them for any signs that they might be faking their grief but saw none. As they all sat in silence waiting for Bo to return, she used the quiet to connect with her sixth sense and see if it told a different story. It didn't. Maggie felt in her bones that the women were truly distraught.

Bo came back in the room and positioned himself in a chair opposite the Cuties. "Tell me everything you know about Debbie Stern," Bo began.

Angela and Suzy let Jan do the talking. Jan filled him in on Debbie's business triumph, loss, and subsequent breakdown.

"Thank you. Did you know she had created a business plan to oust Jan from the Cajun Cutie presidency, take over the organization, and turn it into a profit-making venture?"

All three mouths dropped open at the same time as if choreographed. Maggie scanned each face carefully and saw no signs of artifice. She would put money on the fact that Jan, Angela, and Suzy were genuinely stunned.

"Impossible," Angela declared. "Debbie never would have done that."

"I'm afraid that we have proof," Bo said.

"I was Debbie's best friend," Jan said. "She wouldn't have done that to me. Whatever you have is fake."

"I'm afraid it's not."

Maggie noticed that Jan had started shivering. "But-but-but-but—" she stammered as she searched for a way to rebut Bo's statement.

"We have proof," Bo repeated, his tone kind but adamant.

"I swear to God, if Debbie wasn't already dead, I'd kill her," Suzy spat out.

Bo was about to caution her when Cal Vichet opened the door and stuck his head in.

"Sir, we need you," he told Bo.

"I'm requesting that you not to speak to each other while I'm gone." With that, Bo followed Cal out the door.

*

The next few minutes felt interminable as Maggie waited with the Cuties. Brought together by a common love and now devastated by a betrayal, each woman seemed to be in her own world. Maggie could tell they were trying to process Debbie's duplicity and felt for them, but she was relieved when Bo returned. Cal was right behind him, holding something in a plastic bag. Bo motioned toward Cal, who showed the bag to the women. Maggie saw that it contained a purple ombré scarf.

"Do any of you recognize this?" he asked them.

"It's mine," Jan said. "I've been looking for it. It went missing a couple of days ago. Where did you find it?"

"Stuffed under a bush near the victim," Bo said. "Ms. Slansky and DiPietro, you're free to go right now, but know that I may call you in again for questioning." He faced Jan. "Ms. Robbins, I'm going to need you to come to the station with me."

The three women exchanged terrified glances.

"Am—am I being arrested?" Jan asked. Maggie noticed that her shivering had intensified and felt terrible for the woman.

"No, ma'am," Bo said. "At least not until we get back DNA results on this scarf and see if they're a match for Debbie Stern."

Chapter Twenty-Three

As Bo and Cal Vichet led Jan out to Bo's car for further questioning at the police station, they were followed by Angela and Suzy, who was issuing a stream of profanity that brought a flush to Cal's weather-beaten face. "I haven't heard language like that since my unit was bombed in Iraq," he said, shaking his head in disbelief.

Gaynell left after making Maggie swear to let her know if she needed any help. Maggie, who'd promised to contact Quentin MacIlhoney on Jan's behalf, called the lawyer, but his assistant said he was unavailable due to the fact he was shooting an episode of *For Crime's Sake,* a local show that pitted an ex-DA against a defense attorney as they argued about a Louisiana murder cold case. Maggie stressed the urgency of the situation and extracted a promise of a return call as soon as taping finished. Then she made the rounds of Crozat's guests—at least the ones that weren't in police custody or murdered.

Shane Butler whispered to her that he'd given Emily a sleeping pill to help her get through the trauma of discovering Debbie. The Georgia boys were celebrating the capture of the "Crozat Killer," as they dubbed Jan, by heading back to LSU for a party that they found via social media. The Rykers told Maggie not to worry about them for dinner but didn't share their plans. She blamed herself for their sudden reticence and deeply regretted her crack about treasure hunting.

Maggie went to the front parlor, where she found her father ending a phone call. He looked grim. "That was the *New York Times*."

"Seriously?"

"I'm afraid so."

"Any chance they wanted Mom's recipe for Crawfish Crozat?"

Tug shook his head. "Nope. Apparently you can get away with one old geezer being offed at a B and B, but when a successful Manhattan businesswoman is 'murdered by her best friend,' that's news. In print and online. I've hung up on a couple of Internet bottom feeders this morning."

"How did they find out so fast?"

"I think we can thank the Georgia boys' social media accounts for that."

Maggie groaned and then massaged her temples as she contemplated how to do damage control. "There is a bright side. Print media is dying. And you know how voracious the Internet is. Stories have a short shelf life. Since the police think they caught Debbie's killer, this should blow over pretty quickly." Of course, as she well knew, it would pop up whenever anyone did an Internet search for "Crozat Plantation." But she chose not to burden her father with this ugly reality.

"The question is, will Crozat still be standing when it does blow over?" Tug asked. "We've already had four cancellations for Labor Day weekend. We're always full then. This is bad, Maggie." Maggie gave Tug a comforting hug. Her father held on to her for a minute and then pulled away. "Please, honey, let's keep this a secret between you and me. Your mom certainly doesn't need to know."

"Of course, Dad."

Tug went back to work, and Maggie walked out onto the veranda to think. She stared out at the grassy levee that separated Crozat from the mercurial Mississippi. The river, like a hungry python, had swallowed plantations whole over the centuries. Yet it always spared Crozat, and she couldn't stand the thought that her family home, having survived many a natural disaster, might be brought down by a human one.

She glanced back at the parlor, where her father was hunched over his computer keyboard. Was it her imagination, or had his copper hair dulled? Were there more lines on his face and darker shadows under his eyes? She scrunched her eyes to fight off tears. There wasn't a day in her life when Tug and Ninette hadn't offered love and support in a crisis, no matter how trivial. When mean girls in Maggie's fifth-grade class anointed themselves "the Fashion Police" and made fun of her quirky outfit choices, Tug made sure that the school principal ended the group's sartorial reign of terror. When Maggie threw a childish tantrum at seventeen because she got a bad haircut, Ninette made her feel better by showing how the cut could be fixed by simply flipping her part to the left.

As she watched her dad deal with the fallout brought on by the Crozat Killer—whoever he or she was—Maggie realized she'd reached that moment in a child's relationship with their parents where the balance shifts. Instead of getting support, it was time to give it. She was going to make things better for her mom and dad.

She just had to figure out how.

Maggie walked toward the shotgun and passed the area where PPD CSI was still dissecting the crime scene, although with much less attention to detail now that the potentially incriminating scarf had been discovered. As soon as she got home, she sat on the couch with her tablet and typed in a search for "Crozat Plantation B and B." Page one was nothing but links to e-bites about the murders, as were pages two through five. It wasn't until page six that customer reviews from a travel website appeared—glowing reviews now usurped by the notoriety of recent events. Maggie mulled over something an old roommate, Kristie, once told her. Kristie had been an entry-level executive at a large public relations firm and, as low girl on the corporate totem pole, often found herself assigned the most heinous clients. "But," she said to Maggie one day as she was in the middle of turning a starlet's drug habit into a story of rehab redemption, "I always stick to the basic rule of PR: if you don't like what people are saying about your client, change the conversation." Maggie wished she could call on Kristie to help her out with Crozat, but Kristie's success at changing conversations had led her to an executive vice president position at her firm's LA office, and the last time Maggie had seen her was on television as she led an Oscar-nominated client down the red carpet prior to the Academy Awards.

Maggie lay back on the couch and closed her eyes, trying to think how she could change the current salacious conversation about Crozat into one that would staunch its financial bleeding. She was jolted out of her thoughts by her cell phone's ring. Maggie checked and saw Gaynell was the caller.

"How fast can you get here?" Gaynell asked.

"Huh?"

"You're on for the night tour, remember? The group off the riverboat cruise? They're docking in fifteen minutes. I tried to find a sub for you, but no one else was free."

Maggie jumped up. "Gay, I am so sorry. I totally forgot."

"I know you had a day that was a gift from the devil, but if I have to spend two hours working this group with only Vanessa, I will volunteer to be Crozat's next victim."

"I'm on my way." Maggie texted her parents to let them know that she was due at Doucet and then grabbed her purse and car keys. She ran to the Falcon, jumped in, and headed for Doucet.

*

As she drove, she found herself replaying her conversation with Tug. Something about it sparked memories of the Clabbers' funeral. She had a sudden flash that there was a clue to the murders in an interaction she had that day, but hard as she tried, she couldn't pinpoint the moment. It remained elusive.

Maggie slowed down as she drove through the town speed trap. She saw that Pelican PD had pulled a van over—a news van from the Baton Rouge television station. Cal Vichet was castigating the unhappy driver while handing him ticket. As she drove by, Cal caught her eye and winked at her. She smiled back. Pelicaners had a history of protecting their own, and no news crew or reporter would find themselves welcome in town. Maggie just hoped that Cal's boss Rufus Durand didn't find out about the solid that the officer had done the Crozats.

Five minutes after she pulled into Doucet's pebbled parking lot, Maggie was at the front door of the mansion in full dress, wig, and makeup, calling up her best Louisiana accent to welcome a group of thirty retired teachers from Ohio. She, Gaynell, and Vanessa each toured ten of them through the plantation, and since these visitors were educated and engaged, the evening wound up being a bit of a murder palate cleanser.

The evening tours for riverboat groups always ended with a champagne toast, and Maggie volunteered to lead it. "A toast to Doucet. May we appreciate its beauty while we learn from its history."

There were a few *hear, hears*, they all toasted, and then she, Gaynell, and Vanessa escorted the group back to the riverboat landing. The evening shadows transformed the women's polyester gowns into the illusion of silk taffeta. They waved parade queen waves to the boat as it paddled off down the river and froze like statues so the tourists could snap a few last-minute shots. For a moment, the Ohio retirees could pretend that they were in another century, one where women's gracious manners made them beautiful, horrible injustices were ignored, and murders were the by-product of duels fought in the name of honor.

"I gotta pee like a racehorse," Vanessa announced, breaking the mood. She hiked up her hoop skirt so she could race back to the staff lounge while Maggie and Gaynell strolled behind her.

Maggie filled Gaynell in on the latest developments regarding Debbie's death as they walked into the lounge to change. Vanessa had a head start on them but was slowed down by the difficulty of trying to zip up jeans that were at least a size too small. "Ru called and told me about the *latest* murder," Vanessa said. She sucked in her gut and gave the zipper one last yank. "Y'all keep going like this and the only way you'll have visitors is if you try to sell Crozat as some kinda creepy haunted house."

"You know, Van," Maggie said, making sure to use a hated nickname, "unnaturally tight pants can create infertility in women as well as men."

"You're just mad 'cuz you know I'm right." Vanessa touched up her face with so much makeup that Maggie wondered if she was heading over to Nudie's Princess Palace to pole dance. "And 'cuz you don't have a boyfriend."

Maggie didn't deign to respond. Unfortunately, it was because she knew Vanessa was right on at least one count. Crozat B and B was in big trouble. It was time for her to change the conversation. "Gay, any chance you could cover my shifts for the next couple of days?"

"Sure. I could use the money."

"Thanks."

"Wish I could help you," Vanessa chimed in, "but it's Ru and me's two-month-aversary and I got to plan something special."

"I appreciate the thought, Vanessa," Maggie said, choosing the high road.

She finished changing and said good-night to her coworkers. As she walked to her car, she pulled out her cell and called Tug.

"Hey, honey," he said. "What's up?"

She lowered her voice. "If any of our guests take you up on the offer to find other accommodations, tell them you checked and nothing in the area is available. I need to buy some time."

"To do what?" Tug asked, worried.

"As soon as our guests leave, it'll be that much harder— maybe impossible—to find suspects besides Jan and Kyle. Don't worry; I'm not going to do anything stupid or unsafe. I won't be like one of those dumb cheerleaders in a horror movie who goes roaming around a house where there's a killer on the loose. I'm just going to research some stuff."

"Well, that couldn't be vaguer," Tug responded, his concerns not allayed. She didn't respond. "All right, but be careful. And let me know if you need anything. Just me. We're gonna keep your mom out of this."

"Definitely."

"More secrets, I'm afraid," Tug sighed.

Maggie ended the call and got into her car. As she drove home, she concentrated on clues that would lead in the opposite direction of Kyle and Jan. Gaynell was still waiting to hear from her brother about his negative experiences with the Pi Pis, but an Internet search might also yield some dirt. The Rykers clearly had something to hide. For the sake of their kids, Maggie hoped it wasn't murder. And she couldn't forget the ring and brochures she'd discovered under Beverly's bed. It was time to give those another look and see if they sparked anything useful. She also realized that she'd never put the original brochures and the ring back in the Clabbers' bedroom as she had planned. There was no time for that now; she'd give everything to Bo and just tell him that she'd found it all while cleaning the Clabbers' room.

*

By the time she got home, Crozat was quiet and few lights were on. Guests and staff had retreated for the night, probably worn out by the day's events. Maggie noted that Gran's light was out too, so she tiptoed across the shotgun's floor, eliciting only small squeaks from the centuries-old cypress boards. She retrieved the desk key from its hiding place in her bureau and went to her desk in the living room. She was about to unlock the desk drawer, but as she inserted the key, the drawer slid open. It was already unlocked.

Maggie paused, trying to recall when she last went into the drawer. Maybe she'd forgotten to lock it. But the memory she retrieved was a clear picture of placing the Clabber items under other documents, turning the key, and tugging at the drawer to make sure it was properly locked. In fact, she remembered locking all four drawers on the desk.

She checked them. Each was unlocked.

Her heart heavy with fear, she opened the drawer and pawed through its contents until she found the file marked "Receipts." She was relieved to see the copies she'd made of the Clabbers' brochures and Beverly's ring. Then she dug to the bottom of the pile to find the originals. She saw nothing. Fear blossomed into panic as Maggie yanked out the drawer and dumped everything in it onto the floor. She went through the papers and loose ends over and over again. But the ring was gone, as well as the original brochures.

"My goodness, what is going on out here?" A sleepy Gran' appeared in her bedroom doorway, her lace-trimmed cream nightgown gently billowing from the breeze of the ceiling fan above her. "I was afraid we had mice, or one of those giant flying palmetto bugs had found their way in. I still have the occasional nightmare from when I thought I heard someone in my room and turned on the light only to find one of those disgusting winged roaches wandering through my perfumes."

"Gran', have you been in this drawer? Did you take a ring and some brochures from it? It's okay if you did; I just need to know."

"I would never do such a thing without telling you. Why, are they important?"

"They're what I found hidden in the Clabbers' room. A signet initial ring and brochures from a Scottish castle and English country manor."

"And they're missing?"

Maggie hesitated, hating to admit it. "Yes."

"Oh, dear." Gran' sat on the couch. "That's not good at all, is it?"

"No. It is not good."

Neither of them voiced it, but the same thought was in both of their minds. Someone had come into their home with the express purpose of finding what the Clabbers had hidden and Maggie had rehidden.

And the odds were pretty good that the evidence thief was Beverly Clabber's killer.

Chapter Twenty-Four

"Let's not jump to conclusions," Gran' cautioned. "It could be a common burglar. I'll see if my jewelry is gone and you do the same."

"I don't have anything worth stealing."

"Well, the burglars don't know that."

The women went into their bedrooms and checked on their valuables, which in Maggie's case meant sentimental costume jewelry like a charm bracelet she'd received for her seventh birthday featuring images of the Spice Girls, a pop group she'd idolized at the time. She and Gran' then reconvened in the living room.

"Nothing's missing," Maggie reported.

"Nothing of mine either." Gran' said. "I never thought I'd be disappointed *not* to be robbed."

"So all they wanted was Beverly Clabber's things. How did they even know I had them? Or that *she* had them?"

"I think if we knew that, we'd know who killed the poor woman. By the way, hiding the copies in that 'Receipts' folder was very clever of you. At least you still have something to work from."

"To be honest," Maggie confessed, "I didn't do it on purpose. I just grabbed the nearest empty folder."

"My dear, learn to take a compliment." Gran' stood and stretched. "I'm going back to bed."

Maggie stared at her grandmother. "You can sleep now?"

"Well, I don't see any use in the alternative. I'd much rather be killed in my sleep than lie awake waiting for it."

"Gran', that's so brutal."

"I prefer to think of it as practical. Good-night." Gran' walked to her room but stopped in the doorway. "Although do throw the deadbolt tonight for a bit of extra insurance."

Gran' disappeared into her room and Maggie stared at the mess on the floor. No ring or brochures magically materialized, so she put everything back in the drawer, which she then maneuvered into place. The only item she kept out was the folder with the copies.

She got up, threw the deadbolt, then returned to the desk and turned on the desk lamp. Unlike Gran', there was no way she could sleep. Instead, she pulled out the copy of the McDonough Castle brochure and powered up her tablet. An Internet search yielded the website for the castle, and Maggie studied it carefully. The "About" tab took her to a chatty page that shared the castle's history as the ancestral home of the

Murrays, Scottish-landed gentries who could trace their peerage back to the late seventeenth century. The eldest Murray laid claim to the title Duke of Dundess.

At the bottom of the page was a crest, and under that a monogram. Maggie pulled out the copy of Beverly's ring; the florid script on it was an exact match to the McDonough Castle monogram's calligraphy. Clearly, Beverly had some connection to the place. Was she just a McDonough Castle fangirl? Maggie knew the obsessive love people developed for a certain part of the world. The Cuties were the perfect case in point. Maybe Beverly was a British Castle Cutie. If Maggie was going to discover whatever it was that motivated Beverly to ape the monogram's calligraphy, she needed to learn more about the castle, which meant going beyond the first page of the search.

But first, she stared at the crest. She could swear she'd seen it before but couldn't place where. She closed her eyes, took some meditative breaths, and tried clearing her mind.

*

The next thing Maggie knew, sunshine was streaming through the windows and Gran' was gently shaking her. "Wake up, darlin'. You fell asleep right on top of your computer."

Maggie roused herself and looked at the computer screen. Her castle search was gone, replaced by gobbledygook. At some point, she must have passed out with her head resting on the keyboard and hit a bunch of keys.

"Jan is back," Gran' said as she adjusted the tie on her bathrobe. "The police can't charge her with anything until they get the results from the DNA test. Heavens, listen to me. In my life, I never thought I'd sound like some character from a TV police show. Back to business; the Cuties are staying here with her, but our other guests are preparing to check out."

"No," Maggie said, frowning. "I need more time."

Gran' went into her room to dress for the day and Maggie retyped her Internet search, this time listing it as "information on McDonough Castle and Cobs Manor." On the second page, she found the connection between the two historic sites featured on Beverly's brochures. Cobs Manor was also an ancestral home of the Murrays, sort of a summer place.

She canceled her search and entered "Duke of Dundess—McDonough Hall." An obituary for Hamish Murray, a.k.a. Lord Livingston, Duke of Dundess, filled her screen. A solitary sort, he had passed away only a few months ago at the age of ninety-two, survived by no one. She entered another search specifically for the late duke, and a brief article from one of Scotland's leading newspapers, *The Herald,* popped up. It was titled "American Royalty?" and explained that because Hamish left no heirs in the British Isles, his attorneys had to cast a wide net. They managed to track down a very distant relative in the United States, guaranteeing that the dukedom wouldn't go extinct.

Maggie sat back and digested this information. Was horrible Hal Clabber slated to be the next Duke of Dundess? She had read enough Jane Austen to know that inherited titles only passed to sons, not daughters—at least in the nineteenth century. Maybe things had changed in the last two hundred years. She searched "inherited peerages" and was disappointed to see a long list of articles about an ongoing battle in Britain to allow daughters to inherit when no son was in the picture. Apparently, things hadn't changed, which pointed to Hal Clabber, which made no sense since he had died of natural causes while his wife was the murder victim.

Maggie groaned. Then a sentence under the title of one article caught her eye: "Most Scottish peerages, like the ancient English baronies, allow the peerage to pass to the 'heirs general,' so females can inherit them."

"Oh my God," she said. It was all starting to make sense.

Gran' came out of her bedroom, dressed in a pale blue linen sheath with matching sandals. "I heard that," she said. "Are you onto something?"

"I think so." Maggie filled Gran' in on what she'd learned so far. "What if Beverly, not Hal, was next of kin to Hamish Murray?"

"That would certainly explain the signet ring. Beverly Clabber, Duchess of Dundess. It would also explain why she bragged to Yvonne about having something to lord over me. At the end of my time on this earth, I will have been many things, but a duchess is not one of them."

"What it doesn't explain is why she was murdered."

"Well, why do people kill?" Gran' mused. "There's jealousy. And please rule me out on that score. Then there's money. Lots of people kill for that. I adored your grandfather, but believe me, there was the occasional time when I understood why someone would do in their spouse for the insurance payout."

"Gran'!" Maggie admonished.

"I'm sorry, but the man did have his days."

Maggie picked up where Gran' had left off. "There's fear, there's feeling threatened. There's revenge. And then there are sickos who just kill for fun."

"My goodness, there are so many reasons to murder that it's a wonder any of us live to see another day."

Maggie tabbed back to the McDonough Castle homepage and stared at it. "I *know* I've seen that crest before. This is making me nuts."

"You know what you need to do, dear."

"Yes." Maggie repeated by rote, "Clear my mind and give space for the answer."

"Exactly. I'll see you at breakfast. I believe we're having pecan pancakes. At least Mr. Clabber isn't around to complain that we're predictable." With that, Gran' sauntered out.

As soon as she was gone, Maggie closed her eyes and willed her mind to sift through its memories. Pictures floated through her recollections, some lovely, some not. While she quickly shook off the image of Debbie's lifeless body, she was tempted to linger at the memory of Bo's kindness during her dark moments the night before. Instead, she concentrated all her energy on the image of the crest. And suddenly she remembered. She knew where she'd seen it. Then she finally landed on the significant snippet of conversation from the Clabbers' funeral.

One by one, images clicked into place until they formed a clear picture of Beverly Clabber and Debbie Stern's murderer.

Maggie threw on a clean T-shirt and jean shorts. She ran out the front door of the shotgun and past Gran', who was chatting with the Butlers and Carrie and Lachlan Ryker.

"Gran', have they hauled away the garbage yet?" she called to her.

"No, dear. Late as usual. Someone really should complain to—"

Maggie didn't stop to hear the rest of the sentence. She just ran, ignoring the glances that the Butlers exchanged with the Rykers. She reached the back of the Crozat property, where unsightly items like the B and B's dumpsters were housed, and noticed a log cut from the stump of an old cypress tree. It took all her strength to push it next to the dumpsters, but she managed to maneuver it into place. She then climbed on it, threw one leg over the edge of a dumpster, and jumped in. Fortunately, the Crozats composted as much solid waste as possible, but given the effect of Louisiana's humidity on garbage, the dumpster still smelled wretched. For once, it didn't bother Maggie, which she credited to her olfactory glands having been beaten down by the stench of the Georgia boys' room.

Raccoons had gotten into the trash. Bags were ripped open and stuff was strewn about. Maggie hoped that even given the wide debris field, garbage was still generally grouped together. She wandered through the dumpster until she found an item that narrowed her search. She planted herself in the northwest corner of the dumpster, pawed through god-knows-what, and finally found the crumpled sheet of paper that she was looking for.

"Yes," she cried out triumphantly. "I was right."

"Uh, are you okay?"

A male voice startled her. She looked to see Shane Butler and Lachlan Ryker staring at her with odd expressions.

"I . . . I accidentally threw out something I needed, but I just found it."

"Oh," Shane said. "That's good. Need any help getting out of there?"

"No thanks. I'm fine." Maggie willed them to leave. She desperately needed to get in touch with Bo and didn't want any guests around when she made the call.

For a moment, there was an awkward standoff. Then Lachlan shrugged. "Right then. No worries."

The two men walked off, much too slowly for her taste. She took out her cell phone, but it rang before she could call Bo and alert him to the evidence she'd dug out of the dumpster. The screen flashed "Gaynell." Maggie answered the call with a quick "Hey."

"I have info for you," Gaynell said. "About Pi Pi Iota. I think I know why the Georgia boys are at Crozat." Gaynell filled her in and by the time she reached the end of her story, Maggie was furious.

"Those *creeps*. I'm booting them out right now. Look, Gaynell, do me a favor. I think I know who killed Beverly Clabber. Call Bo and tell him this."

Maggie shared her theory. When she was done, Gaynell was silent for a minute. "It's so hard to believe that anyone would be that demented," she finally said. "But I guess it does make a very sick kind of sense. I'll call Bo, but be careful, Maggie. This is dangerous stuff."

"Don't worry. I'm never without my gris-gris bag." Maggie patted the waist of her jeans, where she thought she had pinned the protection bag Lia had made for her. It was gone. "Great.

It must have fallen off somewhere in here. I don't have time to look for it now. I promise I won't do anything until Bo gets here. I have to go."

"Maggie—" Gaynell said, but Maggie ended the call. She climbed out of the dumpster, hopped to the ground, and took off for the Georgia boys' room. The boys were packing and the door was wide open. She ran in and slammed the door behind her.

"Jesus," Georgia One said. "You almost gave me a heart attack."

"Two words," Maggie said through clenched teeth. "Southern Glory."

Georgia One's face relaxed into a smile. "Aw, dang, you found out. We wanted to surprise y'all."

"I'm chapter president, so I get to tell her," Georgia Three said. He then adopted the voice of a documentary narrator. "Every year, the Beta Chapter of Pi Pi Iota hosts a celebration of our beloved Deep South's glorious history. We rent out a plantation and assume the ranks of Confederate soldiers, from officers on down. We stay in tents on the property and our dates stay in the plantation's housing. We rent uniforms and wear them the entire time and on a Saturday night host the Robert E. Lee Memorial Ball, where our dates get to wear the kind of ball gowns ladies wore back then."

"At the ball, we pretend that the Confederate Army won the War of Northern Aggression," Georgia Three threw in. "It's totes awesome."

"We've spent a lot of time this summer checking out different plantations. And congratulations. We've chosen Crozat as this year's location for our Southern Glory Weekend."

Maggie was so filled with anger that for a moment, she couldn't speak. She felt like she might explode and hoped she was too young to stroke out. "Get. Out."

"Huh?" Georgia Three looked confused.

"Get out now or I swear to God, I will have the police run you out of here. And don't *ever* come back to Crozat."

"Hey, if we leave, we take our business with us," Georgia One said, insulted. "And after what's gone on here, you guys should be thanking us for even still thinking about renting this place."

"Yeah," Georgia Two chimed in. "You're lucky we think a place where there's been murders is cool."

Maggie's face twitched as she tried to calm down. "Let me try to explain this to you," she said working to keep her tone even, despite the rage she felt. "Obviously we celebrate aspects of our Southern heritage here in Pelican, and especially here at Crozat. But there are many aspects of our history that we're not proud of. There's a saying, 'To forget is to condone.' We can't acknowledge the good without paying homage to the bad—something your incredibly superficial event ignores. So we would never sanction it, no less let it happen on our property. Have I made myself clear?"

"I think she's on her period," Georgia Three whispered none too quietly to his cohorts.

Maggie had had it. "If you're not gone in five minutes, I will find rabid dogs and sic them on you," she screamed at the boys. She flung open the door and slammed it shut behind her. As she marched back to the shotgun, she saw the Butlers' car pull out of the driveway. The Rykers were loading up their SUV.

Then Maggie noticed Angela and Suzy carrying suitcases to the Cuties' minivan. She ran up to them.

"You're leaving too?"

"We have to," Angela said. "We'd booked a return flight for tonight and it's really expensive to change."

"We're on fixed incomes," Suzy explained.

"We were going to stay here for Jan, but she wants us to get back to New York and post positive updates about our trip on our website. We need to do some damage control about Debbie and her plans and her murder."

"Well," Maggie said, trying to sound nonchalant, "we'll miss you."

She bid them good-bye, and then as she walked away, pulled out her cell and texted Bo one word: "HURRY!"

Maggie hastened into the shotgun, eager to update Gran' on her theory, as well as the morning's events. The living room was empty. "Gran'?" she called out as she went into the kitchen and got a glass of water. Her throat was scratchy from yelling at the Georgia boys, and the water soothed it. She heard muffled sounds coming from Gran's room, and ran in. But the bedroom was also empty. "Gran'?" she called again.

"Help!" came Gran's voice. Maggie traced it to the closet.

"What the—" She ran to the closet and pulled on the doorknob. "It's locked."

"I know. I was puttering around, minding my own business when someone threw a pillowcase over my head. They made me get the key to this door, then shoved me in here and locked it."

"Was it a man or a woman?"

"I couldn't tell. The voice was very low and rough. It could have been a man, or a woman disguising her voice."

"Don't worry, I'll find the key."

Maggie turned to start the hunt and screamed. Facing her was Emily Butler. She had a Crozat kitchen knife in her hand. Maggie recognized it as one of the sharpest.

"I don't think you'll be finding that key," Emily said in a whisper. "But I'm guessing you did find the stupid drawing of the knight that my stupid husband made."

Chapter
Twenty-Five

Emily poked Maggie with the knife and motioned for her to move into the living room. "I don't want your grandmother to hear my voice," Emily said in a venomous whisper. "She could identify me. Tell her you'll be back when you find the key."

With a knife jabbing painfully into her stomach, Maggie did as she was told.

"Thank you, dear," Gran' said from the closet. "And if you could hurry, that would be wonderful. It's a bit stuffy in here."

Emily prodded Maggie into a far corner of the living room, away from the windows. "So did you find it?" She stuck her with the point of the knife so sharply that Maggie felt it draw blood. "The sketch with the knight and his crest that Shane was supposed to throw away. Did you find it? Did you?"

"Yes," Maggie said quietly.

"That idiot," Emily said through clenched teeth.

Maggie winced as the knife's point pocked her skin. The screw was now painfully on the other foot. "So thanks to him," Emily continued, her tone aggrieved, "I had to figure out a way to fix this. Which, being a problem solver, I'm proud to say I've done."

"Congratulations," Maggie said. "Any chance it doesn't involve my death?"

"Ha, ha. Nope. Now, step one—leave your cell phone on the table. And hand over the doodle."

"That sounded kind of funny."

"Do it," Emily hissed with fury.

"And that didn't."

Maggie took the balled-up scratch paper and her phone out of her back pocket and placed both on the desk. Emily stuffed the paper into the front pocket of her pants and then took out a dog leash and attached it to Maggie's belt loop. "This is to make sure you don't run away." She secured the leash and then used her weapon to steer Maggie down the shotgun's long hallway. "Now let's go out the back door into the woods."

Maggie had always welcomed the shotgun's slight isolation, but now she cursed it. The back door opened into the no man's land of Crozat, a dense area of woods and thicket rarely ventured into by family or guests. "Please," she said to Emily, "whatever you're going to do with me, all I ask is that you don't hurt my grandmother."

"No worries. You're a threat; she's harmless. If she's lucky, someone will find her before she suffocates in that closet. If not, well, she's old. She had her life."

Emily and her knife stayed so close to Maggie as they entered the woods that she could feel the girl's warm breath on her neck. Twigs snapped and scraped her feet. She'd picked the wrong day to wear flip-flops. Then again, she hadn't foreseen being the prisoner of a lunatic.

Her heart thumped so loudly that she could hear it. She needed to calm herself so she could think rationally. "It's interesting how the mind works," she said, keeping her tone as calm as possible. "My dad and I were talking about keeping secrets and it reminded me of something, but I couldn't remember what. When I was looking at Shane's sketch, it came to me. How he said at the Clabbers' funeral that Mrs. C hadn't even told Mr. C she'd lived here before. That's a huge secret. Why would you not share that with your husband but tell a complete stranger? Unless the person you told wasn't a stranger."

"Shut up and keep walking," Emily snapped. Maggie was encouraged by the undercurrent of nervousness in her captor's rough tone. A vulnerable head case might be more malleable than a confident one.

"That's why you were always in your room, wasn't it?" she said. "You were planning the murders."

"A little. And then we'd have sex. The planning got us hot."

"Ugh, gross!"

"God, be a prude why don't you?" Emily said with a smirk.

Maggie silently cursed herself. She'd shown an emotion and now it was advantage, Emily. "Whatever," she said, resuming her casual tone. "By the way, nice move bringing up how the poison could have been planted earlier. Even when they found the old box of arsenic from the plantation store, that thought was still on people's minds."

"Thanks, but I really can't take credit for that one. That moron Jan gave me a gift with her speech about how 'no one here is a murderer.' Which made it hilarious when the cops thought *she* was."

"Hilarious. Not exactly a word I'd use in the situation."

"Jesus, get a sense of humor."

Maggie and Emily continued to trudge through the woods, but their psychotic chitchat had given Maggie time to think. She slowed down, forcing Emily to slow with her. "You know, there are snakes out here," she told her captor, hoping to scare her. "Poisonous ones."

"If you see one, let me know so I can push you on it. Having you die from a snake bite would save me a lot of trouble."

Well, that was an epic fail, Maggie thought. "What exactly is your plan for me?"

"I wanted to surprise you," Emily said, sounding more like she was talking about a birthday party than a murder. "But what the hell. The plan is stab you, then push you in the bayou. By the time anyone finds your body, Shane and I'll be long gone."

"Okay, first of all, the definition of bayou is 'a slow-moving stream,' so don't count on my body being quickly carried away to oblivion. And second, Shane's already gone. I saw him pull out this morning."

Maggie hoped this news would upset and distract Emily, but instead she just smirked. "Sorry, but he just went to town. He's being the wonderful husband who wants to buy some last-minute gifts for his poor wife who got the shock of her life when she discovered a fellow guest's lifeless body. Nobody'll suspect us for a minute."

"Unless they wonder why the same person found two dead bodies—Debbie's and potentially mine."

"Hmmm. Good point." Emily pondered this potential dilemma, and Maggie congratulated herself on derailing the girl's master plan. "Oooh, I know. We'll have Shane find your body instead of me. I told you I was a problem solver."

"Yeah, you're brilliant," Maggie shot at Emily. She was frustrated to find herself thwarted again. "Why did you kill Debbie, anyway? I know you did it. You can tell me; I'm going to be dead soon so it's not like I'll turn you in."

"She heard something she shouldn't have. She told us she'd never tell and actually knew a way to make it work to both our advantages. She wanted to tie our castles into this secret plan she had for the Cuties. You know, create a Castle Cuties group that she could develop and market the same way she planned on capitalizing on the whole Cajun Cutie thing. But she was screwing her own friends, so I didn't exactly trust her."

"Nice move stealing and hiding the scarf to implicate Jan in Debbie's murder."

"You know, you're awfully chatty for someone who's going to die in a few minutes."

"I've never been in this position before," Maggie said. "To be honest, I think maybe I'm in shock."

"I looked up the symptoms of shock when I had to pretend I was in shock after killing Debbie. The way you're acting wasn't on the list. Maybe you still think you're going to live."

Emily stopped, threw her hand over Maggie's mouth, and gave the knife the deepest thrust yet. Maggie let out a muffled cry. A few tears even escaped, despite her determination to hide her fear and pain. Emily pulled her hand away from Maggie's mouth and smiled. "That's better. Now walk."

The two women trudged through the dense foliage in silence. Sweat dripped into Maggie's eyes and burned them. "You know," she said after a few minutes, "there are alligators this way."

Emily stopped and Maggie sensed she'd finally struck a nerve. "You're lying," Emily said.

"Feel free to take that chance."

They walked a few more steps, and then Emily stopped again. "Is there another way to the bayou?"

Maggie nodded and started in a new direction, Emily and the knife right behind her. They pushed back branches and batted off swarms of mosquitoes as they got closer to the bayou. The ground was uneven and both women stumbled occasionally, but Emily still managed to keep the knife in the small of Maggie's back even as she clutched her captive's arm for balance.

"I don't know how you live in this place," Emily grumbled. "I can't wait to get out of here. I can't wait to get out of America."

"So that's the plan? Move into one of your newly inherited estates, Your Highness? Or is that not what you call duchesses? Maybe it's 'milady.' That's what Beverly Clabber would have been if she'd lived. It's what she and Hal called each other the one night they were with us. 'Milord' and 'milady.'"

Emily said nothing. She just continued to push Maggie through the woods.

"You may have stolen the rings and brochures from my house, but what you didn't get were the copies of them that I made," Maggie continued. "And I stared at those copies long enough to remember where I'd seen the Murray family crest before. On the paper scrap in your room. It was the crest on the knight's shield. And I thought, could the person who murdered Beverly be next in line for the Dundess inherited peerage? And could that person be you or Shane? My guess, given your family's background, is that it's you."

"Wow," Emily said. "Way to put things together. I thought you were just some whiny, self-involved artist."

Maggie was surprised to find herself stung by Emily's judgment. "I'm going through a hard time, okay?"

"Like I said, whiny. Yeah, it's me. My dad told me when I was little that we were distantly related to this titled Scottish family, but the odds of us ever inheriting were pretty remote. Then I started doing some genealogy research. The family was a bunch of nut jobs—I mean, literal nut jobs, like they ended up either in loony bins or killing themselves—and there was just one old guy left in Scotland. When my dad died, that meant I was next in line on our side. But then I found out about Beverly, a Murray on her mother's side. She was one less removed than I was, so she'd be ahead of me, which made me really mad. You know why she changed her name from Francine to Beverly? Because Beverly was the name of the first Duchess of Dundess. What a wannabe." Emily peered ahead. "I think I see the bayou. God, I never thought we'd get here."

Maggie stopped short. "Oh, crap."

"What now?" Emily said, annoyed.

Maggie pointed to what looked like a large piece of wood. "There—a gator."

"Bull," Emily scoffed. "That's a log."

"Does a log have two eyes? Let's go—quickly." Maggie turned abruptly, throwing Emily off balance. As Emily tried to steady herself, Maggie threw her weight into her captor. Emily let go of the leash she'd attached to Maggie, and the knife went flying out of her hand as she fell into the hole that the treasure-hunting Rykers had dug. She clawed at the edge as she pulled herself to standing. It was a surprisingly deep hole, and Emily was in it up to her neck. "My leg," she screamed. "Oh God, it hurts. I think it's broken. Help, please. Get me out of here before the alligator sees me."

Maggie knelt down and got in Emily's face. "You can just rot here until I come back with the police. Because, guess what? You were right. That *is* a log."

Maggie stood up, triumphant over her enemy. But Emily still looked terrified. "I'm not talking about that one," she said, gesturing to the log with her hand. "I'm talking about *that* one." Emily pointed beyond it to what looked like another log.

Only this one moved.

Chapter Twenty-Six

Maggie stared, frozen in place, as the alligator hefted his enormous body out of the water onto dry land. Emily whimpered, and the gator turned his head toward the women. He eyed them with curiosity.

"What do we do?" Emily asked in a shaky voice.

"Pray that he's already eaten."

Emily whimpered again.

"Never show fear to a wild animal," Maggie snapped at her.

The gator contemplated his next step, which gave Maggie a chance to contemplate hers. As much as she'd love to leave Emily to her fate, she couldn't bring herself to do that. The gator was moving slowly, as if he had a full belly, but her parents had always warned her not to buy into the misconceptions about a gator's behavior. Alligators had the ability to move fast on land, and while most avoided human contact, others could be aggressive. The jury was out on this one, but the fact that he hadn't retreated back into the water was not a good sign. Maggie regretted not asking her parents for a refresher course on what to do should she actually run into one.

"We need to get out of here," she told Emily.

Emily, who was waist-deep into the hole, tried to hoist herself out of it, and groaned in pain. "I can't."

"Great," Maggie muttered. "I get to save the woman who wanted to kill me. I better get points for this somewhere."

She bent down, hooked her arms under Emily's armpits and with great effort, and pulled her out of the hole. She started to drag a sobbing Emily through the woods but stopped when the gator advanced toward them.

"What's wrong? Why are you stopping?" Emily asked between sobs.

"Our friend there thinks that you're my prey and I'm dragging you off to eat. Which only makes you look more delicious to him."

"Oh my God, I'm gonna die."

"No you're not. At least not here. Hopefully in the jail where you'll be spending the rest of your life."

"Forget it," Emily cried. "I'd rather be eaten by the alligator."

Maggie ignored her and thought for a minute. She and some friends had once gone camping in California's Sequoia National Park. A park ranger warned the group, "If you're confronted by a mountain lion, don't act scared and run. Instead make yourselves appear as large as possible, then yell and scream and act like *you're* the predators." Maggie wondered if the same trick might work with an alligator. She dropped Emily, and pulled herself up to her full height, expanding her physical presence as much as she could.

"Yah!" she screamed at the gator as she waved her arms in a threatening manner. The gator stared at her, and Maggie began to panic that instead of telegraphing "Go away!" her actions were sending the message, "Come 'n get it!" But it was too late to take a different tack, so she continued to yell and stomp around like a lunatic. After what felt like the longest seconds of her life, the gator turned away and slowly slunk back into the water until he was completely submerged.

"You did it," Emily said. "You got rid of him."

"Yup," Maggie said as she started off. "And now I can get rid of you. I'll be back with the police."

"Wait," Emily begged. "Don't. Let me go and I'll give you whatever you want. I have money. Or one of the castles. I don't need both; you can just pick one. They're both awesome."

"You have got to be kidding." Maggie, furious, put her hands on her hips and bent down until she was face to face with Emily. "Can you possibly think that I'd be like, 'Hey, she murdered two people but I get a castle, so no biggie?' That is the most insulting thing anyone has ever said to me in my life. How dare you think—"

Maggie's diatribe was interrupted by the sound of shouting.

"Maggie! Maggie, where are you?"

She instantly recognized the voice. "Here, Bo! By the hole!"

Leaves crunched under the feet of someone running through the woods. Bo yanked some branches out of his way as he emerged from the trees with his gun drawn. Gaynell was right behind him. Both ran up to Maggie.

"Are you all right?" Bo asked.

Maggie nodded yes. "But she's not," Maggie said as she pointed to Emily, who was making a futile effort to crawl away. Bo trained his gun on her and she stopped. "Emily murdered Beverly and Debbie, and she was going to kill me too. We have to free Gran'. Emily locked her in the closet in the shotgun."

She began running toward the shotgun, but Gaynell pulled her back. "Your Grand-mère's okay," Gaynell said. "We found her when we went to look for you. Bo used GPS to trace your phone to the shotgun house. Gran's on the veranda having a Gin Fizz and sharing her story with anyone who'll listen."

"Thank God." Overwhelmed, Maggie sunk to the ground, the drama and danger of the morning finally catching up to her.

Gaynell knelt down and put an arm around her friend's shoulder. "You can relax. It's over."

There was the rhythmic sound of steps in the woods, and they all tensed up. Bo quietly circled, gun at the ready.

"Em?" a voice whispered. "Emily are you there?"

"Shane," Emily called. "Help! I'm hurt and these people won't let me go. They think I killed those women."

Shane shoved his way through a tangle of trees and ran to Emily's side. "What the hell? Boo Bear, what happened?"

Emily burst into tears that Maggie figured were at least half-real, given her busted leg. "It's awful. Maggie accused me of murder and chased me into the woods, and I fell in a big hole and I think I broke something."

Shane whipped around and faced Maggie. "I'm gonna sue your ass off." Then he turned to Bo. "And have you thrown off the force for police brutality."

Maggie snorted. "Nice act, Shane."

Bo held the gun on Shane with one hand and pulled out a pair of cuffs with the other. "You're both under arrest for the murders of Francine-slash-Beverly Prepoire Roubideaux Walker Clabber and Debra Stern." He holstered his gun and turned back to Shane. "Hands behind your back."

"You can't do this," Shane said as Bo cuffed him. "It's false arrest. I'm gonna sue your ass off too."

The others ignored him. "It's going to be hard to get a stretcher through these woods," Maggie said. She motioned to Emily. "Do you think we should carry her or let her put an arm around each of us and have her hop out?"

"Don't you touch her," Shane shouted. "She might be pregnant."

"That's right," Emily said. Maggie could see Emily looking for a way to use this to her advantage. "Pregnant suspects need to be treated very carefully."

"Sorry to break it to you, Emily," Maggie said. "But we happen to know you're not pregnant."

"Yup," Gaynell said. "We found the negative pee stick in your trash."

Maggie saw the relief on Shane's face. Unfortunately for him, so did Emily. And it really ticked her off. "The whole thing was his idea," she cried out. "He forced me into it."

Shane stared at her. "What?! Are you out of your mind? You're the one who came up with the entire plan. You said I'd get my own golf course in Scotland."

"He's lying," Emily sobbed theatrically. "He only wanted me to have a baby as insurance. That way we'd definitely have an heir."

"No, no way, she's talking crazy." Shane's voice and panic level rose simultaneously. "It was all about the golf course. And hunting. I could hunt in England and Scotland at my mansions, but I wouldn't have to wear a skirt unless I wanted to, and then I'd have my own, one of those kilt things." Shane devolved into babbling while Emily continued to hurl blame at him.

Maggie marveled at how quickly the couple had gone from sugary "boo bears" to selling each other out. *Had they ever really cared for each other,* she wondered, *or was their connection solely based on a mutual desire to live out some warped version of a fairy tale replete with duchies and castles?*

An ambulance siren wailed in the distance. A moment later, a police siren joined in. Shane turned to face Bo. "It was all her idea, I swear. I'll tell you anything you want to know, just cut me a deal."

"Don't believe him, he's full of it," Emily said, her tone vicious.

The sirens grew louder as the ambulance and police cruiser drew closer to Crozat. "As easy as listening to you two incriminate each other makes my job, I'm really not interested in some lovers' quarrel," Bo said. "I just want to get your statements and hand you over to the DA."

The sound of sirens was replaced by screeching tires and slamming doors. Someone called Bo's name and he yelled back his location. Soon the area was overrun with EMTs and police officers. Bo and Cal Vichet led Shane to the black-and-white while Artie got in the ambulance to escort Emily, now officially under arrest, to the hospital.

"Let's get you home for some rest and a shower," Gaynell told Maggie.

"That sounds so good right now."

As she followed Gaynell out of the woods, she glanced back at the bayou and saw a pair of black eyes staring back at her. The gator's head then rose just above the water, and Maggie could swear it was grinning at her.

Chapter Twenty-Seven

A warm shower and a couple of croissants revived Maggie, and despite the urging of her family, she refused to take to bed like a distressed damsel. She threw on a teal cotton tank top and shorts and then went to find the Rykers before they and their treasure-hunting gear got away. She'd been relieved to hear that both the Rykers and Cuties had delayed their departures, not wanting to leave until they got all the dirt on the morning's events and arrests.

Maggie found the Ryker kids entertaining themselves on the lawn in front of Crozat. Alice was texting on her cell as the boys tossed a ball back and forth. "Hey," she greeted them. "Have you seen your parents?"

"They went for a walk," Sam said, pointing down the road. "We're sticking around to hear the copper's story."

She thanked Sam and headed in the direction that he'd gestured to. After a short stroll, she saw Carrie and Lachlan resting on a boulder, pulling their damp clothes from where they'd stuck to their bodies. Maggie wasn't surprised to see that they hadn't gotten very far. It was the kind of clammy Louisiana day that could produce perspiration in only a few yards.

Maggie sat down next to the Rykers. "Hi, there."

"Hello," Lachlan said politely.

"You know," she said. "I realized something very interesting about this week. Well, besides the murders, which pretty much top any list of interesting events. Anyway, what I realized is that most of our guests had an agenda for their visit. What Detective Durand would call an ulterior motive. The Butlers, the Georgia boys, the Clabbers . . ."

"We didn't," Carrie said. Her face was red and her voice weak. She was a terrible liar.

"Oh, I think you did. So let's talk about your clandestine treasure hunting on our property."

Carrie and Lachlan exchanged a guilty look. "We're awfully sorry about that," Carrie said. "It's just . . . things have been rather hard for us lately. I owned a needlepoint shop in Sydney, but when the economy crashed, it took my store with it and left us with a pile of debt that we're still paying off."

"And then about eight months ago," Lachlan said, "the daily paper I wrote for folded. You can imagine how hard it is to get a job as a reporter these days. I was born in Los

Angeles, so I'm actually a U.S. citizen. We thought maybe we'd give America a go, you know, start over and all that. We were going to head straight to LA, where I still have family, but when we read about Louisiana and all the rumors of hidden treasure . . ."

"It was stupid, we know that now," Carrie admitted. "Color us desperate, I guess."

Maggie's anger at the couple dissipated. She could certainly empathize with financial hardship. "Well, you're not the first people who got sucked into that fantasy. And the hole you dug did save my life." She paused. "What will you do now?"

"I have a great-uncle I've never met who lives in Sherman Oaks in the San Fernando Valley," Lachlan said. "He's a widower with a nice house, and he offered us a place to stay while we both job hunt. If you can bear our brood for one more night, we'll start off on the drive in the morning."

"We'll pay," Carrie added quickly. "We insist on it."

As much as she wanted to, Maggie couldn't bring herself to take the struggling family's money. "Please, at this point, don't worry about that."

"Thank you so much. Oh, before I forget . . ." Carrie pulled something out of her pocket. It was Maggie's missing gris-gris bag. "I found this by our car. It's yours, isn't it? It must have fallen off when you were rummaging through the dumpster."

"Keep it," Maggie told Carrie. "You need it more than I do now. In fact, I'll ask my cousin to make you each one for prosperity." Right then, it hit her that she hadn't touched base with Lia yet. "I have to go. I'll see you later."

When Maggie got back to Crozat, she saw Lia's car parked in front. She ran up the wide-planked stairs into the house, where she found Lia and Kyle in the front parlor with Tug, Ninette, Gran', and the Cuties, including Jan. Maggie threw her arms around Lia and then took turns hugging Kyle and Jan. "It's over," Maggie said as she sank into a damask chair. "What a relief."

"It wouldn't be over if it wasn't for you," Kyle said.

"Amen to that," Jan declared, thumping the arm of her chair with her fist for emphasis.

"Thanks, but I had plenty of help," Maggie said.

Gran' wagged a finger at her. "Darlin', what did I tell you about learning to take a compliment? I believe this calls for champagne. Tug, please pop open a few of my personal bottles."

Tug did as his mother told him and filled delicate flutes for all. They toasted to Maggie, who tried not to feel uncomfortable with the attention. As they were about to sip, Sam ran in yelling, "The copper's here!" Sam was followed by Luke, Carrie, and Lachlan. Alice lagged behind, trying to pretend that she wasn't interested in what Bo had to report. But she took a seat in front of her brothers and ignored their griping.

Bo walked in a moment after the Rykers. He was still in his official attire of crisp shirt, blazer, and jeans. But when Gran' asked if he was on or off duty, Bo quickly responded "off" and took the flute of champagne that she offered him.

"So," he said as he sipped his champagne. "How is everybody?"

His audience groused, and Maggie chucked him playfully on the shoulder. "Stop being a jerk and tell us what happened. Did they reveal anything?"

"Mack MacIlhoney went from congratulating Kyle and Jan on their releases to signing up Emily as his next client," Bo said. "So he shut her down as quick as possible. But by the time Shane's public defender showed up, he'd given us enough of a story to make a cable miniseries."

"I think I figured out at least part of it," Maggie said.

Bo grinned. "Go for it."

"Beverly Clabber was obviously the original distant relative who inherited the peerage. Remember how they called each other milord and milady? They weren't just being obnoxiously cutesy. They were actually, well . . . milord and milady. That's what Beverly planned to reveal and throw in Gran's face. Gran' may be 'Louisiana royalty,' but that's a joke compared to the real thing, at least in Beverly's eyes. She would have finally one-upped Gran'. I'm guessing her plan was to make a big announcement and then start flashing the ring around. The initials stand for Beverly, Duchess of Dundess.'"

"Like I care about that sort of thing," Gran' huffed.

"You never got the chance to give Beverly that lack of satisfaction because Emily, Miss Next-in-Line-for-the-Title, got rid of her competition."

"Wait, this means Beverly and Emily were related," Lia said.

"Very distantly," Bo said, taking over the story. "In the way that I once met a man whose last name was Rockafellow, and he was distantly related to *the* Rockefellers. 'Rockafellow' was their original name and an ancestor changed it at some point."

"Did Emily and Beverly know each other before this all came up?" Ninette asked.

"According to Shane, no. Emily only found out about Beverly when she was contacted by the Dundess estate solicitors from Great Britain. That's when—again, according to Shane, but we think he's the money in this case—Emily came up with the scheme. She and Shane were both making squat at their start-ups and basically living off Emily's trust fund, which was drying up. She manipulated her way into getting Beverly's contact info from one of the solicitor's assistants and then got in touch with Beverly using 'family history' as an excuse. When she found out the Clabbers were coming here, she booked a trip too. She convinced Beverly to keep their connection on the down low so it wouldn't blow Beverly's big moment of revealing her duchessdom, or whatever you call it, to Mrs. Crozat."

"I told you, it's Charlotte, not Mrs. Crozat," Gran' playfully chided Bo.

"Crawfish Crozat," Maggie exclaimed. The others looked at her, confused. "Shane and Emily—they were the first ones to eat it at Fet Let. Everyone else was worried it might be poisoned, but they weren't. Because they *knew* it wasn't."

"Exactly," Bo nodded. "Emily found a time when the Clabbers weren't in their room, snuck in, and filled Mrs. Clabber's medicine capsules with the poison she stole from your plantation store. The Butlers had brought their own—Shane told us where they disposed of it, which gave us some solid hard evidence—but Emily thought that using yours would focus the investigation on the Crozats, which it did—"

"Yeah, thanks for that."

"—very briefly," Bo continued, ignoring Maggie's sarcasm. "Emily also knew about the ring and brochures because Beverly had shown them to her. When the police didn't bring them up, she figured they hadn't found them, which they hadn't due to Rufus letting CSI get away with a half-assed job."

"And pretty much anyone paying attention—which Emily certainly was—could figure out that I was doing my own investigating," Maggie added, "which led her right to my place when it came to searching for that stuff."

"Shane admitted that he was the one who planted faulty fuses in the backup generator," Bo shared. "They couldn't time when Beverly Clabber would take her medication, but once the storm hit so fierce, it was a pretty safe bet that she'd need something to calm down, and Emily figured a total blackout would kick up the old woman's anxiety level. As it turned out, the whole fuse thing was unnecessary. When Hal had his stroke, you all just assumed that the trauma of the event triggered a stroke in his wife."

"The term 'evil genius' comes to mind," Kyle said.

"That's Emily for sure," Bo agreed. "The DA's office researched her background and she appears to have been troubled from early on. She was asked to leave several schools due to disruptive behavior. It escalated to the point of a violent confrontation with another student in middle school, at which point she was sent to a boarding school for girls with personality disorders."

"Emily once told me that her parents said their lives got more complicated after she was born," Maggie recalled. "I thought it was such a terrible thing for them to say. But now I guess I understand where they were coming from."

Bo downed what was left in his champagne glass. "Her behavior seemed to improve after her time at the boarding school, but in retrospect, it seems that her psychosis didn't disappear, it just went dormant. It was triggered again by the news that she had a shot at becoming royalty. She became fixated on the idea, to the point of it becoming an overwhelming obsession."

"Much like Beverly," Maggie said. "I guess it ran in the family."

"Shane, on the other hand, was mostly in it for the freebies. Although he did say he was looking forward to literally lording it over his blue-collar relatives."

"I thought you Americans didn't care about this kind of stuff," Luke said.

"Most of us don't," Maggie replied. "But we still have debutantes and social snobs in this country. And Princess Kate and Prince William brought sexy back to royalty in general."

The guests continued to pepper Bo with questions, eager to extract every last detail about the case from him. The conversation could have gone on for hours, but Ninette noticed Bo's energy flagging.

"This has been a very long day and I'm guessing everyone here has quite the appetite," she said as she stood up. "I've got a pot of jambalaya warming on the stove. Tug, will you help me serve?"

"Yes, ma'am." Tug exited out of the parlor after his wife. The rest of the group drifted into the dining room, leaving only Bo and Maggie in the parlor.

"Thank you," she said to Bo. "You're the only one on the force who was really on our side. I owe you, Bo."

Bo smiled. She had never noticed that he had a slight cleft to his chin. "You don't owe me anything. But you do owe my kid an art lesson."

Epilogue

The new week brought game-changing developments to Pelican. Ears all over town bled from the scream Vanessa Fleer let out when Rufus caved to her nagging and said, "Fine, I'll put a ring on it. Now shut up and lemme clean my gun." A proposal was a proposal in Vanessa's book, so its lack of romance didn't bother her, especially when she learned that her fiancé would soon be up to his bushy eyebrows in cash. The Durand family had finally received an offer on Grove Hall that even Rufus couldn't refuse. Maggie and Bo crossed their fingers that the perpetually slothful Ru would feel flush enough from his share of the sale to quit his position as police chief. But Rufus had no intention of relinquishing his throne. "Money *and* power, buddy," he gloated to his cousin as he unscrewed the cap on a thirty-two ounce bottle of convenience store beer. "I'm livin' the dream."

Bo took comfort in the fact that his share of the sale would allow Xander to attend Bright Start, the Baton Rouge school dedicated to kids with unique academic needs. And Maggie did get to revel in Ru's outrage when he learned that the LLC that purchased Grove Hall was owned by Kyle Bruner, whose move to Pelican brought joy to Lia and the rest of the Crozats. Any Crozat happiness would always mean Rufus Durand misery. "Tough break, Ru Ru," Maggie fake-commiserated, making sure that she revealed Vanessa's pet name for the police chief in front of delighted department gossips Cal and Artie.

To make up for the hell that Jan Robbins had gone through with her false arrest and Debbie Stern's betrayal, Bo put in a call to the Cuties' airline and arranged a few extra days in Pelican for the group with no change fee to their plane tickets. "You were the only ones who came here without some scheme in your visit plans, and I'll never forget that," Maggie told the women as she hugged them good-bye. Jan promised that when the Cuties returned to Cajun Country in the spring for their convention, many events would be held at Crozat, and with one last cry of "laissez les bons temps rouler!" the Cajun Cuties had taken off for the airport in their rented minivan.

There was news regarding the Ryker clan as well. Gran', who'd set up an Internet alert for Crozat Plantation B and B, was tickled to receive an e-blast containing a rave review written by Lachlan Ryker on a website called aussiesinamerica.com. Carrie and Lachlan had adopted the American entrepreneurial spirit the minute they arrived in California and created a website for homesick Aussie ex-pats that would help them navigate the New World. It was rudimentary and would take time to grow, but Maggie's instincts told her that the prosperity gris-gris bags Lia had gifted the family with would eventually bear financial fruit.

Crozat Plantation B and B slowly began its recovery from the fallout of a double murder on its property. Maggie came up with a "Don't Labor on Labor Day Special" that offered low rates and a Crozat cookout, both of which attracted potential guests. "And we can credit morbid curiosity for a few of the reservations," Gran' said. "It's sold many a ticket to a freak show." The Shexnayders returned from their holiday rested and ready to resume their housekeeping and maintenance duties. From the little winks and butt pinches between them that Maggie observed, the break had also energized their libidos.

With Bud and Marie back at work, Maggie finally had time to market her line of souvenirs, and it was picked up by several of the nearby plantations. This provided the pressure she needed to convince Gran' that it would be in perfectly fine taste to sell the items—displayed discreetly, of course—at Crozat. Once on board, Gran' became a sales powerhouse, and no visitor to Crozat left without a memento, even if the poor soul just stuck their head in the door to ask for directions.

The best news of all came from a visit to Ninette's oncologist, Dr. Felicia Gilbert.

"Negative," Dr. Gilbert told Ninette's family. "Every test."

The Crozats fell into each other's arms and breathed a collective sigh of relief. "But then what was wrong with me?" Ninette asked.

"There was no evidence of an infection, so I'm going to write off the fever and high white count as the result of stress you've been under, especially since your numbers are normal and appear to have stabilized. The night sweats are something else. You're menopausal, Ninette. And given the intensity of those sweats, you might be in for a rough ride."

"Given the alternative, I'll take it." Ninette grinned. Maggie hadn't seen a smile that big on her mother's face in a long time. The family would never be free of worry about Ninette's health, but Dr. Gilbert had given them a respite from it.

With life at Crozat running relatively smoothly once again, Maggie could return to her art. But first . . .

*

It was early afternoon, and the light offered the first golden glint of autumn. Two easels stood side by side on the lawn next to the parterre. Tubes of oil paint covered a small table between them.

"They're arranged by color and shades within each color," Maggie explained to Xander, who nodded, his brow furrowed as he concentrated on the tubes of paints. She was finally making good on her promise to give the boy an art lesson. Bo napped on a blanket next to them while Gopher rested his head on Xander's feet. "But if you want to mix your own shade of a color, you can. Would you like to try that?"

Xander nodded yes. He picked up a few tubes with his slim little fingers and squeezed dollops onto the palette Maggie had given him. Maggie added a big blob of white. "You can make a ton of color shades just by adding a little or a lot of white," she explained. Xander stared at the paints and then started carefully mixing some colors, adding a touch blue, a drip of yellow, a bit more white. When he was satisfied with the result, he showed it to Maggie, who stared at the palette, mesmerized.

"Wow, just . . . wow," she sputtered.

Xander had created a shade of green that was extraordinary. The boy then picked up tubes of yellow and blue and mixed them. He did the same with a range of other colors until his palette was a phantasmagorical rainbow. Maggie watched, amazed. How could a boy who wouldn't eat his hot dog because the mustard and ketchup touched mix the most beautiful, otherworldly colors that she had ever seen?

Xander stopped and looked at her for approval. "Wow," she said again. "Xander, those are just . . . gorgeous. Okay, so, let's paint. I thought it would be fun to try and do the vegetable garden and chicken yard. Do you like that idea?"

Xander nodded and began painting. Maggie picked up a brush but put it down to watch Xander put his vision on canvas. He had a child's surreal view, but it was coupled with an attention to detail that seemed channeled from another realm.

Xander's hour lesson turned into the whole afternoon, which bled into early evening. The young boy finished his painting and wandered off to feed the chickens, followed as always by his canine shadow, Gopher. Bo roused himself from his nap with a yawn. "Has it been an hour yet?" he asked.

"It's been four hours," Maggie answered.

"What?" Bo jumped to his feet. "I didn't mean to pass out." He glanced at the finished canvas on the easel. "Hey, you're really good."

"That's not mine. That's your son's." Maggie pointed to Xander.

"Huh?" Bo rubbed his eyes. "Are you telling me Xander did this? Seven-year-old Xander?"

"Yes. He's got a gift, Bo. Whether it's from God or the universe or genetics, I don't know. But wherever it's from, it's magical and special, and I want to help him."

Bo ran his hands through his thick black hair as he tried to process what Maggie was telling him. "Yes. Sure. Do whatever you have to. I just want him to be happy. And feel good about himself. He needs that. He deserves it."

Bo walked over to his son, picked him up, and carried him back to where Maggie was standing. "Wanna get something to eat?" he asked Xander, who nodded yes. "You wanna come with?" Bo asked Maggie, who shook her head no.

"You two go. I've got something I need to do."

"Okay." Bo rubbed noses with Xander, who gave a slight smile. "Do me a favor, buddy, go wait by the car. I'll be right there." He put Xander down, and the boy ran off around the side of the main house to the front drive where Bo had parked. Bo turned to Maggie. "Not to be crass and inartistic or anything, but the more lessons you give him, the more I get to see you in a way that even Ru can't have a fit about."

"I was so busy obsessing about Xander's talent that I didn't even think of that," Maggie said. "But yes. Yay!"

Bo laughed. Then he bent his head down close to Maggie's and kissed her. It was a kiss as soft and warm and electric as any she'd ever experienced or even fantasized about. Maggie shuddered. But this time, in a good way.

Bo held a finger to her lips and she nodded. The kiss, as well as any that followed, would be their secret . . . for now. No sense in poking the odious bear that was Rufus.

Bo disappeared into the darkness and Maggie soon heard the sound of his car driving away from Crozat. Then she turned back to the canvas on her easel and began sketching. She continued through the night, and when dawn broke, she transported her canvas and art supplies down to her special spot by the bayou, where she painted quickly and fiercely.

When Maggie was done, she eyed the result with a serenity that she hadn't felt as an artist for a very long time. The painting depicted the languid bayou scene, but with a heightened photo-realism. Beyond that, an inquisitive art aficionado would discover something else—the silhouette of a man. Some would argue it wasn't even there, that it was the mind playing tricks on the viewer. This was the artist's intention—to imbue her work with a bit of sensual mystery.

She lay down and rested her head on a thicket of moss. "I know now," she thought to herself. "I know why I came home."

Then she smiled, closed her eyes, and with the soft Louisiana morning air as her blanket, Maggie fell asleep.

Crawfish Crozat

Ninette's signature dish is deceptively simple, but for a good reason. While many recipes bury the crawfish in heavy cream sauces, Ninette's is designed to let its delicious flavor dominate.

Ingredients

1 lb. peeled and cooked crawfish tails
1 cup okra, thinly sliced
1 red pepper, diced
1 lb. regular or whole wheat penne
4 tbsp. olive oil
3 minced garlic cloves
½ tsp. sea salt
½ tsp. paprika
¼ tsp. cayenne pepper (subtract or add more, depending on your taste for spicy)
¼ tsp. ground gumbo filé
½ tsp. garlic powder
½ tsp. onion powder

¼ tsp. thyme
¼ tsp. black pepper
2 tsp. Cajun seasoning, any brand

(Note: if your Cajun seasoning has salt, you may want to reduce
the ½ tsp. sea salt. You can always add more if you feel it's
needed.)

Instructions

Mix the salt, paprika, cayenne pepper, filé, garlic powder, onion
powder, black pepper, thyme, and Cajun seasoning together in a
small bowl.

Warm two tablespoons of olive oil in a skillet on a medium flame,
and add the okra and red pepper. Cook until softened, about five
minutes. Turn off the heat and add the crawfish; stir so it absorbs
some of the vegetable's warmth.

Cook the penne until it's al dente, and drain. Toss it with the
remaining oil and the herb/spice mix.

Add the crawfish, okra, and red pepper, and toss gently.

Note: Don't have crawfish or okra? Substitute shrimp and broc-
coli. Don't like seafood? Substitute two cups of chopped cooked
chicken.

Serves 4–6.

Chulanes

The broadest definition of a praline is a flat sugar candy flavored with nuts. Recipes often call for butter and brown sugar. Here is Tug's somewhat healthier version, named in honor of his alma mater, Louisiana's prestigious Tulane University.

Ingredients

8 oz. unsweetened baker's chocolate, melted

½ cup honey, warmed

¼ tsp. vanilla (you can substitute a liquor like
     rum or bourbon if you prefer)

¼ tsp. sea salt

1 cup mix-ins, like chopped nuts, raisins, dried fruit (Tug's
     favorites are raisins and slivered honeyed almonds)

Instructions

Stir the honey into the melted chocolate. It will be soupy. Don't worry about that.

Add the vanilla and salt, and stir.

Mix in the mix-ins.

Line a baking sheet with parchment. Drop the Chulanes onto the parchment by large spoonfuls.

Place in the freezer until the Chulanes harden. They can be kept in the fridge after that and will have a chewy consistency.

Makes 12.

Bourbon Pecan Bread Pudding

Bread pudding is one of those fun dishes that's easy to adapt to anyone's taste. Lia jazzes hers up with bourbon and that other Louisiana staple, pecans. *Laissez les bons temps rouler!*

Ingredients

4 ½ cups lightly packed bite-size croissant
    pieces (about 4 croissants)
1 cup chopped pecans
3 large eggs
¾ cups granulated sugar
1 cup milk
⅓ cup bourbon, plus 1 tsp.
½ cup heavy or whipping cream
1 tsp. vanilla
¼ tsp. salt

1 tbsp. dark brown sugar
2 tbsp. unsalted butter

Instructions

Preheat oven to 350 degrees.

Dry bread uncovered at room temperature for 12 hours (or dry the bread in a 250-degree oven for one hour).

Butter an 8 × 8 baking dish.

Arrange the bread in the baking dish. Sprinkle the pecans over the bread, making sure they're evenly dispersed.

In a bowl, whisk together the eggs, sugar, milk, ⅓ cup bourbon, ½ cup of cream, vanilla, and salt. Pour it slowly and evenly over the bread.

Cream the butter with the brown sugar and teaspoon of bourbon, then dot the pudding with the mixture.

(Note: you can chill the pudding, covered, for anywhere from an hour to a day before baking, but this is optional.)

Bake the pudding in the middle of the oven until it's slightly puffed and golden and the middle has set—approximately 40 minutes.

Serves 6.

*A Lagniappe** *about* Plantation Shudders

I became fascinated by Cajun culture when I was a student at Tulane University. During a visit to Louisiana after graduation, my friend Jan and I drove up the east bank of River Road, and we were drawn to a dilapidated but stunning plantation. It was glorious architecturally but in total disrepair. Yet a woman was offering tours. Her name was Gaynell Bourgeois Moore, and she worked for the only member of the Hayward family who refused to okay a sale of the plantation, Ashland-Belle Helene, to Shell Oil Company.

---

* Lagniappe: a small gift given with a purchase to a customer by way of compliment or for good measure; bonus. Also defined as "a little something extra."

Even though Gaynell was more than twenty-five years my senior, we struck up a friendship. A self-taught artist, musician, and writer, she was a total delight. But I was in my twenties and living the life of a single New Yorker, so we lost touch.

Fast-forward to 1997: I'm a married television writer living in Los Angeles. I take my husband on a trip to Louisiana, where we wander through the bayous and back roads. We drive up River Road and stop at Houmas House, one of the great icons of Plantation Country. I mention to a saleswoman in the gift shop that I had a friend named Gaynell who once worked at Ashland-Belle Helene. The woman says, "Gaynell? She's working here." She calls for Gaynell on her walkie-talkie, and Gaynell runs in wearing her full tour guide regalia of hoop skirt, ball gown, and accessories. Our friendship is rekindled, now for life.

Houmas House inspired Doucet Plantation in *Plantation Shudders.* Crozat Plantation B and B was inspired by Madewood Plantation, where my husband and I enjoyed a wonderful evening's respite. And Grove Hall was inspired by my beloved Ashland-Belle Helene, which was eventually sold to Shell Oil. Years later, it still sits waiting for a promised restoration. Grove Hall will meet a happier fate in Book Two of the series. (Sidebar: in my mind, Crozat looks like Ashland-Belle Helene and Doucet looks like Madewood. Writer's prerogative!)

When I was writing *Plantation Shudders,* I knew I wanted to name a character after Gaynell. My protagonist is Magnolia "Maggie" Crozat, an aspiring artist who has returned home after living in New York for ten years. I called Gaynell and told her that she could choose between Maggie's grandmother, a mischievous grand dame, or a nineteen-year-old friend Maggie has made while working as a tour guide at a local plantation. And seventysomething Gaynell quickly responded in her inimitable Cajun accent, "Oh, I'd like to be the nineteen-year-old."

So she is.

Acknowledgments

I am eternally grateful to many people for their support and input on *Plantation Shudders*. Thanks to my awesome agent, Doug Grad, and to editorial director Matthew Martz and editorial assistant Nike Power, the wonders behind Crooked Lane Books. Without this trifecta of talent, there would be no *Cajun Country Mysteries*. A big thanks to Rick Copp and Connie Archer for their generosity. Linda Konner, I will forever owe you for your invaluable advice throughout my journey. Thanks to my beloved brothers, Tony and David Seideman, for their love and support. A big shout-out to my patient and gifted TV writing partner, Lissa Kapstrom. Lisa Q. Mathews, you are, and always will be, my mystery BFF. Thank you, Kelly Goode and Lisa Libatique, for putting up with my walk 'n talks—and you, too, Kim Rose! Nancy Adler, Laura Graff, and June Stoddard, my friendship with each of you inspires me every day. Karen Fried and Denise and Stacy Smithers—ditto! Thanks to my Louisiana crew for all their help—that's you, Laurie and Walter Becker, Gaynell Bourgeois Moore, and Jan Gilbert. The same

Ellen Byron

goes for my Texas crew, Pam and Jon Shaffer and Charlotte Waguespack Allen, who does double duty as my source for great anecdotes about her illustrious Louisiana family. Tulane University, you are not a person, but without you, I honestly don't know if I ever would have become a writer.

And finally, words can't express my gratitude to Mindy Schneider for including me when she decided to start a writers group with Kathy McCullough, Kate Schein, and Teri Wagener. I'm honored and blessed to be in the company of such talented women. Thank you.